Trouble Never Sleeps

Trouble Never Sleeps

Stephanie Tromly

Kathy Dawson Books

KATHY DAWSON BOOKS
PENGUIN YOUNG READERS GROUP
An imprint of Penguin Random House LLC
375 Hudson Street
New York, NY 10014

Library of Congress Cataloging-in-Publication Data

Tromly, Stephanie, author.
Trouble never sleeps / Stephanie Tromly.
Description: New York, NY : Kathy Dawson Books, [2018]
Sequel to: Trouble makes a comeback.
Summary: When Zoe gets an invitation to attend the Prentiss School in
New York City, she wonders what will happen to her relationship with Digby
after his sister's disappearance is solved.
LCCN 2017035203| ISBN 9780525428428 (hardback) | ISBN 9780698188754 (ebook)
Subjects: CYAC: Missing children—Fiction. | High schools—Fiction. |
Schools—Fiction. | Dating (Social customs)—Fiction. | Mystery and detective stories.
LCC PZ7.1.T76 Tu 2018   DDC [Fic]—dc23

Printed in the United States of America

1 3 5 7 9 10 8 6 4 2

Designed by Cerise Steel
Text set in Calisto MT

Trouble Never Sleeps

. . .

"So this is what closure feels like," Digby says.

We're standing on the grassy patch where his little sister, Sally, was buried nine years ago.

"Closure sucks," Digby says. "Now what?"

He isn't asking for suggestions. He is telling me something I already know. The search for the truth about what happened to his sister after her kidnapping had been the basis of so many of our arguments, so much of the hurt we'd dealt other people, all the times we'd broken the law, all the times we'd broken our bodies. I'd gone along because . . . *Digby*. He needed to find Sally. But now, for the first time in a long time, Digby doesn't have an angle to play. He doesn't have his next move planned.

"What did I expect, right? It's like they say. The truth is almost always disappointing." Digby turns to me. "But . . . now what? Other than me, talking in clichés."

I watch him wrestle with his paralysis and I think about how different my priorities have become since I met Digby eight months ago. I'd first arrived in River Heights wanting nothing more than to make some friends and have some normal high school fun.

And I did that. I made friends. I even had a boyfriend. But I blew all that up because . . . *Digby*. And now, with a trail of bad blood and narrowly avoided felony charges behind me, I perversely find myself dreading the end of the crazy.

Because it really does look like it is game over. Sally Digby is dead.

I know it's selfish to wonder, but what does this mean for Digby and me? As a wise woman once said, relationships that start under intense circumstances never last.

"This isn't the time to think about what's next," I say, putting the shovel back in his hand. "Now we keep digging."

We are about to get going again when a pair of flashlight beams comes out of the main house's back door and bobs toward us.

"Do we run?" I say. The anguish on Digby's face makes me wonder if he can survive a late-in-the-game plot twist.

But, as usual, I'm starting at the end.

So here it is. One last time, from the top. Meaning, we have to go back to the night of Kyle Mesmer's lake house party.

ONE

My awareness that Digby and I had been standing on the gravel road at Kyle's house kissing for a long time came only from my feet turning into burning balls of agony. I wasn't used to being jacked up on the five-inch heels of Sloane's loaner boots. I tried shifting my weight, but the gravel and rocks under my feet gave way and all of a sudden, I was falling backward.

Only I wasn't falling. Without breaking away from kissing me, Digby had scooped me up and was carrying me to the grassy field off the path we'd been standing on. When he set me down on the ground, I lay back and pulled him on top of me. I hated to compare, but I thought back to the times when I had to stop and ask my recently ex-ed boyfriend Austin to move this and move that so I could breathe. Digby knew just how to rest his weight mostly on his knees and elbows so I was exactly the right kind of breathless under him.

"Ready to have your world rocked?" Digby said. In one

smooth move, he sat up, and then unzipped and pulled off my boot.

I'd started to laugh but the sensation of my liberated toes unfurling was so fricking sublime, I straight-up moaned. I even writhed a little bit. After Digby peeled off my other boot, I pulled him back down on top of me.

I felt his hand creep up my hip and linger on the bare skin of my midriff. It took me a minute to realize he couldn't get any farther than that because the leather clothes I'd borrowed from Sloane were so binding.

"Forget about abstinence education. Let's just start putting people in these sexbot outfits. Teen pregnancy rates would fall through the floor. Nothing's getting past this." Digby flicked his finger against my tight leather second skin. "And why are none of the zippers and buttons anywhere you'd think they'd be . . ."

Wardrobe malfunction or not, this was our champagne-popping moment. Just earlier that day we'd helped Henry get his football coach arrested for distributing steroids to some of the players. Austin had just dumped me to be with my (supposed) friend Allie and while that sounds awful, it was actually a blessed end to two weeks of agonizing over secretly wanting to be with Digby when I was officially still with Austin. Now that I was kissing Digby, it felt crazy that I'd ever considered being with anyone else.

And then, most importantly, Digby had just gotten our local

oligarch and parody of an evil villain, Hans de Groot, to admit he'd kidnapped Digby's sister, Sally. Even better, Digby had gotten him to promise to reveal what had ultimately happened to Sally—in exchange for what de Groot had kidnapped Sally to get nine years ago: Digby's mother's bionanotechnology research.

And with that thought came the memory of something Digby had said to de Groot. I pushed Digby off. "Wait a minute."

"What? Too much?" he said. "Sorry . . ."

"You said you'd trade your mom's research for the truth about what happened to your sister," I said. "You plan to take it from inside your mom's old lab in Perses?"

"Yep."

I said, "But how? Won't it be hard to—"

"Break into an unbelievably secure facility with federal clearance to manufacture sensitive defense-related assets?" he said. "Yep. It sure will be."

I was confused by how calm he looked. "So how—?"

"Should I be worried you're distracted here?" Digby gestured at our intertwined legs. "Because I'm coming at you with my A game."

I tried to relax, but when we started kissing again, his conversation with de Groot continued to replay in my head. I could only get up to lukewarm in my response. Digby groaned and pulled away again.

"Really?" he said.

"Sorry," I said.

"After eight months of frustration, we're finally here on the same page and you want to talk about this?" he said.

"You said 'inside job.' What inside job?" I said. "Who do you know inside Perses?" I could think of only one possibility. "Besides Felix's dad."

Digby sat up.

"Oh, no." I sat up too. "Wouldn't that get him arrested? And put away for treason? Just like you were afraid *your* parents might have been?"

"I mean, it isn't my plan for anyone to get caught," he said.

I said, "Digby. You can't—"

"Wait. Shh," Digby said. "Do you hear that?"

"Don't change the subject," I said.

"No, really," he said. "You didn't hear that?"

I listened and then I did hear it too. It sounded like someone was in the bushes.

Digby jumped up and helped me to my feet. He waited for me to pull on my boots and then we headed into the tree line. We split up and looked around.

When Digby and I met up again, I said, "There's no one here." The truth was that there could've been twenty people standing two feet away from me and I wouldn't have seen them. We were enveloped in pitch-black, far from the party's lights and at least a hundred yards away from where Mesmer's landscaping crew called it a day.

"But I definitely heard someone." Digby pointed at the ground and said, "And look at these footprints."

"Are you sure those aren't our own?" I said.

He walked farther. "We were never over here."

I followed him on the trail of the footprints. "Who do you think it was?"

"Best guess?" he said. "De Groot's security guys."

My phone rang. I couldn't make out the image in the message until I turned up my screen's brightness. "What the hell is this?"

"Typical evil scumbag move . . ." Digby said. "Make a deal with me and then immediately try to cheat me out of my information without having to give me his."

When my eyes finally made out the image, I said, "It might not have been de Groot."

"No, this was definitely de Groot," he said. "This is exactly their MO."

"Then their MO now includes carpet-bombing our school with pictures of us." I showed him the grainy picture of Digby and me rolling around in the grass.

"Whoa." Digby looked at the picture, patted his gut, and sucked in. "I better start getting my ten thousand steps in. Who sent this to you?"

"Charlotte forwarded it." I took the phone back from Digby and typed in, "Where did u get this?"

A second image came through. This one was of us ugly kissing. Or, more precisely, it was a picture of me ugly kissing Digby.

"Oh, my God." Whoever took the picture had caught me with my tongue sticking all the way out.

Digby laughed.

"Yeah, I see it. I have a freakishly long tongue," I said. My phone beeped. "Charlotte just said everyone's getting the pics. She doesn't know who's sending them. Let's go back to the party. I need to figure out what's going on."

Our fingers brushed a few times as we were walking until finally, somehow, we ended up holding hands. But every time I got myself to relax and enjoy the fact that I was walking in the moonlight with Digby, my phone would alert me to another embarrassing picture of us that had been put into circulation.

When we were within sight of Mesmer's house, Digby grabbed my arm and pulled me into the cover of some bushes. "Hey, Princeton. You know, we're having such a good night." He kissed me again. "We could just split. Deal with this tomorrow."

I was about to agree when Digby burst out laughing and said, "Jabba the Hutt. *That's* what that picture looks like." He pretended to throttle himself with his own hands, wagged his outstretched tongue from side to side, and mimicked Jabba's horrifying death rattle.

"That's it." I walked back to the party as fast as my high heels let me.

"Hey, Princeton, wait up," Digby said.

"I'll find you later. I need to talk to Charlotte," I said. I crossed the lawn, wondering what exactly Charlotte had meant when she'd said "everyone" had gotten the pictures. I started to fear the worst, though, when the group of people smoking on the porch snickered as I walked past them into the house.

When I got to the living room I noticed a new, slightly hysterical edge to the party's vibe. There was trash everywhere and I could see at least some of the walls would need to be repainted. A girl tripped right in front of me and didn't manage to put her hands out in time to stop her face hitting the floor. People were getting sloppy.

I helped her to the couch and then bumped into one of Austin's teammates on my way to the kitchen. "Hi, Pete . . ."

"Heeeey, Zoe . . ." Pete made sure I noticed how hard he was trying—but failing—to stop himself from laughing at me. The group he'd been standing with were all laughing at me too.

I finally found Charlotte by the keg in the backyard. "What's going on?"

"Dude." Charlotte led me away from the crowd. "This one's going to be a meme . . ." She showed me the Jabba pic.

"It looks like the pics went up on the yearbook group chat?" I said. "And then they got shared?" When Charlotte nodded, I said, "Then it was Bill. Has to be."

"Well, I mean, it was from an unknown user," Charlotte said. "And tons of people are on yearbook. Including you and me."

But I knew it was Bill.

Both our phones beeped.

"Oh, there's more," Charlotte said.

15

I looked down at my phone to see a shot of my face, scrunched up and unrecognizable in an ecstatic expression I'd never seen myself make. "Oh, my God . . ." That and the unfortunate camera angle of Digby between my legs pulling off my boots made the scene look much more sordid than it had actually been.

"Where's Bill?" I said.

"Inside," Charlotte said. "Crying like you made Digby leave her at the altar."

"You know, I got dumped tonight too," I said as I scrolled through the pictures. "This isn't fair."

No one was saying boo about Austin dumping me to be with my supposed friend who, actually, now that I was thinking about it, probably only hung out with me to get closer to my boyfriend. But more unfair was that my happy ending had lasted a grand total of a half an hour. A half an hour of rolling in the grass in exchange for death by social media.

"Look. Allie snaked Austin away from you. And then you snaked Digby from Bill, and if Bill had snaked a guy from someone else, then *she'd* be the home-wrecking slut we're all talking about, but . . ." Charlotte pointed at me. "Right now, you're it."

"Home-wrecking?" I said. "Wait. Did you just call me a home-wrecking slut?"

"*I* didn't," Charlotte said. "That's just what the comments say."

I went back into the house to find Bill.

16

TWO

Bill was in Kyle's living room, blowing cigarette smoke out of an open window and looking pretty while she cried. Three girls were comforting her. I was just about to wade into her pity party when she broke away and walked to the bathroom.

I rushed over and got there in time to block her from closing the bathroom door. I muscled my way in after her, not realizing how aggressive I was acting until I saw her frightened expression.

"Bill," I said.

"Zoe?" She took a big step back and would've fallen into the bathtub if I hadn't caught her.

"Chill. I'm not going to hurt you," I said. "I don't think."

"What do you want?" she said.

"Are you kidding me?" I said. "I want you to stop sending out those pictures."

Bill tried. "What pictures?" she said.

17

I grabbed her phone from her hand and found dozens of pictures in her album. I started erasing.

"Hey," Bill said. She tried to snatch the phone back from me.

"I can either erase these pictures or just drop the entire phone in the toilet. Your choice."

"Why did you say I could date him if you were just going to snatch him back anyway?" Bill said. "Was it for the extra challenge?"

"Bill, tonight wasn't something I planned."

"Oh, is that why you turned up in those clothes?" She pointed at my borrowed clothes. "This is like last year with you and Henry and Sloane . . . you and your love triangles," Bill said. "Your whole deal is just so *high school*."

That comment in and of itself wouldn't have bothered me, but knowing that by calling me "high school," Bill was giving me what she considered her greatest insult made me want to claw her eyes out. Luckily, someone started banging on the bathroom door before I could.

I yelled, "It's occupied!"

"Zoe? You have to come out here. *Now*."

"Felix?" I opened the door to find Felix hopping around outside the bathroom. "What's the matter?"

"Digby told me to come get you." And then Felix took off running down the hallway and up the stairs.

I said "To be continued" to Bill and followed Felix around

the corner onto the second-floor landing, where we ran into a jam of people in the hallway outside one of the bedrooms. They were laughing, and from their body language it seemed like they were talking about whatever was happening behind the closed door.

"Excuse me, people, make a hole, make a hole." Felix parted a path through the crowd for the two of us. He pounded on the bedroom door. "Digby! Hey, it's Felix."

Standing right up against the door, I could hear the sound of angry talking and scuffling. And then I heard a male voice whimper, "Ouch ouch ouch that hurts."

I asked Felix, "What the hell is going on in there?"

Someone toward the back of the crowd yelled out, "Yeah! What's going on in there?"

Someone else said, "Catfight."

And that's when people began pushing up against me to get within earshot, so I banged on the door and yelled, "Digby! Open the door." By now, the pressure from the crowd was pinning me against the door. I checked that the door opened away from me and saw the lock looked reassuringly old. "Felix, do you have a bus pass? Or some kind of credit card?"

Felix handed me a museum membership pass. "You know how to do that?"

"How hard can it be?" It had looked easy enough when I'd watched Digby do it, so the sound of Felix's card snapping in half surprised me. "Um, do you have another one?"

Felix grimaced but gave me his library card anyway.

I pushed at the person behind me to back up so I'd have room to work the card gently. Click.

"You did it," Felix said.

My brain couldn't make sense of the chaos we saw when the door opened, but eventually the flailing bodies untangled to reveal Digby and Henry standing back to back, trying to keep Sloane from killing Maisie, the sophomore I'd found curled up in an armchair with Henry earlier that night.

The crowd behind me whooped and cheered at the sight of Sloane going crazy. I saw people raising their phones to record, so I pulled Felix inside and slammed the door shut behind us. The crowd outside started booing and complaining.

"Sloane, *ouch,*" Henry said.

Sloane was climbing Henry, windmilling her arms to get at Maisie, who was trying to get around Digby to reach Sloane.

"Princeton. Help?" Digby said.

Neither Henry nor Digby was willing to actually put hands on either Sloane or Maisie, so I grabbed Sloane, wrestled her onto the bed, and sat on top of her. "Get Maisie out of here," I said. After a weird no-hands dance, Digby finally managed to shuffle Maisie out the door.

Once it was just the five of us, I climbed off Sloane and sat next to her on the bed. "Damn it, Sloane, what the hell's the matter with you?"

"It was me . . . my fault." Henry flopped onto the bed next to me and said, "I guess Maisie thought—"

Sloane leaped over me and started hitting Henry.

"Wait, Sloane! Nothing happened," Henry said. "Stop hitting me."

"I know nothing happened. Of course nothing happened," Sloane said. "Would you even be *breathing* if I actually thought something did happen?"

"Then why are you mad?" Henry said.

Sloane grabbed a pillow and hit Henry in the face. "Because you let her think something *could've* happened."

"She jumped *me*. I was just sleeping it off in the chair . . ." Henry pointed at the recliner. "And when I woke up, she was on my lap kissing me."

"Well, who told you to drink so much in the first place?" Sloane said.

Digby gasped. "Are you blaming the victim?"

"That's not funny. Of course she wasn't," I said.

"You know, Sloane, girls need to get consent too," Digby said.

Sloane kept ripping into Henry. "What's wrong with you? Spring workouts start next week—"

"Hello?" Henry said. "I got Coach *arrested* . . . which basically means I personally canceled spring workouts. Actually, I pretty much got next season canceled too, because they're going to check everyone for steroid use and I don't know *how* many of the guys are using." Henry flopped back on the bed. "And anyway, Coach is going to make Austin QB so, really, my whole life is canceled since if the college scouts don't see me play . . . no college for Henry."

"Number one," Sloane said, "it doesn't matter if he *had* decided to replace you with Austin, because as of this morning, Coach Fogle is a criminal. Number two: The season's not over until they tell you it is and *then* we call my lawyers." Henry picked up a random Solo cup from the nightstand. "And number three . . ." Henry lifted the cup to his lips for a drink but Sloane slapped it out of his hand before he could. "*Stop drinking.*"

Felix pointed at the now-beer-soaked wall. "Should we clean up?"

"This house is a gut job at this point," Digby said. "We should just get out of here."

"Yes. Definitely," I said. "Party's over."

"I have to go to the bathroom," Sloane said, and walked out of the room.

"So, is this true? You two now? Maya sent me this." Felix handed me his phone, where the picture of my ugly kissing Digby was captioned with, *Isn't she your friend?*

"Maya. The soccer captain?" I said. "So now all the sportos have it?"

"Oh, the Jabba pic?" Digby said.

Felix clapped his hands. "That *is* what she looks like." He and Digby did the death rattle tongue waggle. "On the pleasure barge."

"Ha-ha. Yeah, yeah, classic scene," I said. And then I realized what was bothering me. "Wait. Where did Sloane go?

There's a bathroom right here." I pointed at the en suite across the room from us. "Damn it."

I left the room just as Digby worked it out and said, "Uh-oh . . ."

I ran down the halls, alternating between asking "Seen Maisie?" and "Did Sloane come through here?" Finally, I found Sloane standing in the living room, holding a beer and looking weirdly calm.

"Oh, hi, Zoe," Sloane said.

"'Oh, hi, Zoe'?" I said. "Did you even need the bathroom? What are you up to?"

"She's talking about me," Sloane said.

I watched Maisie huddled with her friends across the room, being aggressively obvious about mocking us.

"Probably because you're standing here staring at her like a psycho. Let's go, Sloane, you're just driving yourself nuts," I said.

"Fine," Sloane said.

I'd already started for the front door when I realized Sloane wasn't walking with me. I went back through the crowd to find her. "Sloane, what the hell? Get back here."

And then—I swear—I saw her hand moving upward with her cup of beer, so I rushed over to stop her from dumping it all over Maisie. I got in grabbing range just as Sloane yelled Maisie's name and Maisie turned around. I almost had Sloane by the arm but then my left heel got caught in the tassels of the living room carpet while my right foot kept on going. I dove forward and I reached out to break my fall but all I got was a handful of Sloane's hair. Both Sloane and I went down screaming, and I watched her cup of beer arc through the air and hit Maisie in the face.

Still crouched on the floor next to me, Sloane said, "What did you do that for?"

"To stop you from attacking her with your beer," I said.

"You mean like the way you just did? I was only going to cuss her out," Sloane said.

The chorus of OMGs and sympathetic faces gathered around Maisie morphed into angry sneers as people looked at us.

"They're turning on us, Sloane," I said. Sloane and I helped each other get up. "Go say sorry."

"Why?" Sloane said. "You did it."

Maisie pointed at us, with black eyeliner dripping down her cheeks. "You *bitches*." She picked up a random cup and flung the contents toward me but Sloane yanked me backward and took the soaking in my place.

The room burst into celebration. Maisie was coming at me with another cup, so I grabbed Sloane's hand and we ran out the front door and straight to Sloane's SUV.

Hince, her driver, started the engine even before we'd fully gotten in.

"I'll text Digby and the guys to come out here," I said.

24

Maisie stomped out the front door with a stream of people behind her.

"Uh, Miss Bloom?" Hince said.

"The angry villagers," Sloane said. She locked her door. "We can't wait for the guys. Go, Hince. *Go*."

We lurched away, with Hince periodically slamming on the brakes to avoid killing the morons who thought it'd be funny to jump in our path or climb onto our moving car. When we finally shook off the last faux rioter and got under way, I handed Sloane the box of Kleenex she kept in the car and helped her wipe off some of the beer.

"Thanks for the save, Sloane. I didn't need a public beer shower on top of the crummy night I'm already having." And then I noticed her eyes flick down to my legs and I realized what was really going on. "It was your leather pants, wasn't it? You didn't want beer on your pants."

"Those are brand-new. And speaking of . . ." Sloane reached down and straightened my legs. "Knees."

THREE

I wasn't in the mood for one of Sloane's lectures about a poor little rich girl growing up alone in a castle on a hill, so I told her she could spend the night at my place. I put her in the guest bedroom, said good night, and brushed my teeth. But when I got back to my room, Sloane was sitting on my bed, reading one of my books.

"Something wrong with the guest room?" I said.

"Those sheets don't look clean," Sloane said.

"They're clean. No one's slept in them," I said. "I changed them myself after Digby moved out."

"Digby slept on that bed?" Sloane said. "Wait, did you ever . . . with him on that bed?"

I shook my head.

"What about elsewhere? Like, in the dirt outside Kyle Mesmer's summer house?" Sloane said.

"I can see those pictures are going to be so annoying," I said.

"No, we did not." I dove into my closet. "There's a sleeping bag in here you can have."

"Is it clean?" she said.

"No, Sloane, I'm going to stuff you into a dirty sleeping bag and make you spend the night as a filthy proletariat Hot Pocket," I said. "It's *clean*."

"Ha-ha," she said. "By the way, thanks for lending me your clothes, but . . ."

I threw Sloane a set of my pajamas.

She caught them and said, "Are they—"

"*Yes,* Sloane, they are clean," I said.

"Also, I'm thirsty," she said.

After a while, I realized that she was staring at me because she expected me to do something about it.

"Go to the bathroom and get a drink," I said.

"Like a dog?" she said.

"Did I say drink from the toilet?" I said. "I don't know how it is in your house, but we have a sink in our bathroom."

"Is the water filtered?" she said.

"Then just go get a bottle from the fridge already, okay?" I said. "My God, you are exhausting."

Finally alone, I exchanged a few awkward messages with Digby in which I avoided saying what I really wanted to say— *please come over*—before I figured out that he didn't think Henry was in any shape to be left alone.

"What's this?" Sloane came back in the room holding a white envelope.

"Mail? I don't know." I didn't recognize the crest on the envelope at first, but when I finally did, my entire being flooded with dread.

"The Prentiss School? Is this . . . ?" Sloane said.

"The decision letter. It's so late," I said. "I just assumed . . ."

Sloane ran her finger along the envelope's flap. "Open it."

"Ugh. This on top of everything else tonight," I said. "Man, I wish I hadn't let you talk me into going to that party."

"Don't look at me like I *made* you go," Sloane said.

"Literally, that is what you did," I said.

"Wait. Did you tell Austin you were applying?" Sloane said. "When you sent in the application, I mean?"

"I didn't tell anyone I applied," I said. "Not even my parents."

Sloane said, "So, besides the admissions people and yourself . . ."

"You're the only other person who knows," I said. "Yes."

Sloane laughed. "You're mad at Austin and Allie for 'stabbing you in the back,'"—Sloane made air quotes—"but *really*, you were making plans to leave town behind *his* back the entire time you guys were together?"

"To be honest, I only applied out of spite because my father said I wouldn't get in. I didn't actually contemplate what I'd do if I did," I said. "And look, I *didn't* get in."

"You don't know for sure you didn't get in," Sloane said.

"It's the skinny envelope, Sloane," I said.

"But until you open it, you don't *know*," she said.

"You just want me to read the letter so you can watch me get rejected," I said.

"Wow. I'm glad you have such a high opinion of me," Sloane said.

Even for Sloane and me, it was a low blow. I resigned myself to taking a major hit to the self-esteem and tore open the envelope. "Happy now?"

It took me another minute to register what the letter actually said.

"What?" I said. "What the hell?"

"What is it?" Sloane said.

I couldn't think of what else to say, so I just spat out every filthy combination of swear words my exhausted brain came up with.

"I have to see this." Sloane took the letter from me. "Wait . . . you got in. Zoe? You got in . . ."

I took the letter back from Sloane and reread it. A few times. *"Dear Ms. Webster, we are happy to inform you that we have a vacancy at the Prentiss School starting this fall . . ."*

"You got in," Sloane said.

It finally sunk in. "You bet your sweet ass I did."

Sloane was silent. Something weird went on with her face.

Eventually, I just had to ask. "What's your deal? Are you fighting a sneeze?"

Sloane held up a finger to buy herself time and then, when she was more composed, she said, "I'm doing my exercises."

"Exercises?" I said. "Exercises for what?"

29

"They're like this." She breathed in and said, "Zoe has more." She breathed out. "But I don't have less. I am not less." She pointed at me, and said, "You." She drew an invisible perimeter around herself. "Me."

"Okay," I said. "That's weird. Why *would* you be less?"

"What? You don't feel bad when other people get something you wanted for yourself?" she said.

"But, Sloane, you could easily get in anywhere," I said. "Prentiss . . . *wherever*. Why would you feel bad?"

"I can't go to a private school," Sloane said. "My family's Democrat and my father wants to be the president of the United States."

"Then what's the point of feeling bad?" I said. "It doesn't make any sense."

"Of course it doesn't make any sense. I'm competitive. It doesn't have to make sense. Oh, please. Don't even try to tell me you don't get competitive like that." When I couldn't deny it, Sloane said, "Exactly. It started to be an OCD thing with me, so I got help. What do *you* do about it?"

"Well, I don't have eleventy thousand dollars to spend on grooming my feelings . . ." I said. "So I just eat my heart out like a regular person."

Sloane said, "Well, this feels much better." She redrew the invisible perimeter around herself over and over.

"And—*bonus*—it doesn't at all look insane," I said. "Oh, God, I feel kinda good. I think I need to dance." And so I did. "How you like me now, Dad?"

"And *that* doesn't at all look insane," Sloane said. "So, that's who you're telling first? Your father? Are you telling Digby? How will he take it?" She paused. "So that means you're going to accept your spot?"

Each question left me feeling crummier than the one before. "I don't know. I haven't decided if I'm going yet."

"Of course you're going," Sloane said.

I glanced at my phone and saw more posted images of me. Ugly reality beckoned me off my cloud. "Great." Sloane had gotten back on my bed, so I sat down on the floor. "Do you think a lot of people have seen these? The pictures of Digby and me?"

"Sure. They're everywhere." When I groaned, Sloane said, "Sorry."

"Oh, God," I said. "It's so humiliating. I look so . . ."

"Are you and Digby together now?" Sloane said.

"No idea," I said. "Everything happened so fast."

"Although . . . what would 'being together' even mean for a guy like him?" she said.

"I get to carry the bail money?" I said. "I'm his steady alibi?"

I spotted the sleeping bag under a pile of shoes at the bottom of my closet and yanked it out.

"I guess before I worry about whom to tell, I need to figure out what I want to *do* about Prentiss. I'd better do it soon, though. It says here the deposit's due," I said. "I don't know. I mean, is it worth it to go for just one year? What will I even have time to learn in a year?"

"'Learn'? How the real world works, for one," Sloane said. "People don't go to places like Prentiss to *learn*. Stay home and read a book if you want to learn. People go to places like Prentiss for access. Colleges reserve places for Prentiss graduates."

"Is that really true?" I said. "I mean, it sounds like an elitist fairy tale."

"Look. On average, two-thirds of Harvard undergrads come from thirty thousand public schools, *but* five percent of each Harvard class comes from just *seven* private schools." Sloane said. "See?"

"It's four a.m. and you're switching between percents and fractions. I have no idea what you're saying to me," I said. "And I don't even want to go to Harvard."

"Ugh. Harvard's just an example. What I'm saying is . . . a handful of schools like Prentiss sent around fifteen of their grad class to Harvard last year while the public schools averaged point zero five of a person going to Harvard. You're dreaming if you think that's all because of merit and grades," Sloane said. "Trust me, they hold places for the preps."

"Nope. That's way too much math for the night I've had," I said. "God, just thinking about telling Mom makes me want to forget the whole thing already. Is that lame?"

"Lame," Sloane said.

"Plus, I feel like if I went, my father would be winning somehow," I said.

"Double lame." Sloane flopped back on my bed and said, "Your problems make me tired."

"You don't know, okay?" I slouched down onto the floor and propped my head on the rolled-up sleeping bag. "My parents are *divorced*. Everything I do is, like, a huge *choice*. Someone's always offended. New York equals Dad. River Heights equals Mom." I was already staring into the abyss, so I decided to keep going. "And how do I deal with the crap Digby's going to give me? Seriously. Being called 'Princeton' is annoying enough. I can't even think what he'll come up with when I tell him *this*." But when I did start thinking about it, I felt myself getting angry. "I mean, am I supposed to be embarrassed I want to go to a good school? Does he think—what?—that he can just blow into my life and suddenly be the most important thing? And what do I do when he decides to blow back out of town again? It took me, like, an entire week to get my life back together the last time he disappeared. And that was *bad*. It was, like, no-shower-no-food-for-a-week bad." Maybe that last bit was an overshare. "So *whatever*. Bite me, Philip Digby. I did *good*, dammit. I'm going to celebrate. I want ice cream. Do you want some ice cream?" Sloane was silent. "Hey, Sloane. Ice cream?"

All I got back from her was a snore. I sat up to find her sprawled out on my duvet, eyes shut and breathing deeply, already fast sleep. I didn't feel like going through the drama of peeling her off my bed, so I unzipped my sleeping bag and got comfortable.

I'd started the day at the apex of a love triangle and now I was ending it sleeping on the floor of my own room, wrapped in a filthy sleeping bag because I'd given up my bed to the mean girl who'd once stopped Austin and me in the hall and asked him, "Her?"

Things had definitely taken a turn.

FOUR

I woke up still holding the letter from Prentiss. When I rolled over, the first thing I saw was Sloane, looking at me with an intense stare that freaked me out. "What?" I said.

"I've never met anyone who's as good at being themselves no matter what," Sloane said. "You just don't care what people think. I wish I were that tough mentally."

"O . . . kay . . ." I could hear the build-up to what I now recognized as the trademark Sloane Bloom complisult structure. It gave a compliment . . . and then used it to tear a strip off your soul.

"And now everyone in school hates you and thinks you're a slut . . ." she said. "That skill's going to be a huge advantage. I really admire that in you."

"Wow. Stop. I don't think I can handle any more of your admiration right now," I said. "I've only been awake five minutes and I already want to kill myself." I got up.

"Where are you going?" Sloane said.

"I am now going to go cry in the shower until the hot water runs out," I said.

"What?" Sloane said. "What did I say?"

• • •

Later, I found Sloane sitting at the kitchen counter.

"So," Sloane said. "I was thinking."

"Goody. More thoughts." I noticed the full breakfast plated in front of her. "Oh, is my mom here?"

"I haven't seen anyone else this morning," Sloane said.

Weird. I'd just gone into Mom's room and noticed her unmade bed. She would only have left it like that if she'd been in a huge hurry.

"Are you telling me you cooked that?" I pointed at her plate of food. "Wow. That actually looks good."

"Rude," Sloane said.

"You're right. Sorry. Let's start again," I said. "You were thinking?"

"About, you know . . ." Sloane said. "You being the new school slut—"

"Yes, okay. What about it?" Hearing it filled me with renewed dread. "Let's work on phrasing, by the way."

"How do you want to deal with it?" she said.

"You're the school's queen bee. Can't you make it go away?

Give me a royal pardon?" I was half kidding but the half that wasn't kidding hoped she'd say yes.

"Maybe a few weeks ago. Right now . . . socially, things with me have been . . ." She made a rocking motion with her hand.

"Are you okay?" I said. I was surprised that she'd been able to negatively review herself with such breathtaking ease.

"Sure. I needed a break anyway," Sloane said. "It's really high-maintenance being me."

"That's a bold statement . . ." I said. "And a *lie*." When she tried to deny it, I said, "That, apparently, you are telling yourself. Sloane, you love being queen bee."

"I just need to take time off from those harpies," Sloane said. "Hey. I also need gym shoes. You want to come to the mall?"

"The *mall*? Together?" I said. "All right. What's really going on?"

"What?" she said.

"Sloane," I said. "What's going on?"

"Fine. You're not allowed to laugh." Sloane went into her phone. "I saw this and then I couldn't sleep for a week."

She then showed me video of one massive black chimpanzee beating the crap out of another chimp. The narrator said, "From the start it was clear that Frodo would rule through brute force . . ."

"Why are you making me watch monkey fight club?" I said.

"The big one's Frodo. Frodo's brother Freud was alpha until

Frodo pushed him out. Because Freud wasn't a bully when he was the leader, the group took Freud back. But see, Frodo was a bully . . ."

I could see it meant a lot to her but I didn't get it. I started to laugh.

Sloane fast-forwarded the video. "So when Frodo got sick, his group murdered him . . ." She showed me her phone. "There were bite marks on his balls, Zoe. Bite marks. On his *balls*. Think about it."

"I don't want to think about it," I said. "Wait. You're being nice to me so people won't think you're a bully? Shouldn't you go be nice to someone who's less hated than I am?"

"Maybe. But you're what I have to work with right now," Sloane said. "I think we should brainstorm about your situation. Our friend Bill has been posting all night. People are mostly calling you a home-wrecker and—your favorite—" Sloane paused for drama. "Skanky ho."

It was predictable of Bill but it still bothered me.

"You need to get in front of this," Sloane said. "Change the conversation."

"Change the conversation? These are high school kids. Can't get in front of that," I said. "Besides. Don't you have Henry to worry about?"

"Henry?" Sloane said.

"Yeah," I said. "Henry."

"Right." Sloane tsked and then got a wistful girl-let's-talk

38

look. "Well, I mean, of *course* I'm not dumping him. But I need to teach him a lesson. He needs to learn not to set off a bimbo eruption every time he's at a party without me—"

"No, Sloane. I wasn't asking about your love drama. I meant the cops. And the steroids?" I said. "We need to get our cover story in line. Make sure Henry's willing to go along with it."

"Screw him," Sloane said. "Maybe I don't feel like covering for him anymore."

But we needed her to. We'd accidentally taken a gym bag full of steroids from an ex-student named Silkstrom who'd been selling them near our school. To get around having to tell the cops about all the borderline illegal things Digby, Felix, Sloane, Henry, and I had done to uncover the fact that our football team's coach had been behind the entire dealing operation, Digby and I had handed the bag of drugs to Harlan Musgrave. Musgrave, a disgraced ex-cop who was now our school's truant officer, agreed to keep us out of the story when Digby told him he could use the credit for busting Coach to get himself back on the River Heights police force. It was a huge tangle of BS and everyone needed to tell the same story, including Sloane, no matter how mad she was at Henry.

I could see she was in no mood to be reasonable. "Okay, maybe you need a cooling-off period—"

The doorbell rang but I heard the door open before I even got to the front hall.

"Hello?" I said. "Mom?"

"Hi, Zoe." Felix walked past me into the kitchen.

Henry followed him in, all shame and slumped shoulders. "Hi, Zoe," he said.

Digby came in last.

"Did I leave the front door open?" I said.

"I still have the key Cooper gave me when I was staying here," Digby said.

"You still have that?" I said. "Shouldn't you give it back now that you've moved out?" I extended my hand to take it from him.

"I will," he said. "Next time I see Cooper."

"Meh . . . who am I kidding, anyway? You'll just break in," I said. "Once again, though, why is *my* place the clubhouse?"

"Henry's house is full of kids, we can't go to my place, and allergic-to-everything-everything over there tried to give me millet salad the last time I was over at his house," Digby said.

I lowered my voice. "Hey, did you talk to Felix about de Groot?"

"I didn't get a chance to. Henry kept me up all night. So much crying," Digby said. "Please never say the word *football* to me again. Or *future* . . . or *scholarship* . . ."

"You can't do that to Felix, Digby," I said. "His whole family—"

Suddenly, a mug of coffee flew out of the kitchen and smashed against the wall.

"Whoa whoa whoa . . ." I said.

Digby and I ran into the kitchen just as Sloane threw

another mug at Henry. Digby caught this one before it hit the cupboards.

"Sloane, can you teach him this lesson at your house?" I said. I pointed at Henry. "And you, get that stupid hangdog look off your face. It just makes her madder. Nothing happened with Maisie. You don't have anything to apologize for—"

Sloane slapped the kitchen counter. "Excuse me. *Nothing?*"

"Yes, because—I'll say it once more—*nothing happened.*" When she started up again, I said, "That's as good as it's going to get for you, Sloane, so take it." She started to protest again, so I said, "I don't want to hear about how he let Maisie think something could've happened blah, blah, blah . . ."

Digby laughed. "Uh-oh, Mom's maaaaad . . ."

"And *you*." I turned on Digby. "You can't just walk in here."

Digby said, "I rang the bell."

"If you'd called, I could've told you it wasn't a good time to come over," I said.

"But we should coordinate our story before anyone starts asking questions," Felix said.

"Screw it. I'm not lying for him." Sloane stared at Henry and said, "I hope you die. Or go to prison, and then die there."

"Sloane, could you just . . ." I made a mouth-shut gesture. "So, Digby? Do we need to get proactive?" I said. "Go to the police before Coach talks? What if he tells them that we were the ones who brought the bag of drugs to school?"

"I doubt Coach *would* talk. Like I said before, Coach's lawyer will probably tell him not to make things worse by mentioning the fact that on top of everything, he tried to murder four students," Digby said. "Coach won't talk."

"What about Silkstrom?" Henry said.

"What about him?" Digby said.

"Do I need to tell my family to look out for Silkstrom?" Henry said. "In case he decides to come after me?"

"Silkstrom sold drugs for Coach, Coach is in jail, so technically, Silkstrom's unemployed," Digby said.

"So you don't think I need to worry?" Henry said.

"I doubt it. We're not dealing with the mafia or anything," Digby said.

"What about Musgrave?" I said.

"Does Musgrave know we're involved?" Sloane pointed at Henry, Felix, and herself. "What did you say when you talked to him yesterday?"

"Man, that was yesterday," Digby said. "Feels like weeks ago."

I knew what he meant. It had been a dizzy twenty-four hours. I endured weeks of stress about the SATs only for the test to be canceled when Coach almost burned down the school during his attempt to kill us for figuring out he'd been selling steroids to his players. And then Digby's nine-year quest to find his sister came to a head later that night during his conversation with de Groot.

"I never mentioned your names. As far as he knows, it was just me and Princeton," Digby said. "I think."

"So, do you think we might've saved the season?" Henry said.

Digby shrugged. "Maybe?"

"Will we need to talk to the police?" Felix said.

"I don't think so," Digby said. "Musgrave's going to say he cracked the case all on his own."

Felix put his hand on his chest and exhaled. "My mom's still mad at me for what happened last semester . . . I don't think I can afford to get in trouble again."

I gave Digby a hard look but he didn't get the message. "Digby? Isn't there something you need to tell Felix?" When Digby looked away from me and stayed quiet, I said, "Hey guys. Digby's had a breakthrough. With Sally."

"What?" Henry said. "What breakthrough?"

"That's amazing," Felix said.

I gestured to Felix. "But now he needs your help." I wanted Digby to say it.

"Me? How?" When neither of us answered, Felix said, "Tell."

"Okay," Digby said. "I finally figured out who took Sally, Felix."

"Have you told the police?" Felix said.

"Told the police? No. It wouldn't help. This guy . . . let's just say he's untouchable," Digby said. "Felix, he says he'll tell me what happened to my sister. But in return . . ."

"What?" Felix said.

"I have to give him what he was after nine years ago," Digby said. "He wants everything my mother was working on at her lab at Perses."

Digby waited for Felix to fully absorb what that meant.

"Hang on. Your mother's lab is my father's lab now." Felix sat down. "Oh. You plan to steal it from my father's lab." He stared at Digby. "You already know how you'd do it?"

"With a spoofed software upgrade that would install a root-kit on your dad's computer. I noticed you and your dad share videos of dogs doing people things, so I was going to send you one of a dog eating at a dinner table with human hands. I was pretty sure you'd forward that to him," Digby said.

"Who could resist?" Felix said.

"And then once he clicked that link," Digby said, "I'd own his and every computer on his network."

Felix looked stunned. "You weren't even going to tell me?"

"But I would only copy my mother's files, Felix. I wouldn't touch the rest." But then Digby muttered, "Well, maybe I'd look around a little . . ."

Felix snapped out of his trance and said, "A rootkit?"

Digby took a USB key out of his jacket suit pocket.

"You wrote it already," Felix said.

To his credit, Digby looked ashamed.

"Did you at least write a script to clear all the event logs?" Felix said.

"Of course," Digby said.

"Including the router logs? The IDS logs?" When Digby

didn't answer, Felix said, "So the next time they do a security audit, they'd see my father's computer was used in the hack?"

"I could go in and do a bash-history," Digby said.

Sloane looked at me but I was just as lost as she was.

"You don't think a million shredded files would look suspicious?" Felix held out his hand. "Give it to me."

At first, Digby resisted Felix when he tried to take the USB from his hand but eventually, he did surrender it to Felix. And then Felix immediately dropped the USB key on the floor and ground it into smithcreens with his foot. "There's a reason I write all your code for you."

I hated seeing the devastated look on Digby's face. "Isn't there a way for Digby to get in the Perses system and get it himself without involving you or your father?" I said.

"Even the best hacks leave a trail. The most you can do is destroy all the logs, but like I said, that's suspicious too. They'll dig around and eventually . . . they'll find their way back to me and then my father." Felix shrugged. "It's data. It's not a physical object where you can go in, boost it, and then disappear."

"Except when it *is* . . ." Digby said. "A physical object."

A long beat passed before Felix finally caught on. "Because it becomes a physical object—"

"Whenever they perform a backup," Digby said.

"How often do they back up?" Henry said.

"To comply with federal laws, corporations have to back up their data for disaster recovery on the regular," Digby said. "So if there were an earthquake or flood or whatever, they could restore and immediately get going again. Perses still puts tapes into a cold-site storage, right? They haven't started using the cloud?"

"I don't think so. My parents haven't said anything," Felix said. "They would've mentioned converting to the cloud . . . probably . . ."

"Wait. We'd have to steal thousands of tapes, wouldn't we?" Digby said. "Google uses something like fifty thousand tapes per quarter."

"Well, number one, Perses isn't Google—they wouldn't have even one percent of that information," Felix said.

Digby said, "But even one percent is still, like, hundreds of tapes—"

"And, number two, I know for a fact that Perses backs up in silos. They go department to department and my father's is happening soon, because he complained about it recently," Felix said. "A hundred and eighty-five terabytes per tape . . . it shouldn't be a crazy number of tapes."

"How soon will it be?" Digby said.

"I don't know," Felix said. "I could ask—"

"No, don't," Digby said. "He'll know something's up."

"I could check my dad's email," Felix said. "Look for alerts."

"Better," Digby said.

"How's *that* better?" I said. "What if he gets caught reading his dad's emails?" I noticed that Digby was studiously avoiding making eye contact with me.

Digby said, "Felix."

"Yes?" Felix said.

"Don't get caught," Digby said.

"Okay," Felix said.

"Wait. You can break into his email account?" I said. "Why can't you just break into his work—"

"I don't have to break into his email account. I know his phone's four-digit passcode. I wait until he charges it and then I open his email app," Felix said. "I'm excited. Pulling off a heist is number five on my bucket list."

"Wait," Sloane said. "Won't those tapes be hard to steal?"

"The servers back up on a schedule and believe it or not, the tapes are sent to storage using normal couriers. The data of almost four million Citibank customers was left in the open because they shipped their data tapes through UPS, and UPS lost them." To Felix, Digby said, "That's what you're thinking, right? Take them while they're being moved?"

Felix nodded.

"And you're sure they haven't changed that?" I said. "Seeing as how now they know how easy it is to steal?"

"Felix, can you find out?" Digby still wouldn't look at me.

"Yeah. I'll try," Felix said

"Well, this is quite a Sunday. Basically, we went from talking about one crime . . ." Sloane pointed at Henry. "To planning a whole new crime."

"And does either of those crimes involve drunk driving

home from a night of underage drinking at a lakeside party?" Cooper said.

We all jumped. None of us had even heard the front door open. Cooper walked into the kitchen dressed in his cop uniform. My heart still instinctively flip-flopped at the sight of the shiny shield pinned to his chest. He'd been dating my mom since the end of last year and had been living with us for months, but Mike Cooper would always be, first and foremost, a cop. And, more specifically, my arresting officer.

"There were three separate calls out to that party last night," Cooper said.

"No, don't worry. No drunk driving," I said. "Sloane's driver brought us home last night."

"Oh, so that's *your* car out there?" Cooper said.

"What? Is Hince here already?" Sloane looked out the window and shook her head. "Where? I don't see him . . ."

"There." Cooper pointed out the window. "I assume those private security–looking guys bird-dogging the house are here for you."

"Uh, Zoe," Sloane said.

I joined them at the window and saw de Groot's two security guys—the ones I thought of as Taller Guy and Shorter Guy—sitting in a black SUV pretty much directly across the street from my house.

"Most people just hire swolled-up gym freaks who can barely move, much less actually fight. But that little guy"—Cooper pointed out the window at Shorter Guy—"might actually mean business. Are they not here with you?" He turned from Sloane to look at me. I tried not to crack under Cooper's stare but Sloane looked uneasy. "Something I should know?"

I emptied my head of all the incriminating thoughts that might have played across my face.

"Because there's also the matter of your football coach getting busted with a big ol' bag o' drugs. Busted by Musgrave," Cooper said. "*Harlan Musgrave?* Do we need to talk about that?"

"Who, me? I'm shocked. Shocked." Digby took Sloane's plate and filled his mouth with a forkful of her eggs. "Drugs in school? Shocking."

"Because I *know* Harlan Musgrave." Cooper laughed. "He's not smart enough to uncover a drug operation." And then Cooper pointed at Digby. "But you are."

Digby just smiled back and kept eating Sloane's eggs.

"When did you have the time to do it? With your school, job, internship . . ." Cooper said.

"I didn't. And even if I did have the time, do you think I'd waste it helping that creep Musgrave?" Digby said.

"Internship?" I said.

But Digby was still ignoring me.

"Huh. I guess they're lost," Cooper said, looking out the window. De Groot's men had pulled out maps and made a show of pretending to be searching through them. I suppose the three of us lined up at the window looking right at their car wasn't exactly subtle.

Cooper walked to the coffeemaker, poured himself a cup, and sighed. "If I weren't so exhausted, I'd work on you kids a little more about those steroids." Cooper pointed at Henry and said, "I don't think it'd take much work to crack this one." And then he went upstairs.

When we heard the bedroom door close upstairs, Henry said, "He's right. I can't lie for beans. I'm busted."

"Calm down, Henry," Digby said. "You won't have to lie. They're not even going to ask you about it." He took a bite of Sloane's toast and muttered, "I hope."

Sloane stepped away from the window and said, "But what about those guys?"

"Don't worry about them," Digby said. "They're here for me." He brought the plate of food over to the window, tapped on the window with his fork, and waved when Shorter Guy looked up.

"What?" To me, Sloane said, "And you're not worried? They're outside your house."

I thought about it. "No," I said. "I think they're just here to watch."

"'To watch'?" Sloane said. "Seriously, you guys?"

Digby shrugged and nodded.

"Never mind. I don't want to know," Sloane said. "You two live weird lives." She got a text message and looked out the window. "Oh, here's Hince now. Anybody need a ride?"

Felix raised his hand and started to follow Sloane and Henry out of the room. Before he left the kitchen, though, Felix said, "Digby, I will never forget that you changed my life. The bullying was so bad, I was basically ready to give up on regular school. But if you ever endanger my family with another piss-poor plan like that—*ever*—I will *end* you." And then he left.

Digby finally looked at me and said, "He could do it too."

I grabbed Digby's arm as he walked away. "You aren't staying?"

"I should get going," he said.

"You're mad," I said. "Because I told Felix." Digby just stared at the floor. "You want me to say sorry."

"But you won't," he said.

"Because I didn't do anything wrong. He had a right to know," I said. "And if your priorities weren't so messed up—"

"Hold on. You're making me sound like I'm some ruthless deviant," Digby said. "I was just using all the tools in my toolbox."

"That's all we are? Tools?" I said. "Is that what you tell yourself to make things easy when the time comes for you to turn on us?"

"Oh, don't give me that," Digby said. "You know what I mean. And if we're talking about turning on people—"

"You mean telling Felix? Give me a break. That was the decent thing to do," I said. For a second, I wondered if he had a point. I wasn't a hundred percent on solid ground lecturing him on loyalty when I was sitting on quite a few secrets myself.

51

"And anyway—isn't this a much better plan than the one you came up with on your own? Like you said—use all your tools."

"So you want me to say thank you," Digby said.

"But you won't," I said.

And then he walked out the door.

FIVE

I woke up from a night of crummy sleep, still obsessing that Digby had gone radio silent. I debated starting a text fight with him so we'd at least be talking. And then there was the problem of the post-party blowback I knew I was going to face in school. But eventually, I got acclimated to the swirling vortex of dread in my stomach and I propelled myself out of bed and got ready to go.

I was just about to leave when Cooper came in from work.

"Hey, Mike, do you know where Mom is?" I said. "She left yesterday morning before we got up, and I don't think she came home last night."

The series of weird expressions Cooper wrestled with before he finally found his straight face reminded me of his having once said that they never let him go undercover.

"She had a work thing," Cooper said. "Came up suddenly."

"On Sunday? And it lasted all night?" I said. "What kind

of all-nighter emergency comes up for a community college English professor on a Sunday?"

"She said it was complicated," Cooper said. "That she'd explain later."

I couldn't tell from the way Cooper was acting whether he actually knew where she was and was covering for her or if Cooper himself didn't know where Mom had gone and was trying to cover up his embarrassment. Either way, I was just as happy when he ran up the stairs and saved us from having *that* awkward conversation.

• • •

I didn't know how I should dress for my public shaming. After trying on basically everything in my closet, I'd settled on a combination of shapeless and mud-colored clothes I hoped would help me blend into the walls. It didn't work, though.

The staring and snickering started on my way up the walk to the main entrance. Not absolutely everyone I walked past was in on the joke but enough people looked my way that I was sure the students who weren't yet in the know would be looped in soon. I'd be trending by lunch.

I put on headphones and listened to an old favorite as I fixed my eyes before my feet and walked head down to my locker. It was a relief not to hear what people were saying. With the world on mute, the song's lyrics felt even truer. Faces look ugly when you're alone.

• • •

After just four months basking in the warm sunshine of Austin's and Charlotte's and Allie's companionship, being back out in the cold was brutal. I felt profoundly alone walking between my classes.

I spent the morning watching everyone talk about me. I experienced some small, petty things—like when some idiot waggled his tongue at me as I walked past and when a girl laughed at me when I passed a worksheet back to her in class—as face-melting humiliations. But I knew the worst was yet to come.

Lunch. That would be when the truly creative would shine.

I kept my new routine of pulling on my headphones the moment class was dismissed. When lunch rolled around, I gritted my teeth and added a book to my armor. I joined the chow line and read the same patch of text over and over until it disintegrated into a meaningless blur of print.

I succeeded in drowning out the world until I had to move my headphones off my ears to order my food. It was then that I heard one of the kids ahead of me say, "Can I get some cole-slut—*oh, snap*—I mean, coleslaw, please." And then he and his friends all turned and laughed at me.

I put my headphones back on and hastily muttered "Pizza" even though I could see it was covered in slimy roasted peppers that would make me gag.

"Damn it," I said. I walked away from the counter, determined to get a grip.

Old Me would've slunk away and eaten in the library stacks. But Old Me was long gone. And so, as painful as it was to be stared at, New Me sat my butt down at a sparsely populated table of assorted randos and tore into my disgusting pizza.

I was so deep into my act of looking at ease, I didn't notice that someone was at my elbow, talking to me, until he pulled off one side of my headphones and yelled, "Wake up, Miss Webster."

It was Musgrave, looking intense as usual.

"We need to talk about our problem," he said.

"Problem?" I said. I had so many problems I needed time to figure out which one he meant.

"That your notebook is still in police evidence," Musgrave said. "Do you understand what kind of crapstorm there'll be when they find that notebook and you and I end up telling different stories about how it got in Coach Fogle's bag of steroids?"

I didn't feel like engaging but I had to point it out. "Actually, that bag technically belonged to a guy named Silkstrom. Ex-student who did the actual dealing . . ." I said. "Though he *did* work for Coach Fogle."

"*What?*" he said. "It isn't even Fogle's? *What?*"

His voice had a hysterical edge that pierced the dull lunchtime buzz.

"Listen, shouldn't we . . ." I gestured at the dining room around us, where people were starting to turn and stare.

Musgrave said, "Music room. Ten minutes."

• • •

Even though I didn't get an answer when I messaged Digby to meet me, I was disappointed anyway when I walked into an empty room. But I didn't have long to dwell on that, because Musgrave arrived and got right into it.

"I still cannot believe you left your notebook in the bag," Musgrave said. "That was dumb."

"'Dumb'? You mean like clocking in five days a week right next to Fogle and not realizing he was dealing drugs?" I think we were both surprised by how aggressive that came out. "There was a lot going on at the time. It was an accident that my notebook got in there."

"Accident?" Musgrave's eyes narrowed. "Or maybe you two planted those drugs on Coach Fogle?"

"That's not what happened," I said.

"Why don't you tell me how this *did* happen? From the beginning." When I didn't speak up, Musgrave said, "You'll tell me the story if you want me to sell this as my bust."

Where to begin. Should I tell him we'd accidentally stolen Silkstrom's bag during a failed fake drug deal we'd arranged in order to flush out whoever was selling to the kids on the football team? Or should I keep it simple and stick to our story of finding the bag and then using it to carry my stuff and forgetting to unpack my notebook before handing it over to him? I wished Digby were there. But he wasn't, so I made a judgment call.

"Look, we realized Coach Fogle was selling when we found

57

the bag he left in the locker room. We took it to report him. I was holding a bunch of books at the time and one of them must've fallen in when Coach chased us," I said. "That's it. Whole story."

"'He left it in the locker room'?" Musgrave grimaced as his monkey brain processed that. "Are other faculty involved? Were other students involved?"

"Like I said, we just found the bag," I said. "I don't know anything more."

"Well, even the greenest public defender would be able to use the notebook to mud up the case and get Fogle sprung," he said. "And if your name"—he pointed at me—"is anywhere on that notebook . . ."

I thought hard about whether my name was written anywhere in the notebook, and while I was pretty sure it wasn't, I also couldn't say I was a hundred percent sure people couldn't figure out whose it was by reading closely. The thought made me wince.

Musgrave noticed my face drop and said, "Then you need to disappear that notebook."

"It *doesn't* have my name on it," I said. "And, anyway, why can't *you* go get it?"

"I told you. I am *not* getting caught tampering with evidence," Musgrave said. "*You* go get it." He pointed at me again. "Your mother's dating Cooper—"

I said, "Let's leave Cooper out of it."

Musgrave said, "Well then, what?"

"I'll take care of it," I said.

Nothing shuts up a bully like giving him what he says he wants.

"You can do it?" Musgrave said.

I didn't know exactly what I was promising but I nodded anyway. "I should get going. Lunch is almost over," I said.

"Fine. But that notebook better be gone before I give my official statement or I'll tell them a CYA story instead," Musgrave said.

"When are you giving your statement?" I said.

"My lawyer and I are going into the DA's office on Thursday," Musgrave said.

It crossed my mind that CYA story meant Cover Your Ass and that it would have to be a pretty big story to cover that angry man's ass. And that made me laugh.

"You kids think everything's a joke," Musgrave said. "I cannot wait until I'm out of here and far, far away from you morons."

Me too, Musgrave.

• • •

All I wanted to do when I got home from school was to bake up some wings and put on some fake reality so I could watch people survive worse things than my current situation and feel maybe things weren't so bad. I tried to comfort myself with the thought that I'd survived the trek through the desert of high school friendlessness before but the idea that none of the supposed new friends I *had* managed to make were working out made me even sadder. Digby, Sloane, Henry, Felix . . . yeah, okay. But shenanigan friends were different from lip gloss and lunchtimes. A girl needs both.

I was actually starting to feel better halfway through my meat and garbage TV binge, but then the horrible thought occurred to me that I'd have to get up and have the same crappy day all over again. And the next and the next until the people at school found someone else to ridicule. And then I realized if I self-soothed like this after every school day, I'd be headed for a coronary before summer vacation.

The detritus of my pity party filled the kitchen trashcan and when I went outside to dump it, I recognized a familiar logo on a lipstick-stained napkin sitting on the top of our trash. It was from a café in our old neighborhood in Brooklyn. Mom still talked about how much she missed their coffee.

"She was in the city?" I said. Just to make sure I wasn't looking at an old napkin she'd found and only now just thrown away, I rubbed the lipstick mark. The pigment was fresh enough to still smear under my finger. "She was in the city."

• • •

I mumbled my way through dinner. My mother didn't seem to notice I'd put a little extra mustard on my usual hostility dog and, of course, that pissed me off even more. I watched her mouth move as she rattled off some weird account of her day at work without really hearing what her singsong voice was trying to tell me.

I was in bed reading when she knocked, opened my door, and said, "Everything all right?" She had a huge smile on her face that annoyed me even more.

"I'm fine," I said.

"Are you sure?" She ignored my attempt to blow her off and came over to the bed to feel my forehead. "I don't think you have a fever."

"No, I don't have a fever," I said. "But . . . I might have one tomorrow morning." I was sort of kidding when I'd said it, but taking a sick day did sound good.

"Oh?" she said. "Do I need to worry? Are you actually sick?"

"No, I'm just tired," I said. "Worst case, I'll have a mild cold that could last until Wednesday." She made me move over so she could sit next to me on the bed.

"Sounds serious."

"No, no. I'm okay," I said.

"I know what it is. You've checked out of school, right? Mentally, I mean," she said. "I bet you're dying to get out of here." She hugged me. "Oh, Zoe. Thank you for being so *so* good about moving here with me. I'm going to miss you. But this is right. You belong back in the city."

"Mother." I peeled her off me. "Is this about the summer? I'm gone for two weeks."

"Zo-e." Mom bobbed her head side to side in that inside-joke way. "I know. I *know*."

"You 'know' what?" I said.

"I *know*," Mom said. "About Prentiss . . ."

"You do?" I said. "How?"

"I woke up after you got home from the party and when I came in here to check on you, I found you passed out in your sleeping bag, holding that letter like . . ." She mimed how I'd been sleeping with my fist clutched against my chest. "I'm so proud of you. Congratulations, babe." She hugged me. "You see? You didn't even need your dad's help."

"You told him already?" I said.

"Your dad? No. I thought you'd want to tell him yourself." She looked confused. "Why? Is something the matter?"

"I just need time to decide if I'm going," I said.

"Time to decide? What do you mean you need time to decide?" Her smile dropped. "*Zoe*. Of course you are going to that school."

"I don't know, Mother," I said.

"Are you playing hard to get now?" she said. "After all the emotional blackmail crap you've been pulling on me for moving you out of New York City? *You need time to decide?*"

"'Emotional blackmail crap'? So when you said I was really good about moving here, you were just being nice because you thought I was leaving?" I said.

"Zoe, I'm confused," she said. "Is this about that boy?"

"I assume you mean Digby," I said.

62

"How many times have I said it? Never change your life to fit a boy's." She jumped off the bed and said, "The closest thing I have to a regret is dropping out of grad school—"

"Okay, yes, thank you. This is all great advice, Mother. Super helpful. Not at all condescending," I said. "And by the way, didn't you drop out of school because you were pregnant with me?"

"Zoe." She put on her therapy-approved soothing Mom voice. "All I'm saying is . . . I don't want to see you making big life decisions based on hormones and what feels good in the moment—"

"Hormones? And 'what feels good in the moment'?" I said. "Do you mean, like, cheating on your current relationship with your ex-husband?" I got a rush from watching the shocked expression cross her face.

"Is this still about the texts from your dad inviting us on a family trip? I've told you. I was just trying to be friendlier with him . . . for my own sanity. I was sick of our divorce being so predictably petty," she said. "How could I know I'd sweep him off his feet just by being civil?"

"Ohhh . . . I see. You didn't mean to lead him on." Even before I'd blurted it out, I knew what I was about to say was wrong. But I was too angry to stop. "There isn't a little part of you that wanted to mess with his new marriage? Maybe show that skank *Shereene*"—I leaned on my father's new wife's name and enjoyed the cheap thrill of watching my mother's face fall—"that cheaters can't change their spots? How far did you

63

go to show her? Hey, what did you tell Cooper you were doing yesterday?"

"*Zoe.*"

I could see my mother struggling to repress whatever mean comment she had in the barrel to fire back at me. "I can't believe you're doing this again," I said. "You never learn."

"And what, exactly, haven't I learned?" she said.

I didn't feel like getting any further into it but I'd gotten her going, so I didn't see that I had a choice. I sighed.

"If you're going to attack the entire history of my relationships, then you're going to have to do better than a judgmental sigh," she said.

"It's so annoying watching you do the same things with Cooper that you did with Dad," I said. "You withhold, then you're *outraged* when they give up and check out on you."

"*Wait.* I withhold? You think your father checked out on our marriage because I was withholding?" she said. "Are you blaming *me*? For his cheating?"

I suddenly worried that maybe that was exactly what I was implying.

"Careful, Zoe. You are punching way above your weight," she said. "And what am I supposedly *withholding* from Mike?"

I opened my dresser drawer and pulled out the dirty napkin I'd dug out of the trash. I threw it on the bed.

And then, emboldened by my mother's silence, I said, "Did you at least get him to pay for your plane ticket? Or do liberated women go Dutch on booty calls?"

And I thought I'd won the fight when she just turned and walked out of my room. In fact, I'd already moved on to struggling with the guilt of having been mean to her when she walked back in and threw a thick envelope on the bed.

"Open it," she said.

"What is it?" When she didn't answer, I opened it to find money. Lots of money. Money bound in thick bank-fresh bundles. "Is this Dad's money?"

"It's *my* money," she said. "I went to the jewelry place near our old apartment and sold my engagement ring. I wanted to make sure we could pay for boarding at Prentiss."

"What? Why?" I said.

"Why?" she said. "What do you mean 'why'? Your father will definitely pay for tuition, but unless you want to live with him and Shereene . . ." She pointed at the cash on the bed.

"I don't even know that I'm going yet," I said.

"I mean, maybe I misread this situation. But what else was I supposed to think? I assumed you wanted to go. You went and did all this applying . . . in secret . . ." Mom paused. "How *did* you do all this, by the way? Didn't they need paperwork from your parents?"

"The proof of financial ability stuff? Yeah, they did ask for that," I said. "I used the copies you had on file from your mortgage application for this house."

"Wow. Pretty crafty," she said. "But see what I mean? That takes real effort. How was I supposed to know you weren't serious about going?"

"I need to think about it, Mom."

"Do you want to think about it together?" she said.

"No thanks. You know I like to think for myself." I handed the envelope of money back to her. "I'm sorry you went to this trouble."

"You and I need to work on our communication. And of course Mike knew what I went into the city to do. He and I have our ups and downs but we're on the same page for the big things." Mom picked up the dirty napkin from the bed. "You have a big, beautiful brain, Zoe. Don't use it to make yourself miserable."

SIX

I spent the next morning lolling around in bed, trying to convince myself that the excused absence note I got from my mother wasn't totally a lie because I felt legit bad enough to justify skipping school. But then I started thinking about the last time I serial skipped, before my parents got divorced, and I remembered how after two days, I basically felt like I *couldn't* go back to school. I spent so much more energy digging myself out of that trap than I would have if I just hadn't started skipping in the first place. I decided to take my chances and got dressed.

I was oblivious with my headphones on and my head in my locker when Sloane poked me in the ribs.

"Damn it, Sloane," I said. "What?"

"What is all this?" She waved her hand to indicate my clothes.

"What does it look like?" I said.

"It looks like we have a possible school shooter," she said. "What are you wearing?"

"I just thought it might help me gut it out today." I pointed at my all-black-everything outfit. "I kicked a lot of ass in these clothes."

"Then why didn't you wear your prom dress with the glued-on feathers? You blew up an entire house in that thing," Sloane said. "Or have you already released it back into the wild?"

"Can we just move on to the conversation you came over here to have with me? Or was this just a drive-by insult assault?" I said. "Where were you yesterday?"

"I took a personal day," Sloane said. "Actually, I'm surprised you came to school . . . have you seen . . . ? Or are you not doing any social media right now? Because wait until you see what that little—"

"Careful. Phrasing," I said. But then I glanced down at her phone and saw the hashtag below a post of my picture. " 'Ugly ho'?"

"Yes, she sure is," Sloane said. "You know, sometimes, that's just the right word."

"No, I'm reading out the hashtags on these posts about me." I grabbed her phone. "They're calling me ugly now too? What happened? I feel like it's getting worse."

"That's what I'm trying to tell you. It got worse when someone posted that you get off on hooking up with guys who are already taken and that you did the same thing with Henry as you did with Digby," Sloane said.

"'Someone'?" I said. "It wasn't *you*, was it?"

"Ha-ha," Sloane said.

But we both knew who it was.

Sloane rolled her eyes at me and we both said, "Bill."

"She is human click bait," I said.

"She is, like, my greatest fear," Sloane said.

Despite myself, I kept scrolling. "Sloane . . ." I showed her the phone's screen. It was a picture of Henry and me talking very closely. "This post is yours."

"That's an old post of mine that got reposted today," Sloane said.

"Hashtag SwiperNoSwiping, hashtag Skank, hashtag ShadyHo?" I said. "Those are your hashtags."

"Those are old," Sloane said. "It's from back when you were—"

"I know, I know. From back when I was making a move on your boyfriend," I said. "Speaking of whom . . ." I pointed down the hall to where Henry was standing, looking around with a little lost boy expression on his face. "Is he okay?"

"Ugh. He's being super-high-maintenance. He doesn't know who to trust . . . he doesn't want to be around his teammates," Sloane said. "He follows me everywhere. Literally, he tried to follow me into the bathroom this morning."

I gave her phone back.

"But I thought you should know," Sloane said.

"Yep," I sighed. "Now I know."

• • •

I went into the library right at the end of the day. I was hoping to avoid running the hallway gauntlet of people letting off whatever last little bit of meanness and poison they had left in their tanks before heading back to their home-cooked meals and good-night kisses. I'd just walked up to the librarian's desk when I spotted Bill herself sitting at one of the nearby computers.

I didn't even break stride. I just executed a tight turn and walked straight back out the door. I kept a brisk pace in case she'd spotted me. My heart sank when I heard her yell my name. I picked up speed and started making random turns until I cornered myself in a hallway that dead-ended. I turned around to run but *boom*, there she was.

Bill put her hands up and cowered. "I come in peace."

"What do you want?" I said.

"Can we talk?" Bill said.

I said again, "What do you want?"

"Things are getting crazy," she said. "For a while, you and I were trending—"

"Stop acting like you're surprised. You created this monster," I said.

Bill said, "Actually, it only really took off after Sloane's old posts got bumped up—"

"What do you want, Bill?" I said. "Or are you just here to give me a progress report on my garbage fire of a junior year?"

"I have an idea about how we can stop this," Bill said. "Stop all the social media hate." She paused for applause.

"Well?" I was interested enough not to walk away.

"I think we should write something. Together," Bill said. "A she said–she said."

"'Why is it a girl-versus-girl thing?' 'Guy gets a pass when he was the one cheating?'" I said. "Does that sound like the articles you had in mind?"

"Plus a little something about love triangles," Bill said. "Why they happen—"

"Love triangles happen because people get confused about their feelings for the partner they already have," I said. "High school is hundreds of people at peak horniness spending eight hours a day together while being told that absolutely no way can they have sex. There's going to be confusion."

"Hey, now I'm worried your half will be better than mine," Bill said.

"Number one, if I ever *did* write it, it would certainly be better than yours," I said. "But number two, I would never write it because it's a cliché."

"It's a cliché? *You're* a cliché," Bill said. "First Henry, then Digby—"

"I'm not getting into this with you because even though I hate your guts and want to punch you directly in the face, we are both better than this conversation," I said. And then I realized what she'd been implying. "Wait. Are you telling me that you could stop my cybertorture if I agree to write this thing with you?"

Bill looked shifty when she said, "I think so."

"You 'think so'?" I came to my senses. She was full of it. "Dream on, Bill. You might've kicked off this nightmare, but you can't do squat now." I laughed in her face. "I bet you *need* to write something to remind people you were involved in the first place." I turned and walked away. "Why am I even talking to you?"

• • •

Having made it through the school day, I went to the mall to go to work. Or at least, I tried to. The sickening feeling of reality shifting faster than I could handle got even more intense when I arrived to find the bookstore was shut. I got some of my frustration out by kicking the metal grate pulled down over the glass doors. Actually, it felt so nice I kicked it twice. On the second kick, I noticed a flyer for one of the Japanese restaurants in the mall tucked in the slats. The small fish on the logo was circled in red pen.

It felt like a Digby thing. I looked around me, fully expecting to see him standing off to the side with an obnoxious smirk on his face, watching me to see how long I'd take to get whatever joke the fish in the circle was supposedly telling. But he wasn't there. And then I realized the circled fish was probably a message from Fisher.

I got to the Japanese restaurant and found Fisher sitting at the bar. Except the long-haired book-loving secondhand bookstore manager hippie I'd known was gone. This Fisher had a new, high and tight haircut and wore a fitted golf shirt over khakis. This Fisher looked like the kind of guy the Digby family would've hired to negotiate with Sally's kidnappers.

"The store didn't open today?" I said.

"I didn't think you'd want to run the place on your own," Fisher said. "Greg gets promoted to manager starting tomorrow."

"You quit?" I said.

"You think I liked that hair? You think I liked those clothes?" he said. "You weren't home from school yet when I came by your place yesterday to let you know I was quitting the bookstore. I don't want to scare you but I saw de Groot has men watching your house." When I didn't look surprised, he said, "But you knew that."

I shrugged.

"Wow. You're not freaked out?" he said. "That's ten points for poise."

I flashed the menu he'd left for me. "This was pretty cryptic. You could've been waiting here for nothing."

"I knew you'd get it. Besides . . ." Fisher gestured at piles of

73

paperwork in front of him. "I had stuff to keep me busy while I waited."

"What is all this?" I said.

"I have an exit routine I like to do when I leave a place," he said.

"Oh . . . you're out of River Heights, then?" I said.

"I have a new gig." He held up a brochure for seaside condos. "Nice calm corporate gig someplace warm. I'm going in-house for a Big Oil outfit. It's the closest I'll ever come to retirement."

I don't know why, but I felt the urge to tell him. "I think I'm out of here too."

"Oh?" Fisher said. "That Prentiss School? I didn't realize you were applying. Well, congratulations. What does Digby think?"

I shrugged and tried to keep it breezy. "Digby knows I always hoped to finish out high school back in New York."

"So you haven't told him." Fisher laughed when I winced. "That'll be an interesting conversation."

"Yeah," I said.

Fisher was studying my face. "If you're sure it's what you really want to do. You don't look so sure . . ."

"Well, when I applied months ago, I was sure that it was the right thing for me," I said.

"And now?" Fisher said.

"Well, now . . . I'm finally starting to get used to this place. Starting over would be . . ." The thought of it exhausted me.

"Like, 'All my stuff's here anyway'? Sure. Inertia. I get it."
Fisher nodded. "But of course you're going."

"Everyone keeps saying that like I don't know my own mind.
It's kind of rude," I said. "I really don't know if I'm going."

"Okay. Let's come at it from another angle," Fisher said.
"Why did you apply in the first place?"

"It's a good school. They run mock college interviews.
Loads of amazing speakers come in to talk about life after
school. They have two full-time career counselors and because
of who all the parents are, the seniors get rotated through really
incredible work experience," I said. "Between all that, *someone*
might finally figure out what I'm good at."

"Sold," Fisher said. "Sounds good to me."

"Sounds good to me too," I said. "My mother's excited. My
father will be too, when I tell him."

"Just you, then? You don't look that excited," Fisher said.
"And of course, Digby won't be excited."

I shrugged. "Who knows? He might not even care. I don't
think friendship means the same thing to him as it does to
other people," I said.

"Uh-oh," Fisher said. "What did he do this time?"

"He called us 'tools in his toolbox,'" I said. "Pissed me off."

"Yikes. Not the best way to say it. But to be fair . . ." Fisher
said. "Kidnap victims' families endure the worst things. To get
through the things they need to get through, their ethical system kind of gets . . ."

"Eliminated?" I said.

"More like suspended," Fisher said. "He's learned to walk away from the direction his moral compass points him to because most of the time, the satisfaction he's looking for is in the opposite direction. I've seen law-abiding people take out loans they know they'll never pay back. Perfectly normal people hire hit men to murder the people who kidnapped their loved ones."

"Sounds like you're making excuses for Digby," I said.

"I'm not making excuses. But for *your* own sanity, try to understand the kind of psychological stress he's experienced," Fisher said. "Okay. End of lecture."

"When are you leaving town?" I said.

"Next week," he said.

"Does that mean you're quitting Digby's case?" I said.

"Not quitting. I'm just putting it on the back burner for the next little while," he said.

"Fisher . . ." I wanted to tell him everything. About de Groot, about the deal Digby made . . . but the picture of his new apartment's sea-view balconies looked like heaven and I didn't want to ruin it for Fisher with tantalizing news about Sally. Especially since it could all mean nothing in the end.

"What?" he said.

"Nothing. Just . . ." I said. "I hope this isn't the last time we see each other."

"I doubt it," Fisher said. "But since you mentioned wanting career counseling . . . here's some. Think about *my* job." When I laughed, he said, "I'm serious. Consider it. Money's good.

Money's incredible, actually. Lots of travel. Crime is a growth industry . . ."

"I think this is more a conversation you should have with Digby, not me," I said.

"Oh, he's a smart kid, no doubt about that." Fisher's smile wavered and he tilted his head. "But what he really cares about is finding out what happened to his sister. I'm not sure he'd be half as good when he doesn't have that to care about anymore."

"But I think he generally enjoys being crafty and making fools of people," I said. "Why would he ever stop that?"

"I didn't say he'd stop being *that* guy but look, it's like this . . ." Fisher said. "Everything Digby has done has been for Sally. All that focus . . . the stamina . . . would he have that if he weren't looking for his sister? I don't know. All these years, Sally's been his Moby Dick, and nobody ever looks to Ahab for tips on fishing. You, on the other hand are the complete angler." He pointed at me. "I want *you*."

I had to laugh at Fisher's intensity. "Moby Dick, the complete angler." I pointed at him. "*Fisher*. Three fishing references. I get it."

"Actually, I can't stand fishing. Boring." He shook my hand. "I hope I see you around, Zoe Webster."

• • •

I'd just gotten myself a drink at my favorite coffee cart when I spotted Austin coming out of the bathroom. Before I could process what I was doing, I'd already ducked behind an instant photo booth.

Why am I hiding? I thought.

I stepped out feeling brave but when he looked up from his phone and almost caught me creeping, all the cool got sucked out of me and I dove back into my hiding place. Who was I kidding? I wasn't ready for small talk and easy-breezy friend hugs. So I peeked around the corner and resumed spying on him instead.

Austin had gone back to his phone. Watching him, I finally let myself admit that I'd never liked the vacant strings-cut look his face got whenever he was texting or surfing. Like he had enough brainpower to *either* use his device *or* not be a zombie but not to do both at once.

My decision to cower behind the photo booth paid off when Allie came down the hall with some football guys and cheers, skipped up to Austin, and tweaked him in the side.

Austin laughed, they kissed, and my jealousy flared. But after the sting of seeing them together passed, I saw how Austin and Allie looked more of a pair than Austin and I ever did. Allie even got along with all his friends in a way I never managed to. Austin and Allie. Sitting in a tree. Doing all the cutesy things he could never get me to do with him. They belonged together. And I suppose that was fine.

But where did *I* belong?

SEVEN

I honestly wasn't fully conscious of what I was doing when instead of going home that night, I got on the bus to Digby's place. I knew I hadn't done the wrong thing forcing him to tell Felix, but at the same time, I knew that I'd broken some kind of unspoken Accomplice's Oath. I needed to make it right.

I got to Digby's bus stop without yet having formed a plan of how to start this conversation and when I got to his front yard, I seriously thought I should turn around and leave. Maybe he was right. Maybe we needed to be apart for a little while. But I kept walking to his house anyway.

By this time, I'd already climbed onto his porch and I was about to turn and walk away when I heard a loud crash from inside the house. I dithered, trying to figure out whether I should ring the bell. I decided against it and instead went around to the back.

I looked through their kitchen window and saw Digby and his mother, Val, at the sink, having an agitated back-and-forth over a sizzling pan he was still smothering with a charred apron. Val was crying and I could hear her shouting "Sorry" from where I was standing outside. When the fire was fully put out, Digby threw the burned pan in the sink and hugged his mom to calm her down. He eventually got her to stop crying and walked out of the kitchen.

I felt guilty about having stayed there watching them and I was just about to sneak away when I heard banging on the kitchen window. I stood up from my crouch to see Digby's mom smiling at me.

Val opened the window and said, "Sorry, did we miss your ringing the bell?"

"No, I didn't actually ring the bell," I said. "I came back here because I heard a crash."

"Oh . . . I see," Val said. "Do you want to come in?"

"I should get home," I said.

"Did you two fight?" Val said.

I nodded.

"That's what I thought. I notice he's been using his sleeping meds these days," Val said. "He doesn't like taking those and he only does it when something's really bothering him."

I didn't want to start a conversation I couldn't finish about Digby's conversation with de Groot, so I just nodded again.

"The pills don't work, by the way. The sleep he does get is garbage. I think it'd be better if he just solved whatever problem was bothering him." She waved me toward the back door. "Come in," she said. When I hesitated, she said, "Please come in. . . . He's been sad all day, staring at messages on his phone that he refuses to respond to. He definitely won't sleep again tonight if you don't make up with him." I still didn't move, so she said, "And you don't look too happy either."

I finally gave up and nodded. "Okay."

On my way to the door, Val said, "You know, since my daughter was taken, no one in this family has had an ordinary emotion. It's almost a relief to see him pouting over a girl like a normal teenager."

I didn't have the heart to bust the fantasy of normalcy she'd built around me, so I said thank you and reached to take the bottle of water she was offering.

Before she let go of the bottle, Val said, "Not that I want him to have his heart broken. Be careful with him."

• • •

I went upstairs but then lost my courage again outside Digby's room. I stood pressed up against the wall, trying to figure out if I wanted to open with an apology just to get the ball rolling . . .

"Are you coming in or not, Princeton?" Digby said.

I froze.

"I know you're out there," he said. "I can smell your old-lady perfume from here."

"Actually, it's my hand lotion." I entered his room. "You're chewing on a Slim Jim and your bedroom smells like old dirty socks and yet you're claiming you can smell the lavender in my hand lotion?"

"My great-aunt Ruth used to have the same one," Digby said. "I'd know it anywhere."

"So I eat like your great-aunt Ruth and now I smell like her too?" I said. "Considering you just made out with me . . . is there something weird there?"

"Great," he said. "More stuff to bring up in therapy, I guess."

And that was all the small talk we had in us. We both let it be awkward for a long beat.

"So," Digby said. "I guess you're here to . . . not apologize?"

"Something like that," I said. "Did you apologize to Felix?"

"Actually, I did," Digby said. "He gets it. *He* knows what this means to me."

"Seriously?" I pointed at the scar on my chin—my souvenir from the first time he'd gotten me to break into a place with him. "So you're implying that *I* don't get what this means to you?"

"Okay, yeah, that was a crappy thing to say," Digby said. "I didn't mean that." He came closer. "But I'm still angry."

"You wouldn't have been able to live with yourself if I'd let you do a sleazebag thing like that to Felix," I said.

"I'm pretty sure I could have. I've done a lot of sleaze-bag things," he said. I could see I'd made my point, though, because his face softened and he moved even closer to me. "In fact, I'm pretty sure I'm straight-up just a sleazebag."

"You aren't," I said. "You're a better person than you think you are."

"I guess we'll have to agree to disagree," he said.

Another awkward moment passed.

"Are we good?" he said.

"I don't know," I said. "Are we?"

He pulled off my scarf and kissed my neck.

"Digby." I didn't want to spoil the mood but I had to say it. "There's something else. Musgrave came to talk to me yesterday. He wants us to steal my notebook from the evidence locker."

"Stealing from the police . . . that's interesting pillow talk, Princeton . . ." Digby kicked the door shut and led me to the bed saying, "But weirdly, I like it."

I said, "He says the DA—"

"Ooh, now the district attorney is in the mix," Digby said. He eased me down onto the mattress with him. "You know, I've always thought *subpoena* was a sexy word . . . say 'subpoena,' Princeton."

I felt myself losing focus when he started to kiss my collarbone, so I tried to push off him. "This is serious, Digby."

"Okay, sure, keep talking. I can multitask," he said. "This is kind of the fantasy, actually. My special lady friend has a head for business and a bod for—"

"It was my diary." It was such a relief to finally tell him.

Digby was so surprised, he pulled away and said, "Pardon?"

"The notebook I left in the bag with Coach's—"

"Oh, no, I heard you." Digby sat up. "I just can't believe what I'm hearing. That's your diary in police evidence?" When I nodded, he said, "And you're just mentioning it *now*?"

"I was embarrassed," I said.

"Well, is your name in it?"

"Of course not," I said. "Who writes their name in their diary?"

"But they'd be able to figure it out from the other names in there. Triangulate Austin, Allie, Charlotte . . ." he said. "And, of course, *me*."

"I didn't use any names," I said. "Only first initials."

"Wait, I thought you said you weren't keeping a diary," he said. "'Too busy'—isn't that what you said?"

"Shut up," I said. "There's more."

"What? Don't tell me there are pictures in there." When I didn't answer fast enough, Digby practically yelled, "*Pictures?* You and Austin couldn't even sext like regular people?"

"No, calm down. Not pictures," I said. "What I was about to say before you drove yourself nuts just now is that Musgrave is giving his official statement the day after tomorrow. He says that if we don't get my notebook out before then, he's going to tell them that we were the ones who gave him the bag."

Digby's eyes narrowed and he stared out the window for a while. And then he said, "Nope."

"'Nope'?" I said.

"He won't do that," Digby said.

I made skeptical noises.

"Let's enter the Musgrave mindscape and game this situation, shall we?" Digby said. "What would happen if I were Musgrave and I now told the police that, *actually,* I didn't bust Fogle and, *really,* a bunch of high school students had handed me the bag and the bust . . ." Digby pondered it for a second and then said, "Well, first of all, I'd look like an idiot for taking credit for the last three days since the bust. *And.* How's it going to look that I worked with the guy for *years* without realizing what Coach was doing? He'll want to claim he at least had a hunch during that time—"

I said, "Musgrave did *not* appreciate it when I pointed out that exact same fact to him . . ."

"On the other hand, if I were Musgrave, and I *didn't* tell anyone about how I really got the bag . . . all I'd have to do is let the police believe whatever other, more likely, reason they themselves come up with about how a teeny bopper's diary might've gotten into a bag lying around in a high school locker room. Like, maybe it fell in. Or, maybe Coach found it and stuck it in his bag . . ." Digby shrugged and smiled. "I mean, that lie practically tells itself. And then, in return, I get all the credit for cleaning up the school and *probably* I'll get to be a cop again? *Bam.* Easy decision."

"I have to admit, that's a pretty good impression of an incredibly lazy person's thought process," I said. "Now I'm wondering if we're doing the right thing turning him back into a cop."

"Don't worry," Digby said. "He'll screw himself back out of the job even before he has a chance to fail his physical."

"So you really don't think we need to go get it?" I said.

"That notebook is not going to be a deal-breaker, I promise you," he said.

That reassured me enough to let him help me out of my jacket. Then I belatedly heard something he'd said a minute ago. "Wait. Did you really just call me your 'special lady friend'?" I said.

"Uh-oh," Digby said. "You'd prefer that I use 'girlfriend'? Isn't that a little . . ."

I was embarrassed that I did prefer it and was mortified that Digby might think I was getting ahead of myself by assuming we were more than we actually were.

But then Digby just said, ". . . basic?"

"Then what would you call me?" I said.

"Is this us trying to have the are-we-official talk?" Digby laughed but he wasn't mocking me. He was nervous too. "Well. Since we're talking now . . . *are* we?"

It was nice to see him off center too, for once. I just smiled.

"You're messing with me," he said. But he knew the answer to his own question. We both did.

We kissed and by the time I next opened my eyes, Digby had kicked off his shoes, thrown off his jacket, and had half-unbuttoned his shirt.

"Whoa," I said. "You got undressed fast—"

We both froze at a huge crashing sound in the kitchen.

When it was quiet for the next few seconds, Digby said, "She's fine—"

But then his mom yelled, "Phil-ly! Help!" When Digby didn't immediately answer, she ratcheted up the drama and screamed, "Help! Help! Help!"

"You'd better go help her," I said. "Before the neighbors call the cops."

"She suddenly decided she wanted to make her own yogurt but she keeps walking away from the pot and burning the milk." Digby started buttoning up his shirt and stepped into his shoes. When he saw me put my jacket back on, he said, "No, no, don't move."

"I really need to get home," I said.

"Are you sure?" he said.

"I should go," I said.

"Damn it," he said. "So close."

"Yeah, right." I laughed. "It wasn't close."

"Are you sure you have to go? I mean . . ." He leered at me and did a not very graceful body roll.

To which my only reply was, "Wow."

He ran his hands over his torso. "There's all *this* here," he said.

"Ha-ha. Surprisingly, I have not changed my mind," I said. There was another loud crash downstairs. "Better hurry."

"Hey, Princeton. That Felix thing . . . we're good?" He stuck out his hand.

"We're good." I shook his hand. "But the real question is . . . what about you and Felix? Are you sure you two are good?"

"Well, he accepted my apology but . . . actually, he hasn't been answering my messages." Digby laughed and said, "I'm starting to get the feeling he isn't totally on board."

"Can you blame him?" I said.

"Nope. Not at all. *I* wouldn't be involved if I didn't need to be." Digby stared at me for a little while. "In fact, I'm not so sure *you* should be involved. Maybe you should sit this one out . . ."

"Shut up. Don't be ridiculous," I said. But it was the first time I'd ever seen Digby this uncertain.

• • •

Ever since Saturday morning, I'd been living with a low but steady buzz of some unnamed impending doom. But now that Digby and I had made up, the terrible hum had been dialed down a notch. I got home from Digby's place determined to get my life back on track. I squashed down my anxiety about having to return to school in the morning, stayed off my phone, ate my dinner, and wound down with a book rather than exhausting myself with overthinking.

I don't know how long I'd been asleep before I woke up with a sudden stab of understanding. I finally knew what that subsonic hum had been trying to make me remember for the last three days.

"Oh, no," I said. "*No.*"

In a cold sweat, I jumped out of bed and thrashed my way through the pile of papers on my desk even though deep down, I knew what I was looking for wasn't going to be there.

My mind rewound back to the months-old memory of being on the bus, doodling daisies on a piece of paper while I listened to music on the way to work. I remembered being overcome with a momentary insanity that moved my hand to write down the single stupidest thought I have ever had: MRS. ZOE DIGBY. I think I might even have written it down twice.

Just remembering the way the words looked on the page shorted out my mind. It felt like millions of my brain cells suddenly cried out in terror and were suddenly silenced. Except there was actual screaming. I screamed so loud that I woke up my mom and then I had to fake a foot cramp to get rid of her.

EIGHT

I spent half the next morning hoping that by some dare-to-dream stroke of luck, I'd look in my book bag and find my stupid page of doodles wadded up at the bottom. The other half, I spent messaging Digby to meet me. No reply.

By the end of school, I couldn't take it anymore. I took three buses to get to the police station. Even though I hadn't heard back from Digby, I waited out front for a few minutes, hoping he would turn up. After a while, I went inside and approached the desk sergeant.

"Oh hi, Zoe, what's up?" the desk sergeant said. "You know Mike doesn't come on until tonight, right?"

"No, actually, I'm here to see Officer McPheeter," I said.

Young and handsome gym enthusiast Officer Abe McPheeter had introduced himself to me at the department's Christmas party and I would've been more receptive to his flirting if I hadn't just started dating Austin. Cooper hadn't been happy when he spotted us talking in the corner and he'd made sure everyone at the party had heard him yell at Abe to "back off them high school girls." Which of course meant that I was busy for the rest of the night because Cooper's warning had made him even more determined to get me to agree to go out with him.

"Abe McPheeter?" he said. "What for?"

"Um . . ." I swallowed down my embarrassment and said, "It's personal."

"Personal, huh? With McPheeter?" The desk sergeant looked worried and said, "Mike is not going to like *that*." But he pointed the way to the uniformed officers' bullpen anyway.

"Excuse me," I said. A few of the cops looked up from their desks. "Is Officer McPheeter around?"

Amid the laughter that my question got, one uniformed officer said, "He's on his break. Or as you might call it . . . *recess*."

"Hey, Aaaaabe . . ." another uniformed officer said. "Another one of your little groupies has come a-calling."

Abe peeked out of the break room, smiled, and waved for me to come over. I crossed the bullpen and joined him in the otherwise empty room.

"Hi, Abe." I tried to evoke jailbait vibes and said, "Do you remember me?"

Abe said, "Of course. Chloe."

"Close," I said. "Zoe."

To compensate, he turned up his smile another notch. "Of course."

I said, "I was just wondering. Remember at the party when you noticed my hands . . ." And then I noticed that his hands were covered in dye. "Why are you purple? Oh. And it's all over your shirt too."

"It is? Oh, man." Abe looked down and groaned. "Idiot intern accidentally deployed an entire stack of dye packs on me."

I'd just said "Idiot intern?" when from the corner of my eye, I saw the jerky shuffle of a very familiar pair of long legs enter the room and walk to a spot directly behind Abe. I didn't need to peer around Abe to be sure that Digby had walked into the room but I did anyway. I momentarily dropped the smile I'd put on for Abe and gave Digby my best nasty look. That's when I noticed the yellow lanyard around his neck was holding an intern badge. Digby raised his coffee cup and toasted me.

"You were asking me about something I said at the Christmas party . . ." Abe said.

But I'd been totally derailed by Digby's unexpected appearance. "Uhhhh . . ."

"Something about your hands?" Abe said.

I watched Digby take a banana from the fruit basket, lean against the counter, and start peeling it in the most annoyingly pointed way. *Go on,* Digby gestured.

"Um . . ." I fought to get my face to relax back into an inviting expression. "You said I could test out the new biometric equipment with the mobile fingerprint scanner?"

"I did?" Abe said. "Wow. I must've been drinking on an empty stomach, because that is majorly inappropes."

"I could ask Mike, I guess." I hated having to give this performance of fake petulance in front of Digby, who, by the way, was now nodding and giving me a thumbs-up.

"No, no, it's okay. I can do it," Abe said. "I mean, this is for school or something, right?"

"Um . . . yeah," I said. "For a paper."

Digby suddenly spoke up, saying, "What class is that for?"

Abe jumped and grabbed his chest. "Geez. I didn't even see you come in here. Like, *at all*." Which tells you a lot about the quality of policing River Heights was getting.

"Excuse me?" I said.

"What class?" Digby said. "What's the paper about? It sounds like a *cool* class."

"Um, we're having a private conversation here," I said. "Abe, can we . . . ?" I gestured out the door.

"Sure. But I should go wash this off first." Abe leaned in, rubbed my arm, whispered, "*That's* the idiot intern," pointed at the mess on his hands and shirt, and then left the room.

When we were alone in the break room, Digby whispered, "Really? This is where we're at?"

"Shut up . . . he's right there." I pointed out the door.

"Oh, sorry. Wouldn't want to ruin your date," Digby said.

"Shhh," I said. "Anyway, now that you're here, do you maybe want to help me?"

"What for? You have it under control," he said. "Give him some accidental contact in the bathing suit area and he'll probably just go fetch it for you."

"Are you jealous? Is this you being jealous?" I said. "Seriously?"

He pointed at my mouth and said, "And is that lipstick? You never wear lipstick for *our* dates."

"When have you *ever* taken me on a date?" I said.

"What about that time in Olympio's?" he said.

"I paid," I said.

"No. The other time," he said.

"I pay every time," I said.

"And how un-feminist is it to get hung up on who paid?" Digby said.

"This is not the time for that discussion," I said. "Are you going to help me or not?"

Digby took a bite of banana and smiled. "You don't need me. He will be very, very easy to steal from . . ."

"Unbelievable." I turned to leave the room.

I was so annoyed, I almost missed Digby's saying, "I mean, I've already stolen from him once today."

When I finally absorbed that and turned around, Digby was reading from an open notebook I realized was my diary.

"You have it? You had it the whole time?" I tried to take it from Digby but he held it high above his head and out of my reach. "Give it to me," I said. "That's private, you sociopath." I finally just hit him in the gut and caught my notebook when he dropped it. I flicked through the pages, hoping hoping hoping I'd find the sheet of incriminating doodles.

"All December long . . . will they? Won't they?" Digby said.

"I hate that you read my diary," I said. But I couldn't find that damned piece of paper.

"Looking for something?" Digby said.

"No, uh . . . I guess I didn't . . ." I smiled at Digby. "Nothing."

Abe poked his head back into the room and said, "Is everything okay?"

I was about to answer when Digby said, "It's okay, man. She says she'd rather go on the intern tour." And then Digby grabbed my hand, spun me, dipped me, and then kissed me.

I heard Abe say, "Oh . . . I guess I'll see you later, Chloe?"

Abe was gone by the time I opened my eyes again.

"You're such a jerk," I said. "He's nice and he didn't deserve that."

"Oh, yeah? I saw him wait until you had your back turned to him and then pop some Tic Tacs," Digby said. "He's not *nice*."

Gross. "Okay, fine." I tucked the notebook into my purse. "Let's go."

"What? I can't." He pointed at his intern badge. "I'm working."

"Are you kidding?" I said.

"Until six thirty," he said.

"Are you coming over for dinner after?"

"Will you wear lipstick again?" he said.

I rolled my eyes and said, "Walk me out so I don't have to walk past Abe alone."

• • •

I went home and called out from the front door, "Mom, Digby is coming to dinner." But then I entered the kitchen and realized right away that I'd made a horrible mistake. From the width of the smile Mom gave me, it was obvious she'd made dinner with a goal. It was the exact wrong time to be bringing home a complication like Digby.

Mom smiled and sang, "Family dinner." She turned her horrifyingly sunny expression on Cooper and stared until he forced a similar grimace onto his face.

"You know . . . studies say the benefits of family dinners include higher self-esteem and better academic performance." Cooper looked like he was in physical pain as he tried to remember the exact phrasing my mother had clearly fed him.

"Whoa," I said. "Are you okay, man?"

Cooper said, "And speaking of better academic performance—"

"Oh, God, Cooper. I can see why they never let you go undercover," I said. "I have *not* made a decision about Prentiss, Mom."

"The deposit is due soon, Zoe," Mom said.

"I'm aware, Mother," I said.

"That was a little tone-y." Mom looked at Cooper and said, "Did you hear a tone, Mike?"

"Yes, I'm sure he did. Because I put a tone in there," I said. "Mom. I need to figure it out for myself."

"And Digby? I'm sure he's had a lot to say about it," Mom said.

It was none of her business and I was still struggling to find a way to tell her so with a level of outrage that stayed on the right side of dignified when the doorbell rang. "That's Digby," I said. "Can we argue about this later? In fact, can we just not talk about it in front of . . ." I pointed toward the front door.

"What? Why not?" Mom said. "He doesn't know?" When I didn't answer, she gasped. "He *doesn't?* Why haven't you told him?"

"Just." I didn't have the words, so I put my hands together and made a pleading gesture. "He doesn't know. Yet. I will tell him soon. For now, could you please . . . ?"

"Certainly. I will *withhold* that information," Mom said. "Oh, wait. Now I'm confused. Should I be withholding? Or will that cause him to check out?"

I ignored her, opened the front door, pushed Digby back out onto the porch, and closed the door behind us. "Hey, I need you to promise me you won't say anything."

"Anything about what?" Digby said.

"It's just, like, a blanket request. Don't talk about anything real," I said. "Keep it casual."

Digby laughed. "This is going to be a fun dinner, I can tell," he said.

I was already turning the doorknob to go back in the house when I remembered to say, "And I should just apologize right now. My mother is—"

"'In need of chill'? 'All about herself'? 'So drama'?" Digby said.

"You have to stop quoting my diary back to me, okay?" I said. "It's deeply creepy."

"Relax. It's just dinner." Digby kissed me on the cheek, handed me the bottle of sparkling water he'd brought as his hostess gift, and pushed open the front door.

We walked back into the house but before we could turn the corner and enter the kitchen, Cooper peeked out of the living room and gestured for us to come over to him. He was on the phone, though, so he held up his finger to signal us to wait quietly for him to finish his conversation.

"No, Phipps, I don't want to hear the expired Chinese food story again," Cooper said. "Just text me the picture you *did* get of the guy." Cooper hung up the phone and said to Digby, "Did you hire someone to look at your sister's case files?"

"Why?" Digby said.

"Remember my old partner, Stella? Well, she put an alert on your sister's files. Anytime a FOIA request gets processed, we get a message. Well, someone requested the file and left word

to have the material up at the front desk for pickup today,"
Cooper said. "Now, I told the desk sergeant to take a photo
when they came in but unfortunately, Sergeant Phipps was
indisposed when the pickup happened. All he got was a cell
phone picture of the guy leaving."

"Can't you just look at the CCTV?" I said.

"Broken," Cooper said.

And then Cooper and Digby both said, "Budget cuts."

Cooper's phone beeped. He showed us the photo he'd just
been texted. "Recognize this guy?"

Digby shook his head and said, "No . . ."

But Digby and I both knew we were looking at the back of
Shorter Guy's head. De Groot was definitely up to something.

Cooper zoomed in on the picture and tilted his head. "Does
that maybe look like the little guy I thought was watching the
house the other day?"

I could tell Digby was as surprised as I was that Cooper
might not be completely oblivious after all. "Uh . . . I don't
know. I don't think so. Zoe? What do you think?" Digby said.

"Um. I guess that's the back of some short white dude's
head, so . . . maybe?" I said.

Mom called out to us from the kitchen. "Hey, are you guys
coming to dinner? Or am I eating alone?"

When we all walked in, Mom said, "Hello, Digby. Welcome
to dinner. I made your favorite." She waved at the dining table.
"Food."

I rolled my eyes and started eating, figuring that the less

I spoke, the less opportunity there would be for me to spark some horrible chain of comments that would lead to any of the many Awkward Subjects I was hoping to avoid. Eventually, though, it became *too* quiet and it was a relief when Digby opened the mineral water and pierced the silence with the explosion of carbonation.

"So," Digby said. "How's it going?"

Mom sighed and said, "Thank you. Zoe said we weren't allowed to talk and I was starting to think I'd have to sit here just listening to you all masticating for the rest of the night."

Digby smiled and said, "She told me not to talk too. I can't tell if she was worried about me offending you or you offending me."

"Zoe?" Mom said. "Which is it?"

I shot the two of them dirty looks and ladled myself some more soup. "You're both equally offensive," I said.

"'Equally'?" Digby said. "Well, since you're already offended . . ."

"I think she just declared the season open," Mom said. She and Digby smiled at each other across the table.

"Lightning round?" Mom said.

"Five apiece?" Digby said.

"Hit me," Mom said.

"Oh, God," I said.

Digby said, "Did you ever want to be anything besides a professor?"

100

"No. I went to grad school because I like reading and I didn't know what else to do after college," Mom said. "Come on, kid, you can do better than softball questions like that."

Digby said, "Did you ever think Zoe's father was your soul mate?"

Mom said, "Not even for a second."

Digby said, "Then why did you marry him?"

"Because he took me on an all-expenses-paid trip to Turks and Caicos but he wouldn't pay hotel shop prices for condoms," Mom said. "I got pregnant."

Cooper did a spit take with his soup and had to go to the sink to clean off his shirtfront.

Digby said, "Do you regret it?"

"No, because from that, I got this beautiful creature who brightens every single one of my days . . . and will, hopefully, wipe off my drool when I'm senile," Mom said.

"Does it bother you that she and I are together?" Digby said.

Mom smiled and said, "So it's official now?" She took a deep breath. "No. It doesn't bother me that she's with you. Austin was very hot . . ."

"Mom," I said.

"But he used to pronounce *cojones* 'cow-jones' and he used to say 'yous guys,' so I knew it was doomed," Mom said. "This is actually a better fit." She waved at Digby and me. "Okay, that's five. Now switch. First question . . ." She reached over, took Digby's hand, and gave it a squeeze. "Are you doing okay?"

Digby nodded, blinking at the break in the tone. "Uh . . . I'm okay."

Mom took her hand away from Digby's and the interrogation resumed. "What are your intentions with my daughter?"

Digby said, "All honorable but still fun."

"Have you two . . ." Mom wiggled her eyebrows.

"*Mom.* You could've asked *me,*" I said.

"Okay, Zoe, are you and Digby having sex?" she said.

"That's none of your business," I said.

Mom threw up her hands.

Digby said, "No. We have not."

Mom looked relieved. She said, "How serious are you guys?"

"We're still figuring it out but . . ." Digby pulled a piece of paper from his jacket pocket and unfolded it. I was instantly horrified. Digby was holding my MRS. ZOE DIGBY doodle. I'd forgotten the garland of hearts and flowers I'd drawn around it.

Mom clapped and yelled, "Oh, Zoe . . ."

"Princeton, I just wanted to say . . . yes. Yes. Yes. A thousand times, *yes,*" Digby said. I snatched the paper out of his hands.

"And, finally, an easy but important one," Mom said. "Okay, Digby, as far as I can tell, your life is a hot mess—"

"Mom."

"But I'd like to think there's a plan under all this," Mom said. "What do you want to be when you grow up?"

Actually, I didn't know how Digby would answer that. And apparently, he didn't either, because Digby put down his spoon and thought long and hard before saying, "I think this might get my street certification revoked but I plan on going to college, doing, like, a combination computer science and actuary degree . . . then heading out west after graduation . . . if there's anything left out there after the robots take over . . ."

"So, you're saying 'there's a great future in plastics'?" Mom looked as unimpressed as I felt.

"No one under forty knows that movie, Liza," Cooper said. "I actually think that's a good plan, Digby." He patted Digby on his back.

"Wow. I would've thought you'd be happy because I didn't say art thief or conman," Digby said.

"I just didn't expect you to say something so bourgeois," Mom said. "I mean, going from your current lifestyle . . ."

"It's not like I chose the hard-knock life, Miss Finn," Digby said. "The hard-knock life chose *me*."

I tried to imagine Digby in a nine-to-five and it thoroughly baked my noodle. For the next few minutes, I watched Mom, Cooper, and Digby talking easily and felt like an alien at my own dinner table. I was so thrown off that when Digby told me he couldn't stay for long because he needed to help his mother with her nightly medication ritual, I actually felt relieved.

NINE

I was at my locker the next morning, trying to use the "almost there" Thursday feeling as motivation to get through the day, when Sloane sidled up.

"Hey, are you all right?" Sloane said. She sounded so worried, she got me going too.

"What do you mean? I put on makeup. I even kind of did my hair," I said. "I thought I was doing well."

"That *is* what I mean. You almost look happy," Sloane said. "Clearly, you are still not looking at your social media. Because they are dragging you through the garbage today . . ."

"Did you come over here just to bum me out?" I said.

Sloane said, "No, actually—"

"Oh, God, here comes Bill," I said.

Then, just in case there was any doubt that she was coming for me, Bill folded her hand into a finger gun and shot it at me.

As she'd calculated, some of the people milling around in the hallway noticed and started to stare at me, waiting to be entertained by my reaction.

"That's, like, a level-two lookalike firearm violation. She'd be suspended if we told," Sloane said. "But she'd probably love it. She could cry on camera about her constitutional rights. She probably already has an outfit all picked out and good to go because she thinks a CNN interview is, like, her destiny."

"I can't even look at her," I said.

The second I turned away from her direction, though, Bill yelled out, "Zoe. We need to talk."

Now *everyone* in the hallway was looking at us. I saw phones go up to record and some people made the loathsome and yet entirely predictable series of cat hisses and growling.

"Ugh. They want a catfight," Sloane said.

"I just cannot deal with this girl right now," I said.

"Then don't," Sloane said.

It was lucky my locker was already locked because Sloane suddenly grabbed my hand and took off running down the hall with me.

"Sloane?" I said. "Where are we going?"

"Who cares," Sloane said. "Away from *her*."

Bill got closer and we heard her bleat, "Come back, you guys. Wait."

"Ew . . . she's catching up," Sloane said.

Sloane pushed me through the doors of the woodshop

room. We ran through, out of breath from running and laughing now too.

"I think we lost her," I said.

Bill again called out, "You guys. Zoe?"

"She's getting closer." Sloane pointed at the open window and we started running. We were almost at the window when Sloane slid on a grease patch. She would've hit the deck hard if I hadn't caught her. More adrenaline surged through us, which meant more uncontrollable laughter. By the time we rolled ourselves out the window onto the lawn outside, we were laughing so hard, we couldn't talk. We walked around to the other side of the building to catch our breath.

"That was a little mean," I said.

"Seriously?" Sloane said. "After what that girl has done to you, you can't even hold on to a grudge?"

I laughed. "Digby said exactly that to me about *you*." I immediately regretted saying it.

Sloane's laugh died down. "Right."

"Sorry. Another thing I can't hold on to is a feel-good moment," I said. "Hey, how are things with Henry?"

"I informed him he was on boyfriend probation, I yell at him all the time, and he really feels lousy about what he did, so . . . things are going according to plan," Sloane said. "The training continues."

"Wow . . . that sounds super healthy," I said.

"I think your judgey tone would get to me if we hadn't just

climbed out of the window to get away from one of *your* relationship casualties," Sloane said.

"Yeah, you're right," I said. "What do I know?"

"I don't feel like going to civics," Sloane said. She gasped. "We should go to the mall."

"I want to . . . but I feel like I've been cutting a lot of classes lately," I said.

"Who hasn't?" Sloane said. "They just teach the textbook—"

The window beside us opened and Miss Riddell, Principal Granger's secretary, leaned out and said, "Zoe Webster, right? You're wanted in the conference room."

"Ugh. Shop blocked," Sloane said.

Miss Riddell had already retreated back into her room but popped out again, "Oh, wait. You too, Sloane Bloom. Conference room."

Sloane rolled her eyes. "I am so done with high school already."

· · ·

We opened the conference room door and found Digby sitting alone at the long table. Our faces all changed when we saw each other.

I closed the door behind me and said, "We thought we were getting called in for cutting classes. You don't think this is about Musgrave, do you?"

"Are the police here?" Sloane said.

"I doubt it," Digby said. "The police don't usually put out cookies for an interrogation."

"What cookies?" I said.

He pointed at a plate of crumbs in the middle of the conference table.

"I read that the CIA gives torture victims Big Macs to get them to talk," I said. "It makes them relax their defenses."

"Well, that is effective, because all I can think of now is how I could go for some milk," Digby said. "God, I would kill for a cold glass of milk."

"Should we worry?" Sloane said.

The sound of footsteps approaching shut us up. All three of us sat back in our chairs and steeled ourselves to what might come through the door. Soon, we heard whispering voices and the doorknob started turning.

"So, to be clear . . ." I said.

"Deny deny deny," Digby said. "As usual."

I heard Sloane's sharp inhale when the door opened. But it wasn't the police at all.

Allie stepped into the room, saw my face, and physically recoiled. She turned around, tried to run, and plowed into Austin and Charlotte, who were walking in right behind her.

"Oh," Austin said when he saw me.

"Oh," Charlotte said when she saw me.

Austin ducked back around and checked they'd gone to the right room.

"No, buddy. This is the place," Digby said. "Have a seat."

Clearly, Digby had felt the same relief, because he'd gone right back to being a jerk. I unclenched my fists and mentally unwound.

From under the table, Digby kicked out the chair across from us and sent it sliding toward Austin . . .

. . . who caught it, carried it back to the table, and pushed it under Allie, before doing the same for Charlotte.

I turned to see Digby watching me notice what Austin had done and felt self-conscious.

"You know, they say Jack the Ripper also had excellent manners," Digby said.

"What's wrong with you, man? It's over. You got my girl," Austin said. "All the rest of us are moving on."

"Look at us . . . I miss this," Digby said. "I miss *us*."

Austin looked at me and said, "Are you having fun, Zoe?"

"Hey, Zoe," Allie said. "I feel like I haven't seen you in years."

That's because you've acted like I was invisible every time we've crossed paths for the last four days, I thought. But instead, I said, "Things have been crazy."

The door opened again and our guidance counselor, Steve, came in. Steve wore the acid sweet I-care-so-much expression on his face that set my teeth on edge as he guided—who else— Bill into the room and to the seat next to him.

"Hello, all," Steve said. "Is everyone comfortable?" We didn't answer but anyway, he said, "Good. Because we are about to get real today. Everybody ready?"

Digby muttered to me, "This is what I get for coming to school."

"You're not being punished, Philip," Steve said. "And if I do my job well, we will all leave here today feeling *great*." He clapped his hands. "This is going to be a positive experience."

Charlotte put her hand up. "Steve? Is this going to take a long time? I have an algebra test in half an hour."

"I've spoken to your teacher and got you an excused absence, Charlotte," Steve said. "You can arrange to take the test later."

"I can't believe I actually studied for it," Charlotte said.

"Maybe we should get to the point of this meeting," Sloane said. "Is this about you?" Sloane pointed at Bill.

Bill slid pink referral slips across the table to Sloane and me, and said, "I was trying to give you these when you two took off running." She sneered at us. "How immature was *that*?"

Sloane flipped Bill the bird.

"So." Steve put his hand on Bill's shoulder and said, "As she just said, Bill requested this guidance session—or actually—I would call it a guidance intercession . . ." He laughed a little at his pun and made us wait while he wrote it down in his note-book. "But before we start . . ." Steve handed out little booklets. "Here are some guidelines to make sure we create a safe space for our conversation today."

The first page was a list of rules like be respectful, don't single out any one person, no cross-talk, no accusations—

"Steve, it says here 'Don't be defensive' but it doesn't say anything about being offensive," Digby said.

"Well, I think that's implied." Steve started flipping the pages of his booklet. "Or maybe you're right. Maybe I should write an addendum about that . . ."

I kicked Digby under the table and whispered, "We'll be here forever if you don't stop it."

Sloane raised her hand and held up her pink slip. "Is this going on my record as a referral?"

Steve snapped back to attention. "*Anyway*. Let's not get off track. We are here today because Bill has pointed out that some hurtful and abusive comments have been posted online—"

"*By her,*" I said. "*She's* posting hurtful and abusive things about me."

Steve held up the booklet and said, "We're trying to build a no accusation zone here, Zoe, so maybe let's rephrase that?"

"I can't really think of another way of saying it because there were posts. She made the posts," I said. "The posts are against me."

"No one knows who posted those," Bill said. "Tons of people here have access to the yearbook account—"

"Oh, please," Sloane said.

Bill started sobbing. "And now everyone is blaming me—"

I said, "You did that to yourself, and now I have to sit here and watch you act like you're somehow the victim—"

Steve said, "Actually, this is precisely the kind of unproductive—"

"Well, maybe I *did* do this to myself in a way because I let myself get into it with *him*." Bill pointed to Digby.

"I'm just sitting here," Digby said.

"Oh, please, Bill," Sloane said. "You are milking this soap opera—"

"Milk," said Digby.

Steve said, "Sloane, why don't we let Zoe and Bill negotiate their conflicting perceptions." From his booklet, he read, *"People view the same incident in dramatically different ways—"*

"This is a stupid waste of time." Steve gasped as Sloane ripped her booklet to little pieces.

"Wait. If this is about me and Bill, what are *they* doing here?" I pointed at the other side of the table, meaning Allie, Charlotte, and Austin.

"They're here because this morning, one of them put this up." Bill showed me her phone. The screen showed a photo of Bill with her shirt lifted provocatively. Nothing crucial was actually showing but the face she was making was probably embarrassment enough.

Charlotte rolled her eyes and said, "Like I told you already, we don't know whose account that is."

"Where did that photo come from?" I said.

"She sent that to me while I was going out with you, Zoe," Austin said.

"What?" I said. "You didn't tell me she did that."

"I didn't want you to get upset," Austin said.

"That was private," Bill said.

"So was Zoe kissing Digby," Charlotte said.

"But I didn't take those photos," Bill said. "And I don't know who posted them."

We all groaned. It took me a second to process the fact that if Bill's accusations were right, Allie, Austin, and Charlotte were on my side.

"And this"—Bill held up her phone again—"is from the AC-DC account, which I was told means Allie and Charlotte Don't Care."

"I heard they called it that because the poster is LGBTQ," Charlotte said. "You know . . . AC-DC, goes both ways . . ."

"Oh, my God. Bill, just admit you posted the Zoe pics and then you two"—Sloane pointed at Allie and Charlotte—"admit you're AC-DC and we'll be done already."

"Actually, Sloane, that's an example of what not to do in terms of cross-talk," Steve said. "Let's allow them to play out their feelings instead of trying to fix them."

Digby, who had been scrolling through his phone the entire time we'd been squabbling, said, "*Nobody* admit to any of those things. AC-DC—*whoever* that is . . . and whoever forwarded the picture to AC-DC in the first place"—Digby glared at Austin—"might have child porn distribution problems."

"No. We definitely don't want that," Steve said, and reached into his backpack for an index card case. "Maybe we could try a little role play—".

All of us shouted, *"No."*

"Look, Steve, I think we're fine," I said. "Can't we just figure this out among ourselves?"

"Well, actually, maybe we should talk a little more about how *you're* doing, Zoe," Steve said. "Because that's something that's getting lost in all this."

"Me?" I said. "I'm fine."

"Zoe, part of my job is to observe and intervene when I spot internalizing behavior in my students and honestly, every time I see you in the hall with your hood up and earphones on, my heart breaks for you," Steve said. "You look so isolated and angry."

Sloane said, "I told you you have all the warning signs."

Steve sat up even straighter. "Did you just say 'warning signs'? Warning signs . . . of school violence?"

"No, no . . ." I said. "That's Sloane's way of saying my clothes are ugly."

Digby did one of those dramatic sighs followed by a conversation-halting tabletop hand slap. "She's not a security threat, Steve," Digby said. "Stand down."

Steve leaned over, took my hand, and said, "Zoe. I know you're switching schools in a few months, but I don't want you leaving us with a bad taste in your mouth—"

"You're leaving?" Austin said.

"Where? Back to NYC?" Allie said. "Fun."

"Wow," Charlotte said.

I looked over to Digby but realized I'd make it worse if I apologized for not telling him earlier in front of everyone.

"You didn't know." Austin pointed at Digby.

Digby didn't answer but it was obvious he was struggling to *not* have a reaction.

"He *didn't* know." Austin laughed and leaned over the table toward Digby. "You're right, bro. I *do* miss this."

"Um, I'm sorry, Steve, how did you find out?" I said. "I haven't accepted or anything."

"The Prentiss admissions office asked me to forward your records," Steve said. "I just assumed it was a done deal."

"Of course she's going," Sloane said. "She'd be crazy not to go."

"I haven't decided if I'm going," I said.

"What happened?" Sloane said. "I thought you'd already decided."

Austin laughed. "Oh my God, even *Sloane* knew before you."

Digby's face darkened even more.

Thank God Bill couldn't take the focus being pulled away from her for too long. "Congratulations, Zoe," Bill said. "But can we please just resolve this?"

"Yes, you're right. Let's refocus our session." Steve referred back to his booklet. "What can we do to make things right? How can we make sure this doesn't happen again? Any ideas, thoughts, suggestions?"

Digby snapped his fingers at Austin. "Give me your phone."

He pointed at Allie and Charlotte. "Yours too." When all three of them instead tightened their hold on their phones, Digby said, "You want to get out of here? Unlock your phones and hand them over."

Charlotte, always the pragmatist, handed hers over first. "What are you doing?" she said.

Digby said, "Deleting." And then he did the same to Austin's and Allie's phones.

Steve said, "But this isn't really how we're supposed to—"

"It's okay, Steve. This is section seven," Digby said. "*Teaching joint responsibility ultimately means leaving it up to them.*"

"That isn't on this handout, is it?" I checked my booklet. "Mine only goes up to section six."

"But it sounds familiar," Steve said. He flipped his booklet over, scouring the text.

"It's written in your notes, Steve." Digby finished deleting, tossed the phones back, and leaned over and tapped a scrawl-filled page on Steve's notebook. "Between *buy tuna cheese Friskies* and *check tire pressure.*" Digby stood up. "Everything's been deleted. Can we agree—no new posts? If, somehow, there are more pictures out there, can we just assume they'll get deleted?" Digby looked at Bill to make it clear she was the object of that admonition.

"What about the ones on *your* phone?" Bill said to Digby. The between-you-and-me intimacy in her tone was annoying enough but then she went on to say, "But I guess you're in them with me, so why would you post them?"

116

Sloane said to me, "Ignore her." To Bill, Sloane said, "Ugh, you are so thirsty."

"Zoe gets it," Bill said. "She knows she doesn't have a right to get upset that Digby slept with other girls before they officially got together."

Steve butted in. "Okay, I think that's—"

"Cross-talk," Charlotte and Allie said to Steve.

"Let Zoe respond," Charlotte said.

I hoped Digby would say something that would help me make sense of what Bill had just said but he was silent. I felt gut punched.

"I don't have anything to say." I got my bag and said to Steve, "Are we done here?" But I left before seeing what his answer was.

TEN

I was kind of disappointed when Digby didn't follow me out of the meeting. I was running fast, but not *that* fast. I went to the bathroom and got myself together before deciding to head to the library. I made some returns, picked up some more books I had on hold, and went around the corner, where I found Digby waiting for me at my favorite desk.

"Ask me how I knew you'd be here," Digby said. "You wrote the due dates for your books on your wall calendar. And I know how much you hate to miss a due date."

When I didn't answer, he said, "You're upset."

Someone from the next stack over shushed us.

I ignored Digby and sat down. I started looking through my planner.

"You're upset about what, specifically?" he said.

I didn't feel like I had to explain myself to him but I glared at him to say, *You know*.

"I'm getting the silent treatment?" He tried again. "I can't believe you let Bill get under your skin."

"And I can't believe you slept with her," I said. Since I was talking already, I also said, "And I mean, I never even understood what you were doing with her in the first place. Was that just to bother me?"

We got another shush from behind the next stack of books.

"Not everything I do is about you," he said.

"So you're telling me you *wanted* to date her . . ." I said. "For her personality."

"Well? Maybe I liked hanging out with her," Digby said. "A little more of a chill hang, maybe."

"That's about me, right? She's 'a chill hang'? Meaning I'm . . . what?" I said.

A sophomore girl I didn't know but had seen around school stomped out from behind the shelves next to us and said to me, "Hey. Maybe Bill has a cool side she saves for her boyfriends. Maybe you don't know *him* as well as you thought . . ." Sophomore Girl was unhinged. "Maybe he needed to date her to realize he never wanted to date her. *I don't know*. None of us could figure out why they got together, either." Sophomore Girl clenched her fists and I really wondered if she was going to attack us. "But maybe you two could discuss it somewhere where there isn't someone who either passes her chemistry test *or* has to lifeguard at the YMCA all summer instead of going to Chicago to hang with her party girl aunt."

I whispered sorry and Digby and I packed up and left the library.

• • •

Once we were in the hallway, Digby said, "So. Where were we?"

"I believe you were telling me about you and Bill and how you had so much fun hanging out with her," I said. "And how you didn't just date her to be annoying."

"Date her to annoy you? And, actually, why *does* it annoy you so much?" Digby said. "As I remember it, you were with Austin at the time."

"Don't give me that," I said. "From the minute you came back to town, you made it your whole mission to break up Austin and me—"

"'My whole mission'?" Digby made mock gagging noises. "Not 'my whole mission,' surely. Um . . . I think I've been doing other stuff too."

"You know what I mean," I said.

"I think maybe someone's being a little conceited," Digby said.

I knew he knew what I'd meant, but I was embarrassed anyway. I turned and walked away from him.

"Aw . . . Zoe, where are you going?" Digby said.

I kept walking and picked up the pace.

"I thought we were done with the silent treatment already," Digby said. "Oh, come on."

This time, Digby followed me when I started running again. I sped up and bolted blindly around the corner, where I smacked straight into Austin. He tried to catch me as I fell backward but I just ended up taking him down with me. Austin and I were still tangled up on the floor when Digby rounded the corner and found us.

"You okay?" Digby put out both his hands and helped Austin and me up.

"I'm fine," I said.

Digby looked at Austin and then at me and said, "Let's talk later."

But when Digby turned to leave, Austin said, "Wait. Actually, Digby, I was coming to find *you*."

Digby was confused for a beat before he said, "Fine." Digby took off his jacket, handed it to me, and started rolling up his sleeves. "I'm good to go right here but if you want it to the death, we should go outside—"

"No, bro, *no*," Austin said. "I'm here because we need your help."

Farther down the hall, Pete, one of Austin's obnoxious teammates, spotted us and did a sneaker-squeak stop and ducked back around another corner and yelled, "Guys! Austin found Digby."

"The team needs to talk to you," Austin said. "They're waiting for you in the AV room."

I was glad to have gotten out of there and turned to leave.

"No, you too, Zoe," Austin said.

"Me too?" I said. "What for?"

Digby turned to Austin. "What is this about?"

Austin looked uncomfortable. "Henry said he'd explain it to you when you got there."

"You better come." Digby put on his jacket and we started walking.

Austin nudged me and said, "Are you okay?"

"I'm fine," I said.

"Was he chasing you?" Austin said.

"Only because she wanted me to catch her," Digby said.

"I never understood these mind games." Austin shook his head. To me, he said, "At least now you found someone who'll play them with you."

"Is this about Coach?" I said.

Austin nodded. "But we shouldn't talk about it here—"

"Austin . . ." I had to know. "Did you tell Coach Fogle I brought the gym bag to school?"

"Are you kidding me?" Austin said. "Not this again."

"Just answer me this time and I won't ask again. Did you tell Coach about the bag knowing he'd make you quarterback if you got Henry out of the way?" I said. "Because you almost got all of us killed by doing that."

"No. I. Did. *Not*. Tell Coach about the bag," Austin said. "And that would've been a stupid thing to do, by the way, because we all knew Coach was dealing. I wouldn't get people killed just to be QB. But thanks for believing in me, Zoe. Gee, I wonder why we didn't work out."

"So, are you QB next season?" Digby said.

"Whatever game plan Coach might've had for making me QB went to jail with him," Austin said. "Henry's QB still because that's who the assistant coaches know how to play."

We walked the rest of the way to the AV room in silence. A few more football players joined us on the way and by the time we reached the AV room on the third floor, we were rolling eight deep.

Just as Austin had said, the rest of the team was waiting for us when we arrived. Some players were sitting at desks and the ones who couldn't get a seat stood leaning against the back wall. Henry was standing in front. It was weird to see them all look to us with such hope and expectation when Digby and I walked in.

"What's going on here?" Digby said.

"We have a major fricking problem, guys," Henry said. "The High School Athletics Association sent a Drug-Free Sport inspector over. They're running no-notice tests on us." Henry showed Digby a form asking him to report to the main boys' bathroom.

"Wait. New York State public high schools don't allow random tests . . ." And then Digby realized. "But it's not random because Coach got arrested. Reasonable suspicion." Digby cursed.

We all froze when the door opened and a tackle named Lyle walked in. His face looked completely drained of blood and his hand trembled when he held out his form for Henry to read. "They had me pee in a cup and then gave me this."

123

Henry read the form and passed it to Digby. "Holy crap."

"Student-Athlete Notification Form. They'll be testing his urine for anabolic agents, diuretics, peptide hormones, anti-estrogens, and Beta-2 agonists." Digby turned to Lyle and said, "I take it from your face you're going to fail this test?"

"I didn't want to take those pills but Coach said they were just supplements," Lyle said. "I mean, after a while, I started to think maybe something weird was going on . . ."

"You mean when you developed a square head and started being able to bench-press a compact car?" Digby looked around the room. "How many people are going to fail this test? Let's see you put your five high."

Henry put his hands up to stop people from answering. "No, no, it's okay, guys." To Digby, Henry said, "Doesn't matter. If one of us gets busted, the whole program gets shut down. Even for the clean players."

"I need to play, man," one player said. And then the rest of the room started chiming in with their own anxious pleas for help.

"Okay, guys, he gets it," Henry said. "What do you think, Digby?"

"I just need to say now that I *don't* approve of steroids," Digby said. "Cheaters never win, boys."

"Most of the guys who took them didn't even know what they were taking, dude," Henry said. "They just trusted Coach."

"Which is why I am going to handle this," Digby said. "It's a one-time deal."

Someone in the back said, "Did he say he's going to handle this?"

I heard at least two high fives and one celebratory "Yes."

"*But,*" Digby said. "I'm going to need something in return."

"I will give you literally every cent I make this summer," one player said.

Another one said, "How much do you want?"

"He doesn't want money," Henry said. "You don't want money, right? Wait. *Do* you want money?"

I recognized the look on Digby's face. "Nope. It's going to be a lot weirder than that," I said.

"I want a human sacrifice," Digby said.

"For example," I said.

Someone in the back said, "You can have my brother. No one's going to miss *that* idiot."

"I bet my mom would even pay you to get my dad out of the picture," another player said.

"Digby. Explain yourself before they make me lose what tiny amount of faith in humanity I have left," I said.

"I need someone here to die on social media," Digby said. "And it has to be a big death."

"How big?" one player asked.

Digby pointed at me. "Bigger than hashtag Homewrecker hashtag UglyHo," he said. "And it has to happen right now or I'm not even going out that door."

"I got video of my girlfriend getting out of her skinny jeans," one player said. "I mean, her body be bangin' but no one looks good getting out of those . . ."

"Nope. I don't want any more shaming of other people," Digby said. "What I want is some of that 'take one for the team' sacrifice stuff you guys are always talking about."

Silence. And then Jim—one of the beefy linesmen—pointed to his phone. "I have video of me hooking up with my cousin over spring break."

As worried as they were about the drug tests, the players still had it in them to mock Jim.

"You took video of that?" Henry said.

"Dude, she's so hot." Jim played it for us to see. "And she's so wild, I bet she'd be into going viral."

I couldn't help it. I said, "Are you serious? You are such a pig."

After watching the video for a few seconds, Digby deflated. "No. We can't. I can see the top of her boob. No child porn."

"Dawg," Jim said. "She's twenty-two. And yes, I'm serious—she won't mind."

Digby perked up. "Well then, that'll do, pig. Send it to them." He pointed at Jim's buddies. "And then you all post it CousinLove, IncestIsBest, AllInTheFamily . . . tack on all the hashtags."

And then Digby looked at me like I ought to be on my knees thanking him. He threw his arms open in a flourish.

"What are you smirking about?" I said. "You're just undoing the crapstorm you unleashed on me."

"Are you guys okay?" Henry said.

"She's mad about the Bill thing," Digby said.

"Why? Are you jealous?" Henry shook his head. "Don't be. Bill basically spent most of her time with Digby asking about you." Henry pointed at me.

"She did?" I said. "How do you know that?"

"They'd come into the diner," Henry said. "And Bill would be like, *What does Zoe get? What did Zoe say? I bet Zoe did this—*"

"Wait. Come into the diner?" I turned to Digby. "You brought her to Olympio's?"

"Oh, dude," Digby said to Henry.

"I at least had more class than to bring Austin to Olympio's for our dates," I said.

"Yeah, I always did think that was awkward, dude," Henry said.

And then I turned to Henry and wiped the sympathetic look he was giving Digby when I said, "And you knew this whole time? What, were you couple-friends with Bill and Digby?"

"Uh . . . no," Henry said. "Sloane hates her."

"Oh, but *you* don't hate her?" I said.

"Let's leave Henry out of this," Digby said.

"Yeah, let's leave Henry out of this," Henry said.

"And like I said, why do you care? Why do you care where we ate?" Digby said. "You were with Austin at the time."

It was only when Digby pointed at Austin and the two of us turned to look that we realized the entire football team was watching us bicker.

"I'm so happy," Austin said.

"But seriously . . . can you help?" Henry handed Digby a summons form. "Because my test is in fifteen minutes."

Digby took the form and said, "Yep. Anything to get a break from this mess."

That annoyed me. "Do you even have a plan?" I said. He got a look on his face that I recognized. "Besides walking out of there with a million jars of urine stuffed in your pockets."

"That was just one of the many worthy ideas I was blue-skying," Digby said.

"If you steal the samples, Drug-Free Sport would come back tomorrow to run another round of tests but this time, they'd bring an extra tech to watch the cart," I said.

"Okay, I see where you're going. Same goes for contaminating the samples," Digby said. "They'd test them, figure out what happened, and come back with better security. And some of the things Coach was giving them will test positive for a month."

"We can't mess with the actual samples," I said. "This is like half of my father's cases. Can't argue with the evidence, so he goes after the process instead. These guys are going to have to lawyer the crap out of this."

"I don't care if you guys are fighting," Henry said to Digby. "You are definitely taking her with you."

With a sigh, Digby turned back to Lyle and said, "Did a same-sex monitor watch you give the urine sample?" When

Lyle nodded, Digby said, "Did he have an assistant or was he working alone?"

"He was alone," Lyle said.

"Were the samples all kept in the bathroom with you guys?" Digby said.

"No," Lyle said. "He had a big cart of stuff with him and he said the bathroom stank, so he rolled the cart to Principal Granger's office. He did all his paperwork in there too."

"So the cart's in the office with Granger?" Digby said.

"No," Lyle said. "The lab guy kicked out Principal Granger."

"Oh, okay, I get it." Lyle looked worried and Digby clapped him on the arm. "Smile, man. That's good news. Your day's starting to look up." Digby thought for a long second and then walked to the trash can and kicked it over to Henry.

"What's this?" Henry said.

"When it's time to give your sample, I need you to hold up the lab tech in that bathroom for the maximum amount of time while Princeton and I see about that cart. It'd help if you went in with an empty bladder," Digby said. "Now back up, Princeton, unless you want to gamble that Henry's a no-splash kind of guy."

I stepped outside.

ELEVEN

The team was borderline ecstatic when Henry, Digby, and I walked away from the AV club's room. As far as they were concerned, they were home free.

"They give away their trust plenty fast," I said. "Hmm . . . I wonder how they ended up accidentally taking steroids."

"Yeah, dude, they really shouldn't be so optimistic," Digby said to Henry. "I have no idea what I'm doing."

"You don't?" Away from his team, Henry let himself express something less than confidence for the first time. "Digby? Are we screwed?"

"It's okay, man. I'll get it together. First, we need to get to that cart. Princeton, I might need you to distract the lab guy at some point," Digby said. "Maybe get out your lipstick?"

"What am I supposed to do, exactly?" I said.

"I don't know," Digby said. "Just be distracting."

When we got down to the first-floor landing, I took off my hoodie so I was down to my tank top. I pulled out my ponytail and fluffed up my hair.

"Whoa. Not *that* distracting," Digby said. "Hoodie on, zip down, hair up."

I'd just gotten my hoodie back on when Henry said, "Really? I'd think more, like, hoodie off, hair up."

"Split the difference?" Digby said. "Hoodie on, zip down, hair down." But then he thought about it and said, "But don't you think hair down would push it over the edge?"

"Maybe over the edge is good?" Henry said.

I pulled my hair back again. "Can you two just—"

A voice said, "Henry Petropoulos?"

"Yes." Henry raised his hand.

We hadn't noticed the tech, an officious jerk in a short white lab coat, walking up to us. He was holding a clipboard that he pointed at Henry. "Let's get going. Follow me." The tech then pointed at Digby and me and said, "Are you two boys on the football team too?"

Digby and Henry looked at each other and said, "Hair down."

Digby and I rounded the corner but ducked our heads back around to watch the tech leave Henry outside the principal's office while he went in to retrieve the paperwork and specimen cup. Then, after taking Henry's information, the tech locked the principal's office door and escorted Henry to the bathroom just two doors down. We waited, but the sound of the bath-room door closing never came. Instead, the loud sound of the tap running echoed in the hallway.

"He didn't close the door," I said. "What do we do now?"

But clearly, Digby hadn't counted on the tech leaving the door open either.

"O . . . kay." Digby put away the little lock-picking tool he'd already unfolded. "I guess we won't be going in through Granger's door, then."

The hallway's geography worked against us. The principal's office was the butt of a cul-de-sac, and the bathroom was close enough that the lab tech would see us if we tried to walk in Principal Granger's door. The only other office on that end of the hallway belonged to Miss Riddell, Principal Granger's sec-retary, but it was right across from the open bathroom door and was locked up for lunch anyway. There would be no rea-son for us to be down at that end of the corridor.

In the long silence while we considered our lack of options, Digby said, "I wouldn't have dated her if I'd known it would upset you like this."

"I think what bothers me is the idea of you sneaking around," I said. "When did you and Bill have all this time together? Like, did you use to run over and see Bill after hang-ing out with me?"

"You're driving yourself crazy," he said.

And I did feel myself getting angry all over again. So, I instead said, "Could we go in through the window?"

"Granger's window is on the same side as the bathroom window," Digby said.

"We could be very quiet," I said.

Digby didn't look convinced. "I've never broken glass quietly before . . ."

Just then Principal Granger walked past and caught us cowering behind the corner, clearly up to no good. He stopped and I prepared a few excuses before it occurred to me that Principal Granger too looked like he was up to no good.

Digby and I squared up to him and we watched one another in silence, trying to figure out who would show their cards first. And then, nice and slow, Principal Granger raised his hand and pointed in the direction of his office. Digby nodded. Principal Granger's face relaxed into an almost-smile and he gestured for us to follow him around the corner and into a supply closet.

Once we were tucked behind the closed closet door, Principal Granger said, "You hear about this no-notice BS? I get a 'courtesy' phone call . . ." Granger made angry air quotes around the word *courtesy* to make sure we got that he considered the courtesy call to have been more like, "screw you." "And not five minutes later, this twerp with his lab coat walks in wanting blood and urine. I drew the line at blood, but apparently he has the right to take urine." Principal Granger was agog. "How weird is that? Precious bodily fluids, know what I mean?"

I looked to confirm Digby was as shocked as I was at Principal Granger's manic demeanor.

"Do you know? Are they going to find banned substances?"

When Digby didn't answer, Principal Granger said, "Oh my God . . . I just can't . . . I'm so stressed as it is. That superintendent's breathing down my neck . . ." And then I think Granger sobbed before he grabbed Digby's arm and said, "If only there were some way those results would just vanish. That really would be ideal." Granger pulled Digby closer and said, "Isn't that the kind of thing you do?" And then Granger looked at me and said, "Or is that what you two are doing already?"

I should just point out that up to this point, neither Digby nor I had uttered even one word since walking into the closet.

"Is it a full moon tonight, or is the whole school just spontaneously coming undone?" Digby said.

"Maybe the water's contaminated," I said. "Poison mold or something in the ventilation system . . ." I realized what I'd just said when the crazy light turned on in his eyes. "Oh, no."

Digby nodded. "That is a *great* idea."

"What?" Principal Granger said.

"Not again," I said.

"What?" Principal Granger said. He grabbed Digby's lapels. "You know what to do?"

Digby unhooked Principal Granger from his lapels and said, "Try to be cool, okay? When the AC is on, does your office smell like the bathroom or food?"

"Food," Principal Granger said. "Why?"

"Finally, we catch a break," Digby said. "Cafeteria, Princeton."

I opened the door and made sure no one was around before

134

I stepped out of the closet. Digby, Principal Granger, and I ran the short distance to the cafeteria, where we blew past the objections of the dining room staff working the chow line and went straight into the kitchen.

Digby and I studied the two parallel duct systems running along the ceiling and into the wall. One had an opening over the oven while the other had a vent directly above a row of deep-fat fryers.

"Pizza or French fries?" Digby said.

Principal Granger, finally clued in to the program, was pulling out the deep-fat fryer from under the duct's opening as he shouted, "French fries. I smell French fries."

To the two prep cooks in the kitchen, I said, "Principal Granger has to check for some possible problems in the HVAC. Could we just have the room?"

One of the cooks looked like he expected as much. "About time. I reported those mouse droppings weeks ago."

Digby slam-dunked the pizza slice I hadn't even seen him swipe in the garbage and spat out the bite he'd been chewing. "Yes. But don't tell anyone right now," Digby said. He guided the kitchen staff out the door. Once we were alone, he said, "Mouse poop? I want to scream."

"*You* want to scream?" I said. "I've been eating here every day."

Principal Granger waved me off. "Mouse droppings—big deal. Every single restaurant has mice. Michelin Star places have mice." At Digby's scandalized look, Principal Granger said, "We'd have to close down the whole school to fumigate, because once they come in for the mice, they're going to find the roaches too. We already lost a bunch of days to snow this year. Do you want the semester to go even longer?" He pointed at me. "And especially you. You still have to complete your junior year here before you're eligible to start senior year at your fancy new school. Do you want to be stuck here until July?"

"I don't know if I'm going yet," I said.

"What?" Principal Granger looked outraged. "After all those letters you made me write? All those essays of yours I had to read and assess? All November long, you stalked me in school. I'd open my email and there you were—"

"November?" Digby said. "This was going on in November? I was here in November."

"She didn't tell you? Well, you did say not to tell anybody," Principal Granger said.

Digby gave me a round-mouth shocked face.

"It's not the same thing," I said.

"What? You sneaking around making plans?" Digby said. "Not at all the same thing."

"Do you two have to do this right now?" Principal Granger said. "Because unless you find a way to stop these tests, we're going to have a big problem here."

"Oh, we already have a big problem, Granger," Digby said.

I looked up at what he was pointing at and after a beat, it

dawned on me. "That air duct going into your office is too flimsy. It won't hold our weight."

"Unlike the last duct we crawled through, they didn't build this one to air out a meth lab. I thought we could do a *Die Hard*," Digby said. "But if we got in that thing, we'd be doing *The Breakfast Club*. Except we'd go straight through that sheet metal and it would shred our hands like pizza cheese. Know what I'm thinking, though?" he said. "I think it's time to go back to *Shawshank*."

"*The Shawshank Redemption*? Wait. What are you going to dig?" Principal Granger said. "Do we have that kind of time?"

TWELVE

We made a brief stop back at the supply closet, where Digby snagged us a hammer and a screwdriver. We then went into the faculty lounge and after Principal Granger cleared out two teaching assistants having a coffee klatsch flirtation and locked the door, Digby got to work.

He peeled off a WORKING FOR THE WEEKEND poster from the common wall between Granger's office and the faculty lounge and stabbed the drywall with the business end of the screwdriver. He turned the screwdriver until it got all the way through to the other side. Digby then added a twist to the screwdriver's revolutions so that its entry hole widened enough for him to insert the hammer's claw.

In less time than I would've thought it should take to destroy a wall, Digby had carved out a large enough hole for me to help him pry away at the dry wall with my bare hands.

"Not too much," he said. "No bigger than the poster."

Digby had already climbed on a chair and gone through the hole into Principal Granger's office when someone outside started turning the doorknob to the faculty lounge.

"It's occupied," Principal Granger said.

"I need coffee," the voice said.

"Wait until we've gone over, cover the hole back up, and then let them in," Digby said.

I climbed through the hole behind Digby, and after Principal Granger put the poster back up, I heard him open the faculty lounge's door to let the coffee-deprived teacher into the room.

Once we were alone in Granger's office, Digby whispered, "You were scheming to go to Prentiss that entire time? So, what was all that drama with your father in the hospital room?"

I ignored him.

"What I don't understand is . . . why didn't you just tell me?"

"Are you asking why I didn't tell you about wanting to go to a school you call Prissy-Priss Academy? After you gave me the 'what you learn doesn't depend on where you go' lecture?" I said. "God, who even knows why I was hesitant to tell you."

"I'm touched that you care what I think," he said. "But can we just agree it was a shady move to keep it from me? And I didn't enjoy finding out in front of everyone like that."

"And speaking of finding out hurtful stuff in front of other people . . ." I said.

"It's not the same thing," Digby said. "You lied about something important—"

"You don't think it's important for me to know that you slept with Bill?" I said. "She's *killing* me on social media because I didn't know I was stealing a guy she was sleeping with—"

"No, no," Digby said. "I never slept with her."

I thought back to the intervention. "But she said . . ."

"Not with her," Digby said.

"Oh," I said. The "with her" part of his answer needed further investigation. "But you have . . ."

"Yes." And then Digby held up two fingers.

"Two people?" I said. "Twice?"

"Yes to both, I guess," he said. "Two women. Once each, so twice total."

Even while I was doing it, I'd known that I was making a huge mistake pushing him for details. Hearing him say "two women" felt horrible. And so I turned to the lab cart in front of me and studied the equipment. The compact medical-grade refrigerator, the box of unused specimen bottles, the files of paperwork. I opened the door of the portable refrigerator and then shut it. And then opened and shut it again.

Digby picked up the box of unused specimen collection bottles and looked through some of the paperwork.

"So?" I said.

"So now we go after the process," he said. Digby took out his utility knife and inserted the hook attachment through the cooling unit's fan grate. He poked around until he was able to yank out a stray wire, which he then sliced with one of his blades.

I said, "But it can't look *too* broken inside because—"

But Digby was already putting the wire back in through the grate so that it was visible but not immediately apparent to someone who wasn't already looking for it. "Because then he'll just transfer the samples to another fridge," he said. "Right there with you, Princeton."

When the wire was concealed yet visible, I nodded. "Perfect."

"Okay, let's clean up," he said.

I took the hammer from Digby and got to work taking an oversized framed Matisse poster off the opposite wall. I pried off the nail and, as lightly as I could, I hammered it back into the wall right above the hole we'd climbed through. I felt particularly proud of the fact that I'd had the foresight to unspool the picture wire attached to the back of the Matisse so we'd have more play when it came time to hang the poster back up from the other side after we'd climbed through the hole.

Meanwhile, Digby was gathering up the pieces of drywall debris we'd created and was stuffing it into Principal Granger's larger bottom desk drawer.

"Hey. Did you just take something?" I said.

Digby put his finger to his lips and pointed in the direction of the faculty lounge to remind me Principal Granger could hear.

"Did I hear pills rattling?" I said. "Did you take pills from his desk drawer?"

"Why would I take his pills? I already get all the good ones." He picked up Principal Granger's pill bottle. "These are for acid reflux."

"Put them back!" I said. "Focus. Come on."

Just then we heard the sound of footsteps coming down the hall. Whether Principal Granger was ready for us or not, Digby and I were coming through. I handed the Matisse poster to Digby and knocked down the WORKING FOR THE WEEKEND poster on the faculty lounge side. I climbed through to find Musgrave standing beside Principal Granger at the coffee machine.

"Oh, great," was all I could say.

Musgrave almost dropped his coffee mug. "What the hell—" Principal Granger clapped his hand over Musgrave's mouth.

And then Digby dove through the hole after me, reached back into Principal Granger's office for the Matisse poster, and then pulled on the picture wire so that the poster lay flat across the back against the hole on Principal Granger's office's side. Digby grimaced as the heavy poster made the metal wire dig into his fingers. I pulled my sleeves low over my hands and helped him hold it up.

From where we were, we could hear the lab tech open Granger's office door and fiddle with the objects on his cart. Clinking sounds. A sneeze. A second sneeze. And then a whole series of sneezes.

"Jeez. This place is *dusty*," the lab tech muttered to no one.

He sneezed a few more times and then we heard the sound of the cart rolling out of the room and the door closing behind him. After a minute, I finally allowed myself to exhale. Digby and I fiddled with the poster until we got the wire to catch on the nail.

We turned around to find Musgrave gawping at us.

"Harlan. As your principal, I'm telling you to let it go," Principal Granger said.

"Did they . . ." Musgrave said. ". . . *tamper* with the urine samples?"

"Really, Harlan? After everything we've been through together?" Digby took a paper towel, soaked it with water from the cooler, and wrapped it around his sore palm. "By the way, how's the DA doing? Have you seen him lately?"

"I'm seeing him later today." Musgrave looked terrified. "Why?"

"It's all good in the hood, Musgrave. Go to your meeting and have fun being a hero. But right now, we really do need the room," Digby said. "And about that hole . . ."

But now Musgrave had been brought to heel. "What hole?" Musgrave said. And then he left.

Principal Granger watched Musgrave obediently leave the room and said, "Wow. You have *got* to share some of whatever you have on him with me."

But Digby was all business. "Okay, Granger, you're in charge of part two of this plan. Before that tech leaves today, you have to photograph the back of his portable medical fridge without tipping him off that you're taking the picture. You got that? It's subtle but it's important. Make sure you get the wire poking out of the ventilation grille, understand? And make sure it's time- and date-stamped. Maybe email it to yourself."

We waited for him to acknowledge us, but Granger just looked stunned.

To me, Digby said, "I don't even know if any of this is getting through to him."

"No, no, I got it. I can do it," Principal Granger said.

Digby didn't look fully convinced but continued anyway. He unfolded the Student-Athlete Notification Form he'd taken from Lyle. "It says here they'll be testing the samples right away. There are going to be a few fails and then the Athletics Association will probably notify you to shut down the football program for a year to clean up—"

Principal Granger gasped.

"*But,*" Digby said. "What you need to do is immediately call your lawyer. Send him your pictures of the fridge. Tell them to use the pictures to challenge the results."

"Then what?" Principal Granger had his hand on his chest, looking like he was about to keel over. "How do I challenge the results? What do I do? Tell me the exact wording I should use—"

The sight of Granger flailing disgusted me. I needed to slap him back to sense. "Look," I said. "There will be rounds of paperwork, and then negotiation, negotiation, negotiation. By the time that's all done, the players' bodies will have broken down whatever junk Coach had given them. So, when they get retested, the results will come back clean. For now, though, you have to keep it together. Can you do that? Or are you still not done being a baby?"

Principal Granger just stared at me. And then he looked at Digby and pointed at me.

Digby nodded and said, "What she said."

THIRTEEN

I felt like there was drywall powder covering every inch of me and anyway, there was no way I'd be able to concentrate, so I accepted the excuse slips Digby got Principal Granger to sign for us and both Digby and I left school early. Not for the first time since moving to River Heights, I worried about exactly what kind of education I was getting.

Digby and I kept things light on the bus. He talked smack about the music on my phone. I gave him a hard time about the recent changes he'd made to his appearance—his slightly nicer black sneakers, the obviously itchy stubble he was trying to grow.

The script flipped the minute we got inside my house, though. Before I'd even gotten my shoes off, Digby said "So" in that let's-talk voice.

"Yeah," I said. "Do you at least want a snack first?"

He saw through my stall tactic and just looked at me, silent.

"Great. Nothing like fighting hangry," I said. "Come on upstairs."

Once in my room, Digby took off his jacket and sat down at my desk. "I don't want to fight."

"Neither do I," I said.

"We both lied," Digby said. "So could we maybe call it even?"

I didn't know what I was going to end up saying even after I'd started talking. "My mom teaches a class called The Ruined Woman. Novels about women who have no future after they lose their virginity. She jokes about how women lose their value the second they lose their new-car smell. I always thought that was dumb. But now . . ."

"It bothers you," Digby said.

"It bothers me," I said.

Digby said, "Because you don't think it'd be as special for me if or when you and I . . ."

I didn't say anything but he got my drift.

"It'd be special for me, Zoe," Digby said. "If or when you and I ever did . . ."

He got up and approached me, watching my face so I'd know I could stop him with a look.

I tried to soften the part of me that had grown brittle imagining him and Bill together, but I felt my defenses going up even as he kissed me in the ways that usually disarmed me. "Digby. No," I said. "I'm too upset."

"No, of course." Digby stepped back and said, "But we can hang out, right?"

I nodded. "Yes, I just don't feel like . . ."

"No, no. No need to explain," he said. "Hey, how should we celebrate?"

"Celebrate what?" I said. "Saving Henry's season?"

"*How* long have you been talking about going to this school?" Digby said. "You did it."

"I haven't decided if I'm going," I said.

"Right. Because how could you leave all this . . ." He sat back down in my chair and spun around to sweep his hand across the view outside my window and sighed. "Of course you're going. You were always bigger than this town. I'm happy for you."

"Are you sure you're happy for me?" I said. "Because you don't look—"

"I'm happy for you, Princeton. Seriously. Learn to take yes for an answer." Digby looked out my window with his sad downturned eyes for a long second. And then he plastered on a smile and said, "Let's go pig out at Olympio's. My treat!"

"Do you really feel like going out?" I said.

"Of course," Digby said. "I'm happy for you, Zoe."

I said, "Yeah . . . you said that already—"

He pointed at something outside my window. "Hey. Look who's watching."

I joined him at the window and saw our nosy neighbor staring at us from across the way. "Oh, hi, Mrs. Breslauer."

"No, down there." Digby pointed down to the street, where I saw the by now familiar Honda sedan parked a few doors down from my house.

"Oh, yeah, them." I myself was surprised at how blasé that sounded. "They come and go. They never actually *do* anything . . ."

"What?" Digby said. "It wasn't just the day after the party?"

"Monday night, they were here. Tuesday night too . . ." I said. "I don't think they were here Wednesday . . ."

"Are you sure?" Digby said.

I said, "Well, it's not like I was keeping a record—"

But Digby had already grabbed his jacket and stormed out of my room. I chased him down the stairs and out of the house.

• • •

"Hey. Hey!" Digby started shouting at the guys in the car even before he'd gotten to the bottom of my porch stairs.

The de Groot security guy I'd been mentally referring to as Shorter Guy was alone behind the wheel of the old Honda, dressed in a T-shirt rather than one of the lumpy suits he and his Taller Guy partner were usually wearing.

Digby jogged over and started banging on the hood of Shorter Guy's car. "What do you want what do you want what do you want?" he said. Digby didn't seem to care that my whole street could hear him screaming.

Shorter Guy got out of the car and proceeded to do a weird

149

dance in which he reached out as though to restrain Digby only to pull back and gesture reassuringly that he'd keep his hands to himself. Finally, he got Digby to calm down enough so he could talk to him. "Please. I'm not here to hurt you," Shorter Guy said.

"Then what are you doing here?" Digby said. "Why are you spying on us?"

"Just . . ." Shorter Guy looked confused. "I . . ."

"Where's your partner?" Digby said. "I bet he's the brains."

And then it occurred to me. "Is he breaking into my house right now?" I said.

"No, no. We're not here to hurt you. We just . . ." Shorter Guy said. "We need to talk to you. We just . . . haven't found a way to say what we need to say."

"What?" Digby said.

Shorter Guy ran a hand through his hair, agitated. "Look. All I can say is, don't trust de Groot. He's going to get what he wants from you and then . . . *please*. Walk away."

I was expecting threats. I was even prepared for some physical violence. But I wasn't prepared for what looked like genuine concern.

"What?" Digby said. "Does de Groot know you're here?"

"Of course not," Shorter Guy said. "I swear to God, kid, I'm here as a friend. I came here to tell you that making deals with de Groot is not going to get you any closer to the truth."

"'Friend'?" Digby turned to me. "Did this clown just try to tell me he's my *friend?*"

"Hey!" Taller Guy came running around the corner carrying a plastic bag loaded with junk food. He pointed at his partner. "Shut up and get in the car."

"I told them," Shorter Guy said.

"Told them *what?*" Taller Guy said.

"Well, for starters . . ." Shorter Guy smiled and stuck out his hand. I was so surprised that I actually shook it. "My name is Art. Hello." He turned to Digby but Digby had the where-withal to cross his arms and decline Art's handshake. "This is my partner—"

Taller Guy said, "Don't do it—"

"Jim," Art said.

Jim groaned, climbed in the car, and slammed the door shut.

"We're not here to hurt you two," Art said. "But please think about what I told you. Get away from de Groot. He's dangerous."

From behind me, I heard Mom say, "Zoe?" I hadn't seen her drive up and park and now she was standing on our driveway across the street. "Everything all right?"

Our busybody neighbor, Helen Breslauer, was standing beside her, yap-yap-yapping away.

I waved at my mom. "Everything's all right, Mom."

"We should go." Art jerked his chin in my mother's direction and said, "When she asks, tell her I was asking for directions." Art climbed into their car and drove off.

Digby and I just stood there, too stunned to speak for a long beat.

"What was that?" I said. I watched Digby struggle to compose himself and started to wonder if maybe he wasn't a little less happy about my getting into Prentiss than he was saying he was. Instead of answering, he pointed at Mom, whose conversation with Helen Breslauer was amping up.

"Better see if your mom's okay," Digby said.

And then his phone rang with a text.

I ran back across the street to Mom in time to hear her half shout at Mrs. Breslauer's retreating back, "Mine is a sex-positive household, Helen. But thank you very much for your concern."

"Mom?" I said.

"What the hell?" Mom said. "What was Digby doing to that car? That was crazier than usual, even for him. Do I need to worry about your safety?"

"No, uh . . . they were just arguing about parking," I said.

"You and Digby in the house," she said. "Now."

"Mom," I said.

"Zoe," Mom said. "*Now.*"

I ran back over to Digby. "Can you come in? My mother wants to talk to us."

"It's tomorrow, Princeton," Digby said.

"What's tomorrow?" I said.

"Felix texted. Perses has a scheduled backup tomorrow. The data storage place emailed a reminder to his dad." Digby showed me his phone. "It's tomorrow."

"It's tomorrow. Right. Okay," I said. "Why don't you come in? Have some dinner? We could talk about it"

"No, uh . . . I should go," Digby said. "Make sure everything's ready for tomorrow."

"Okay," I said. "Are you sure you can get home all right? You look a little distracted."

"I'm okay," he said. Digby walked away but before he got too far, he said, "Hey, Princeton. You don't have to come on this one. It could get real."

"Isn't it always real?" I said.

"I mean it could get really real. If we get caught tomorrow, it'll be the Feds, and the Feds won't care that you're a minor," he said.

"You've never let that stop us before—"

"Princeton. Listen to what I'm saying. The Feds this time. Everything we did before is child's play compared to what I'm going to do tomorrow," he said. "Really think. Sleep on it."

And then Digby left.

• • •

Mom didn't even wait for me to get my shoes off before she laid into me. "Are you having sex? Helen Breslauer says she saw you two having sex in your room. Because I took Digby at his word when he said you weren't." Before I could answer, Mom started up again. "Then again, that might've been true yesterday and one day's practically a lifetime for a teena—"

"Mom. Stop. No," I said. "Still lousy with virginity, okay?"

My mother, being so drama, made me watch her do one of

her breathing exercises before she said, "Then please put your bra back on."

I hadn't even realized that Digby had unclasped it.

Once I'd done it back up, Mom said, "I think it's time to talk."

"No, it's okay, Mom. I know the facts," I said.

"*Do* you?" she said. "What do you know about Digby's sexual partners—"

That came too close to the fight I'd just had with Digby. "That's really between him and me," I said.

"Just a few days ago, you were digging around in the garbage, hysterical about who I might or might not be sleeping with, and now you're going to look me in the eye and pretend you think sex is just about the two people having it?" Mom said. "This is not you versus me. Don't start lying to me, Zoe. You don't have to damage our relationship to develop your relationship with Digby."

I wanted to smart-mouth something about her making everything all about her but actually, I could see the sense in what she'd said.

"Plus, I need to do this so if I end up becoming the youngest grandmother in my Facebook group, I can at least honestly say I tried," Mom said.

Mom poured us coffee and we moved into the living room. The nightmare began with her uttering the line, "Zoe, sperm are sneaky. They are like Spartans. They only need to send one—"

I said, "Mom. I know how it works—"

"STDs, condoms . . . do you want to go on the pill?" she said.

"No, Mom—"

"Do you know what to do if you have an accident?" she said. "Do you know that you should check for yourself if he's put it on right—"

"*Mother*," I said. "I am able to go on the Internet."

"Fine. Then we can skip ahead to part two." Mom put her coffee down and put her hands on my shoulders. "Feelings."

"Oh, no," I said. "Mom. I think we know what our feelings are."

"But have you thought about how you're going to feel *after* the sex? Some people enjoy sex without commitment. Is that what he wants?" And then a thought occurred to her. "Or is that what *you* want since you might be leaving this summer?"

I shook my head but I did wonder.

"Hm." Mom laughed. "Maybe I should have asked you what *your* intentions are."

• • •

Because I'm a masochist, I crawled into bed and checked my social media accounts for the first time in days. To my surprise, Jim and his kissing cousin—not my words—had already taken my place as the engine of our school's disgust/delight dream machine. The fact that Jim had captured some of their murmured hookup conversation was an added bonus and his telling his cousin "Don't tell my mom" had acquired a meme-life of its very own. I scrolled up and from the time stamps, I concluded that my supposed home-wrecking had become stale news.

And then I started thinking about what Digby had planned for the next day. "Meet at gym at noon if you want to come," he'd texted me. To be honest, it'd never occurred to me that I could choose not to.

I fell asleep but jerked awake in the middle of the night. I hopped on my phone and texted him back.

"C U at noon."

FOURTEEN

I could barely concentrate during my morning classes and by the time I went to our arranged meet-up at the back of the main gym, I was practically vibrating. And this without even a sip of the muscled-up coffee I'd brought in my travel mug.

Felix and Digby were already there and they both looked relieved when I showed up.

"Oh, good, she's wearing her sack again today," Digby said.

"Excuse me?" I said. I realized he meant my hoodie. "This is my favorite one."

"Here. How many of these can you hide on you?" Felix held up a couple of four-inch square cartridges that had the Perses logo on their cases.

"Are those the tapes we need to switch out?" I said.

"Yep. These are super tapes," Felix said. "They back up on tapes like this." And then in a much lower voice, he said, "I think."

"Digby, did Felix just say he *thinks* they back up on these?" I said.

"Yes, I have to admit . . . the intel on this is not a hundred percent," Felix said.

"It's not like there's a subtle way to ask, Princeton," Digby said.

"Okay, please don't use your dumdum voice on me," I said.

"But that's the beauty of this whole thing. We can just consider this a test run since the backups happen regularly," Felix said.

"Test run?" I said.

"Yeah," Digby said. "So we don't have to commit to doing it unless we both feel good about the situation when we get there."

"But how do we decide?" I said. "We can't freeze time and have a meeting."

"We could have a safe word," Digby said. "We'll only make our move if we both say it."

"If you both concur," Felix said. "Ooh, like executing a nuclear strike."

"A safe word?" I said. "It'll either be too common and I'll accidentally use it or it'll be too weird and I won't be able to think up a way to use it. I'll panic—"

"Okay. You're kind of panicking right now," Digby said. "What about a signal?" He made a windmilling motion with his arm.

"What's that?" I said.

"That's the baseball signal for go all the way home," Felix said. "Come on. Even *I* know that."

"Wait. So does that mean we should do it or go home?" I said.

"Go *for* home. That means we do it," Digby said. "What's the confusion?"

"No. She's right," Felix said. "I think that might confuse me too."

"Well, since you won't be there, it's okay," Digby said.

"And won't that be really obvious if you're swinging your arm around like that?" I said. "Hold on. I'm already confused again. Does that mean do it or not do it?"

"Oh. My. God. What is there to be confused about?" Digby swung his arm around and around wildly. "Doesn't this just look like *go, go, go*?"

I noticed his bloodshot eyes were even more manic than usual. "Have you slept? When was the last time you slept?"

"I know! Thumbs-up! Now *that's* a good example of a simple signal." Felix did a thumbs-up to emphasize his point.

"Fine. Thumbs-up or thumbs-down," Digby said. "Happy?"

"I don't think *happy* is a word I would use to describe my feelings about this situation," I said. "But I'm good to go."

Digby had brought Val's car to school and the three of us set off to the lot to find it. I could tell Digby was nervous because it took a good five minutes of our wandering around the parking lot for him to remember he'd parked it on the street. But I didn't want to screw with the morale, so I just smiled and got in the car.

Digby turned off the freeway and pulled into the parking lot of a mall made up of a collection of big-box stores beside the bus depot.

"What are we doing here?" I said.

Digby said, "I need to pick up a few items."

"Items?" I said. "Okay, weirdo. Do you need money?" I'd already taken out my wallet because he always needed money.

But Digby said, "No, I got it covered." And then he shut the car door and jogged into the store.

"He has it covered? He never has money," I said to Felix. "Meaning he's been thinking ahead. That's not his steez. *And* he lost the car . . . he's nervous. He hasn't been sleeping, you know."

"He told me that," Felix said. "Are you worried his thinking isn't straight?"

"Well, I mean, when is it ever straight?" I said. But I did wonder if maybe the stress of getting so close to finding out about Sally, plus the lack of sleep . . . "I might need your help if he's too loopy and we have to pull the plug."

"But I'm not going with you two to the server room, remember?" Felix said.

Right. The plan was for us to drive onto the Perses lot together and while Felix sat in his mother's office, Digby and I would sneak into the server room and switch out the tapes.

"Then we should make a decision before we split up," I said.

160

"Okay. But now we have the same problem again," Felix said. "How do we confer, with him right there with us?"

I stuck my thumb up and then down. "Thumbs-up, thumbs-down?"

Felix nodded. "Okay."

"You know, Felix," I said. "You don't have to do this. I know what Digby means to you, but . . . you don't have to do this."

"*You* don't have to do this," Felix said.

I knew what he meant.

"I was thinking the other day about why exactly we all keep getting involved with Digby and his insane capers," Felix said.

I said, "And?"

"And I remembered some PSA about telling your teacher if you found out your friend was using drugs. 'Friends take responsibility for friends,' it said," Felix said. "I don't think this is what the PSA writers had in mind but it feels like the right explanation."

"Well, let's hope we get away with it again this time," I said.

"Yes. Otherwise, it's life in prison for treason." Felix shivered. "Whoa. I just scared myself."

"Scared me too," I said.

"My mouth is dry." Felix pointed at my travel mug of coffee. "May I have a sip?"

"Sure," I said.

Felix then proceeded to drain the entire cup. He smacked his lips. "Whew. I think I like coffee."

"Don't tell me that was the first time you tried coffee," I said.

161

He nodded.

"Really?" I said.

He nodded again.

"*Felix,*" I said. "That was a double red eye."

"What's that?" he said.

I was trying to figure out a way of telling him I'd fortified my coffee with two extra shots of espresso without freaking him out when Digby emerged from the store and started running back to the car.

"Just say something if you start to feel funny, okay?" I said.

"Feel funny?" Felix said.

Digby had two huge bags in one hand and an enormous cake box balanced on the other.

"What did he buy?" I said.

I looked through his bags when Digby got back in the car. "You bought yourself a suit?" I looked in the other bag. "Party supplies . . ." There were hats, streamers, tape, and random party-related junk in the bag. "All Star Wars." There were Star Wars action figures, a DVD of *A New Hope,* and boxes of tubed icing I assumed was intended for the enormous sheet cake he'd bought. "What is this cake? Will we be going to a children's party later? Or is this optimistic pre-planning for our Not-Going-to-Jail party?"

"It's a reminder that there's no such thing as a free lunch," Digby said. "Speaking of . . . use the icing and write *MAY THE FORCE BE WITH TEAM FONG* on it."

I frowned at him.

162

"It's not because you're the girl. It's because Felix . . ." Digby passed his phone to Felix and started the car. "Has to call his mom."

"Oh, boy." Felix looked really nervous and held his stomach. "I am not good at this."

"Just keep it casual. Your mom's paranoia will do half your work for you." Digby looked in the mirror and saw Felix reading from index cards. "Learn the lines and put them away. If it sounds canned, she'll know you're lying."

"I'm terrified I'll forget what to say," Felix said.

"Terrified is good," Digby said. "Terrified is exactly what you need to sound like."

Digby pulled into the bus depot and killed the engine.

"The bus depot?" I said. "Why are we at the bus depot?"

"We're picking up our responsible adult." When I didn't understand, Digby said, "We need someone to drive on the Perses campus and say he's our teacher."

"We're picking out our responsible adult from the people at the bus depot?" I said. I looked out the window. "Literally everyone here looks like they're on the run from the law."

"No, I already have a guy," Digby said.

I gave him a skeptical look.

"He was the best I could do last minute," Digby said.

"He who?" I said. And then I saw who was walking toward the car. "*Aldo* is our responsible adult? No offense to him, but who is this going to fool?"

I mean, I'd first met Aldo when Digby had hired him to

wreak havoc in an OB-GYN's office so we could steal patient files. At the time, Aldo seemed to be of no fixed address and took his payment in the form of chocolate chip cookies.

"It's just like Hamlet said, 'The apparel oft proclaims the man.'" Digby pulled the suit out of the plastic bag. "Clothes make the man, Princeton."

"Hamlet didn't say that," I said. "That Polonius guy did."

"Whatever," Digby said. "If the suit fits . . ."

"No one is going to believe he's our teacher," I said. "I mean, is Aldo working for cookies again? Or is he the one getting this cake?"

"Oh, chill. I have cash for him this time." And then Digby got out of the car.

"That wasn't the point I was trying to make," I said.

"Okay, Felix, it's time to call your mom," Digby said, and then left.

"Felix, you see what's happening here?" I said.

But Felix's mom had picked up on the other end. "Hello, Mom?" Felix said. "Yes . . . this is my teacher's phone. So, uh . . . it's lacrosse for gym today and I left my gym clothes at home to get out of it like you told me to but now they're making me use the sweaty unwashed stuff from lost and found . . ." Felix pulled the phone away to put distance between his ear and his mom's yelling. "No, Mom. You don't have to send anyone. I faked a stomach cramp and my physics teacher offered to drive me to your office. If you leave a drive-on pass at the gate, I can be there soon." Felix hung up and flopped back in

164

his seat. He wiped off the sweat from his top lip. "Whew. That went well." He punched the back of my seat in celebration. "I have a good feeling about today."

I'd been looking out the window, watching Digby help Aldo get dressed. There, standing in the open and without a thought about who might be watching, Aldo dropped his trousers.

"Me too," I lied.

FIFTEEN

We made one more stop at the 7-Eleven, where Digby and I got ID photos taken at the instant photo booth. Afterward, Aldo got in the driver's seat and Digby took the front passenger seat while I got in the back with Felix.

"It's been a while," Aldo said.

Watching Aldo getting the hang of being behind the wheel again made me nervous, so I tore my eyes away from the windshield and got to work piping icing onto the sheet cake instead. When I finished, I realized I'd done a good job writing in a straight line largely because Aldo was a great driver. I didn't even mind the '70s easy listening station he chose for his driving music.

By the time we got to the security check at the entrance to Perses, I was feeling much better about our plan and I'd relaxed to the point where I didn't immediately sense danger when the security guard asked Aldo, "Says here you're dropping off Felix Fong at Admin Building B?"

"Yeah," Aldo said. Clearly, though, Aldo hadn't really understood the guard's rapidly spoken question, because when he tried to parrot it back, Aldo said, "Feelings Fog. Adam Biddle Bede."

But the guard was absorbed in looking over the paperwork, so he missed it. "This drive-on pass is only good for two people." The security guard pointed at us with his pen and counted us off. "One, two, *three, four.*" He threw his hands up. There was a long moment of silence. "I can't let you drive on the campus with these extra passengers."

Digby leaned over across Aldo and said, "Actually—"

But Aldo suddenly spoke up. "I'm dropping off these two at home after." Aldo pointed at Digby and me and shrugged. "I'm doing the sick run today." The security guard still looked dubious, so Aldo said, "Hey, man, I'm happy to leave *this* kid here at the gate." He pointed at Felix. "But his parent probably wouldn't—"

"No, no. Don't do *that.*" Under his breath, the security guard said, "Susan Fong's kid. Hell, no." And then he waved us through.

We got to Admin Building B and Aldo parked Val's car.

"Okay, Aldo. That was great," Digby said. "Now, come in and have some lunch."

But Aldo didn't get out of his seat.

"Aldo?" Digby said. "Everything okay?"

Aldo ran his hand over the steering wheel. "I used to have a Saab." Aldo removed the keys from the ignition and held on to them for a long beat before handing them back to Digby. "I didn't realize how much I missed having keys."

Digby looked momentarily knocked out of his orbit but reset and said, "First this, Aldo, and then we'll talk about your situation, okay?"

We walked Aldo to the cafeteria and after Digby gave him a few twenties, we made our way to Felix's mom's office. Once we got to her floor, Felix brought Digby and me into the men's room and texted, "Mom I'm lost. What is Armes 35?"

"That's all the way across the campus," Felix said. "It's also where they process hazardous waste. She hates the place and if she thinks I'm in that building—"

Felix put his finger to his lips. We heard footsteps run past the men's room. And then we heard the sound of a stumble and the heavy thump of his mother falling down. But then we heard her get up and walk away. Finally, we heard the elevator doors open and close. Seconds later, Felix's phone got his mother's panic-typed text message: "Im xominh Frock."

"I think this means 'I'm coming, Felix.' We have at least ten minutes if she takes the golf cart. Fifteen if she runs," Felix said. "But we have to be careful. Mom's assistant's office is right next to hers."

Once we were in the office, Digby and Felix assembled Perses ID badges for Digby and me using blanks they took from a box in Mrs. Fong's desk drawer and the photos we took in the booth at the 7-Eleven.

"These won't open any doors because I can't activate the mag stripes or the RFID," Felix said. "But it'll look like the real thing, so at least you'll be able to walk around without getting stopped."

"Okay. Thanks, Felix." Digby took the badge from him and clipped it to his lanyard.

"You guys go on without me from here. This is it." Felix held my card out to me. "What do you think?"

This was his unsubtle way of asking me if I thought Digby was up to it. I tried to decide. Perses was a serious step up from the last place we broke into. Every time the computer tapes rubbed against each other in my backpack and clacked, I thought we would be busted for sure.

But then again, this was going more smoothly than any of our stupid shenanigans had ever gone.

"Test run, right?" I said, and then I gave Felix the least enthusiastic thumbs-up in the history of thumbs.

• • •

With our fake IDs, our big bag of party supplies, and the sheet cake, we really did look like the interns we claimed to be. The one guard we passed waved us through when we said, "We're setting up at Dr. Fong's."

Once we got to the restricted floor where Dr. Fong's clean room labs were, Digby found the conference room and hid our party gear with the cleaning supplies under the minibar's sink. We got back down to the lobby and exited the building without anyone looking at us twice.

After a few minutes of walking, Digby said, "We're getting close to the data center. Are you ready?"

"Are *you* ready?" I said.

"Are you kidding?" Digby said. "I've been waiting nine years for this. I am *so* ready."

"Then maybe do up your fly before we go," I said.

As he zipped up, he said, "Made you look."

"I didn't even know they made Thomas the Tank Engine boxers for grown-ups," I said.

"Sure. I think I can, I think I can," Digby said. "Grown-ups need inspirational stuff too."

"Sure they do," I said. "Except it was The Little Engine That Could who said, 'I think I can. I think I can.'"

"Isn't The Little Engine That Could the one where if you believe, a magic train would appear on a secret platform?" Digby said.

"If you believe? Secret platform? What?" I said. "Wait. Are you talking about the Hogwarts Express?"

"And now that we're talking trains, who the hell is Casey Jones?" he said.

"The driver of yet another train," I said. "*That* dude died, by the way."

"God, trains are tragic," he said.

"How are you confused about the Hogwarts Express?" I said. When Digby still looked blank, I said, "Hogwarts Express? It takes Harry Potter and his classmates to Hogwarts?" He still looked blank. "Their magic school?" I said. "Wait. Have you never read Harry Potter?"

"Oh, sure, sure, a page or two here and there," Digby said.

"That's not really how books work. But it does explain the word salad rattling around in your brain," I said. "I can't believe you've never read Harry Potter."

"I was robbed of my childhood. What do you want from me?" Digby said. And then he turned and saw my face. "Of course I read Harry Potter. I was just winding you up. Relax, Princeton." When I still didn't say anything, he said, "Oh, God, are you going to cry? Of course I had a *childhood*—"

"No, it's not that." I pointed at a sign on the building in front of us. SERVER ROOM, it said. "We're here."

But it wasn't actually a room. It was instead an enormous blue metal-sided warehouse. Windowless and built atop a rise from the road, it looked more like a monument or art installation than a working office building.

As he and I walked up to the door, Digby said, "So, high school paper, right?"

"What?" I said. "Didn't we say lost interns?"

"No. Interns in there but school paper in here, remember?" When I looked confused, Digby said, "That way it makes more sense that we're hanging around asking pointless questions."

"Oh, my God," I said. "Maybe we're rushing this . . ."

Digby felt me wavering and suddenly quickened his pace up to the door. He walked in before I could talk him out of it.

Well, I thought to myself, you *did* worry that he was over-thinking things . . .

I caught up with Digby right as he got to a lone desk tucked into a corner. Across from the desk was a glass wall, behind which stretched racks and racks of servers. We stood there on our own. After a while, Digby called out, "Hello?"

There was no sign of the owner of the desk, so I started looking around. Unlike the beautifully ordered glass-and-steel high-tech facility of film, TV, and my imagination, this place was filled with mismatched drives of varying decrepitude connected by expansive clumps of multicolored wire spaghetti. Everything looked old and overloaded.

Finally, we spotted one guy rolling up and down one of the aisles on a wheeled office chair with a laptop balanced on his lap. I thought it was weird he was wearing his coat before I realized that the air-conditioning fans in the server room blew much colder air than was comfortable. The tech got out of his seat and started walking toward us.

I felt Digby nudge me and I saw him put his finger on an envelope sitting on the table. It was one of several pieces of mail addressed to Milton Wright.

"Milton?" Digby said.

"Are you the interns HR sent?" Milton said. Before either of us could answer, Milton said, "Where's your camera?" Digby and I both took out our phones. Milton harrumphed and said, "Yep. That's about what I expected." And then he sighed. "Aren't you going to take the pictures?"

"Of course. Sure," Digby said. "Um . . . ?"

"Well? Are you or aren't you here to take my photo for the retirement announcement?" Milton said.

"Oh, yeah, we are," Digby said. "Where do you want us to do it?" We all looked at the cluttered hobbit hole Milton had built around his desk. There were shelves of collectibles and still-boxed action figures and the walls were papered over with posters and what looked like schematics for a spaceship.

I felt Digby nudge me again and this time, he flicked his eyes to direct my attention to a box sitting on Milton's table, flaps wide open and almost full of data tapes.

"Not here at my desk?" Milton said.

I knew we had to get him away from the box for us to make the switch, so I said, "Not enough . . ." I picked up a figurine I realized was of Milton himself dressed as a Jedi. ". . . gravitas?" The alarm on his phone sounded.

"Oops. Wait here. I'll go get the last one." Milton paused. "The last one." He shook his head. "I still can't believe it." After another second, Milton pointed at the open glass doors between us and the humming server racks. "Just in case . . . don't let these doors close, okay? I know I'm not supposed to keep it open, but after those poor bastards in Thailand—"

"Doors locked, halon fire suppression deployed, a bunch of techs suffocated? I saw the episode on *60 Minutes*," Digby said. "But isn't halon banned now?"

"Our system's been grandfathered in," Milton said. "That's how old this place is." And then Milton walked back through the doors and disappeared into the maze of whirring drives.

"What is going on?" I said. "Did he just leave us with all this sitting out?" I pointed at the box of tapes.

"Never question a freebie, Princeton. Let's get going." Digby walked toward me and started to unpack the tapes from my backpack.

"What if the real interns show up to take his picture?" I said.

"Princeton." Digby paused and let the sound of the throbbing hum of the servers fill the silence. "No one is coming to take this dude's picture."

He spun me around and dove into my bag again.

"Digby, no, wait. Stop." I pointed at the contents of the box Milton was filling. "These aren't the same data tapes Felix gave us to switch out."

Instead of the yellow lightning bolt of the Perses logo, the boxed data tapes on the desk had a red logo of clasped hands.

"Damn it," Digby said.

SIXTEEN

"Should we—" I was going to say "call it and try again another day" but Digby took off and started hunting around the shelves and cupboards.

And then I heard him curse softly and when he turned back around, he was holding up two of the red-logoed data tapes.

I breathed out some of the tension.

"How many do we need?" he said.

I emptied the box and counted out twenty-five super tapes. Digby turned back to the cupboard to retrieve the new tapes while I gathered up the tapes Milton had already put in the box. I guess I'd underestimated how quickly Digby would be working, because when I turned back around to cross the room to him, he was already standing right there behind me. We collided.

We were both speechless after our armloads of tapes clattered down onto the floor into a commingled pile of exactly identical tapes. And, of course, that's exactly when we heard Milton's footsteps approaching.

"You get rid of him. I'll put these back away," I said. "We can't go through with this today—"

Digby said, "No, no. Get rid of him. I'll figure this out—"

"Figure this out? Just put it away." I gave Digby the thumbs-down. "Mission abort—"

Digby said, "No, I can—"

"Abort. Abort," I said. It was so annoying that he was just ignoring me.

Digby had just started kicking the tapes under the desk when the tech walked back around the corner carrying the last data tape.

"What was that?" Milton said. "I heard crashing."

"Oh, uh . . . he tried to cop a feel just now and I knocked some stuff off your desk when I hit him," I said.

"Not my stapler, I hope." Milton picked up his pace and was now almost within sight of the desk and the box we'd emptied. "That's an original Swingline number four. From when they were made on Long Island."

Digby was still trying to push some of the scattered tapes under the desk without tipping off Milton, so I said, "The stapler didn't fall down. Don't worry." I stepped forward to block his view of the box and said, "You know, I just had the best idea for a picture."

"Yes?" Milton said.

I played it extra casual as I eased the last tape from Milton's hand, passed it to Digby, and steered Milton back into the stacks of servers. "Let's get a picture of you in your natural environment," I said. "With the servers."

"Oh, that is a good idea," he said.

I said, "It should only take a minute." But then I looked back and saw Digby staring at a data tape and then bringing it up to his nose to sniff it along all its edges. "Or maybe a few minutes while I find the good light."

I took my time finding a spot tucked away from sight and made a fuss about positioning Milton to get an interesting picture. When I finally settled on a spot, he cleared his throat and said, "My name is Milton Wright. I've worked at Perses Analytics since I graduated from college. I built this data storage facility. I love my job. I don't want to retire." And then he snapped out of his trance and in a more conversational voice, said, "I just feel like I had to say that aloud."

I found myself brought close to tears by the obvious pride Milton took in having built the place. "Are they forcing you to retire?" I asked. "You don't look old enough to retire."

"Oh, I'm retirement age, all right," he said. "But I don't have any sun damage or expression lines because I've been inside and alone for thirty years."

"So, you've been . . ." I pointed down at the floor because I didn't know how to say "in this same place for *thirty years*?" without sounding like I was questioning the basis of his entire existence.

Milton did a combination shrug and look-at-this-place

gesture with his hands. He did look sad but more than any-thing, he looked cast adrift by the impending loss of his legions of servers. I'd initially thought I'd have a hard time buying Digby time to switch the tapes but that worry faded when I saw the way Milton flared to life when I asked for a tour.

•••

Forever and a thousand facts I didn't need to know about cool-ants and fire suppression later, I looked up and saw Digby standing at the end of the server room's main aisle watching me trying to sound fascinated while Milton explained why the building had double-depth walls.

When Digby and I made eye contact, he pointed at my back-pack slung over his shoulder, and gave me a thumbs-up. "Uh . . . sorry to interrupt," Digby said. "But we should get back."

We all walked back to Milton's desk, where—thank God—he closed up and sealed the carton of tapes with packing tape without verifying its contents.

"I didn't mean to come off bitter back there," Milton said. "I've been lucky. Lifer jobs like mine don't exist anymore. It's a good time to quit, actually." He finished packing and patted the box. "I'm glad I'm not going to have to work on tearing this place down."

"Tearing this place down?" I said. "They're tearing down this facility?"

"Yep. They're moving to cloud backup. They think the cloud

is safer. Can you believe it?" Milton said. "After all the hacks, how can the cloud be safer than tape backup?" He patted the box again.

"Right," Digby said. "Tape's the safest."

"I tried to tell them it's crazy not to have both tape and the cloud but . . ." Milton threw up his hands. "So this is the very last round of tape backups Perses will do." He sighed. "Like I said, I helped build this place. I'm glad I don't have to stick around and watch it get ripped up."

I could hear Digby start to breathe faster. "That was the last round of tape backups?" he said.

"End of an era, all right," Milton said.

"I guess it's a good thing we came when we did." Digby seemed overwhelmed. He took a step back and when he bumped into a cupboard with my backpack, the tapes inside clacked together loudly enough that Milton noticed.

I don't know what possessed me to say it, but to deflect Milton's attention from Digby, I said, "Actually, Milton, they're throwing a party for you today in Dr. Fong's lab. Nanorobotics lab."

Milton and Digby both said, "They are?"

"I hope I'm not spoiling things, but nobody said it was a surprise party," I said.

"Nanorobotics?" Milton tapped the box. "That's the department I just backed up."

I made an expression like, Aha, and said, "Probably why they decided to have it up there."

"Wow," Milton said. "That is seriously great."

I immediately moved on to wondering if I'd just set Milton up for more disappointment when I saw his Jedi figurine and was struck with another idea. "Milton, can I take this?" I held up the little plastic Jedi. "Temporary loan."

• • •

Digby didn't even wait for the door to shut fully before he whooped and did a little victory dance.

"I take it you got what you needed?" I said.

All I got in response was a few triumphant pelvic thrusts.

"Okay, that's nice you're happy," I said. "But we've still got the crumbs on our chins, so can we at least walk away from the cookie jar before we celebrate?"

"Speaking of cookies . . ." Digby said.

I handed him one of the granola bars I carried around for his sudden onset hunger emergencies. "What happened to your game face? We're only halfway there."

"You heard him, Princeton. The *last* day. We got it out on the *last day*," Digby said. "I feel it. Fate is on my side today." He pulled out his phone. "I better text Felix."

• • •

Digby and I returned to the nanorobotics lab and set up the conference room for what was now going to be Milton's retirement party. I started to understand what Digby meant about feeling like fate was on our side that day when someone from the lab poked their head around the door to ask who we were and we both automatically said, "Interns from HR." Everything felt in sync.

While Digby loaded the Star Wars DVD into the machine, I opened the cake box and squished down Milton's Jedi figurine where I'd iced *TEAM FONG*. I piped in his name so the cake instead read, *MAY THE FORCE BE WITH MILTON.*

Felix walked into the conference room, read the cake, and said, "Who the heck is Milton?"

"Whoa. You got here fast," I said. "And you're very sweaty."

"Milton's the guy in charge of data storage. Princeton made a friend," Digby said. "Good old Princeton. Always the good girl. Even when she's doing bad things."

"Well? Are we done here?" Felix looked around the conference room. "Because we need to get going. Let's go let's go let's go."

The sweating, the motormouth, the uncharacteristic rudeness. "I see the red eye has kicked in," I said.

"Coffee? You gave him coffee?" Digby said. "Princeton, we don't get extra points for increasing the difficulty."

"Felix, are you all right?" I said.

"Yeah yeah yeah," Felix said. "But I do feel like my heart's going to explode. It's not going to explode, is it?"

"It's not going to explode. You should just maybe have a sip of water or something," I said. "Now what? You guys never actually told me what happens next."

"I told my dad I was coming up to borrow a laptop to do some homework," Felix said. "Digby will start the movie and there'll be a stampede into the conference room when people hear the fanfare. No one will notice when I go into the lab's stockroom for a computer and come out with a tape reader too. Then we make copies of his mom's files."

"But how are we going to decrypt the files?" I said. "Won't we still need passwords?"

"The decryption keys are assigned to the machines, not the people." I guess I didn't look like I understood what he was saying, because Felix said, "Meaning—"

"All the equipment assigned to this lab can decrypt all the data this lab encrypts," I said. "Thanks. I got it."

"So, are we ready?" Digby said. When we nodded, he turned on the TV and pressed play on the DVD. The three of us scurried out of the conference room.

SEVENTEEN

Digby and I went into the handicap stall of the women's bathroom, where he pulled down the baby change table, unpacked our loot of data tapes, and waited for Felix. The sound of his fingers tapping a rapid beat against the table made me nervous.

I put my hand over his and said, "Are you all right? You haven't blinked in a while."

Digby machine-gunned a few dozen blinks.

"I don't want to ruin your concentration mid-shenanigan but . . ." I said. "I've never seen you so off your game."

"You mean I'm holding on too tight? I've lost the edge?" Digby said. "I'm nervous."

"Because you're so close." I nodded. I understood.

"No, Princeton, I'm nervous because I don't have an out planned for you," he said. "If we get caught, that's it for you. And Felix."

"Do you *ever* have an out planned for me?" I said.

"I always just plan to plead guilty in exchange for your immunity." Digby pointed at the data tapes. "But they won't offer a plea deal for this."

I felt a quick splash of panic but I calmed myself down. "You're right. This is by far the stupidest crap we've ever pulled. But we're right in the middle of this tight-rope walk and it's not the right time to start looking down," I said. "I know what I'm doing. A really smart dude once told me that friends take responsibility for friends."

"Felix said that to me too," Digby said. "What do you think it means that we're getting our wisdom from the same guy who spent half an hour arguing with himself whether I was the Archie or Jughead of our little group. I mean, of course—"

I said, "You're Jughead" the exact same moment he said, "I'm Archie."

And then we both said, "What?"

"*Henry* is Archie," I said.

"Henry is *Moose*," Digby said.

"But Sloane is Veronica," I said.

"If I'm Jughead, then you're Ethel," he said. "Although that does kind of make sense because Ethel's always giving Jughead food."

"I'm actually shocked how much you and I know about Archie," I said.

"And I'm shocked I'm only just now realizing how much of that Taylor Swift song is Archie," Digby said. "Betty is like, can't you see that I'm the one who understands you. Been here all along, so why can't you see you belong with me . . ."

"But in the Jughead comics"—Digby and I jumped at Felix's suddenly joining our conversation—"Jughead and Betty get together . . ."

Digby opened the stall door for Felix and let him in.

"And even in the Archie comics, Jughead is always the shoulder Betty cries on whenever Archie chooses Veronica. Of course, if you want to talk about the TV version, then we have to start this conversation over completely." Felix put down the laptop on the baby changer. "And, Digby, I'm running out of polite ways to tell you. I know it's your favorite song and you thought Zoe should've been going out with you instead of Austin, but not every relationship can be explained by 'You Belong With Me.'" Felix started opening the tape boxes. "In fact, you guys are more like 'I Knew You Were Trouble.'"

"It's Princeton's favorite song," Digby said.

"It came on the radio *once* when we were hanging out," I said. "I sang along to some of it and you've been talking about it ever since."

Felix held up a handful of the tapes. "Pick a tape, any tape. That's where we'll start." He inserted the one I chose into the tape reader.

"How long will this take?" I said.

"Well . . . it depends." Felix spent a few minutes scrolling through the tape's directory before ejecting it.

I handed him my second pick of tape.

"It takes a long time to search these backups one by one," Felix said. "But the data's sequential, so I just have to get in the strike zone of Dr. Digby's years of employment at Perses and it'll be super fast from there," Felix said. "Oh, hey, I hear I should be congratulating you?"

"You told him about Prentiss?" I said.

Digby nodded.

"I haven't decided yet," I said.

Both Felix and Digby said, "Of course you're going."

"Just let yourself say it already," Digby said.

"It's a seriously good school," Felix said. "Well, if you want to do the whole 'job' thing."

"The 'job' thing? Who *doesn't* want to do the 'job' thing?" I said. "I mean, if they want to do the whole 'eat and have a place to live' thing . . ."

"Well, yeah, if you want to have a job, sell your time, then, yes, you should go to a good school, get good grades and all that," Felix said. "But, you know, if you want to sell your ideas, it matters a whole lot less where you go and what you score on a test. Or, in fact, if you even want to go to college at all."

"Are you saying you *aren't* going to college?" I said.

My jaw dropped when Felix smiled and said, "Nope."

"Do your parents know?" I said.

Felix said, "Every time I contemplate having that conversation, my brain freezes."

"What are you going to do?" I said.

"I have an idea for a data security start-up." Felix pointed at what he was doing and said, "Clearly, there's a market for it."

"Felix? Didn't you tell me your parents are buying an apartment in Boston so your mom can live with you when you start going to college?" Digby said. "That's happening soon, isn't it?"

"It's going into escrow next week," Felix said.

"Felix. If you're sure you don't want to go to college, you have to tell them before they waste a bunch of money," I said.

Felix muttered something about not wanting to deal with it before he got back to searching the files.

I watched Felix work but after a while, I found myself staring at a screen of rapidly scrolling gibberish dizzying. I stepped outside the stall and washed my hands.

Digby followed me out.

"What are you doing? This is the ladies' room. What if someone came in?" I said. "Get back in the stall."

"We could just start making out and say we're jacked up on hormones and science," Digby said.

From behind the stall door, Felix said, "Please don't do that."

"Relax. No one's coming in." Digby pushed the door open so I could hear everyone at the party reciting the dialogue along with the characters onscreen. "I don't think they'd even notice if I went in there for a slice of cake."

Again, from behind the closed stall door, Felix said, "Please don't do that."

"But I'm starving," Digby said.

I threw him a granola bar. "I don't have any more food, so you'd better make that last."

"Hey!" Felix said. "This tape is blank."

I watched Digby's face suddenly slacken with panic. "I never did ask you how you decided which tapes were which," I said.

"Your old-lady lavender smell gets on everything you touch. I could smell it on the tapes you took out of the box," Digby said. "Remember how your mom smelled it on me that time I was over at your place?"

Felix said, "And *this* one's blank." There was a series of pla-sticky clacks as Felix ejected and threw yet another blank tape aside. "This one isn't empty but it's not the right one," Felix said. "What happened to you two down there?"

Digby gave a summary of the fiasco in the data storage center that ended with, ". . . I mean, at one point, I tried to clear my nose by sniffing the cup of coffee sitting on the desk but the guy adds cream to his."

Felix kicked open the stall door to check if Digby was being serious. For the few seconds between the door swinging open and swinging shut again, Felix gave us a look that perfectly combined pity and disgust. And then the sound of Felix inserting and ejecting tapes resumed.

"Princeton. You don't think I took the wrong ones, do you?" Digby said. I didn't think I could come up with a cheery answer, so I kept my face neutral. "I should've known. It was too easy."

There wasn't anything I could say, so I just hugged him.

Digby said again, "It was too easy . . ."

"Nothing about the past year has been easy," I said.

"I wish life were just a straight suffering for results swap," Digby said. "Then I'd be golden. Because I've already done the suffering part—"

Felix kicked open the stall door and walked out, stiff-legged and wild-eyed.

"What?" I said.

Felix didn't say a word.

"What is it? Nothing?" I said.

Felix and Digby just stared at each other.

"What?" I said. "Come on, you mute bastards, say something."

Felix held up a data tape, his face bathed in triumph, and in the five seconds that followed, I don't think any of us even thought about the risk of getting caught. We screamed.

EIGHTEEN

I felt a deeper relief than I'd ever experienced in my life when we passed the imaginary red line I'd drawn around Perses without hearing a single alarm or siren. Once my over-stimulated brain stopped telling my body it was in crisis, I slipped into a post-adrenaline state of shock. Time stretched and shrunk in weird places. Digby drove Aldo back to the bus terminal and I smiled and said good-bye, all the while feeling like I was underwater.

Next thing I knew, we'd arrived at Olympio's. Digby was slow to get out when we parked the car and when he caught up with us, I pretended I hadn't seen him wipe tears from his eyes.

I didn't blame him. We had his mom's research. Everything de Groot wanted. We were going to find out what happened to Digby's sister. It was a big freaking deal.

Sloane and Henry were waiting for us when we got inside but before we had a chance to sit them down and explain what we'd just done, Henry said, "You guys. A little help? Tino's not here because his wife broke her foot at Jazzercise, Wanda won ten grand on Lotto—won't be seeing her for a while—and the register is acting screwy," Henry said.

I took the plate he handed me. "Wait. Shouldn't your parents come in, then?"

"It's the first time they've trusted me with a busy dinner shift," Henry said. "But I guess I could get them to bail on their movie . . ."

I pointed at the plate and said, "Where does this go?"

Henry said, "This goes to the woman by the window. You'll know which one she is."

Sure enough, an angry woman was craning her neck in our direction.

Right as I served the food, I heard a crash and saw Sloane swabbing at a puddle of spilled soda at a table of noisy kids and their frantic mom. I grabbed a rag and headed over to help Sloane and before we knew what was happening, Felix was in charge of pouring drinks and plating desserts, and Digby, Sloane, and I were running the dinner service while Henry went back into the kitchen to help out the one short-order cook who had shown up for work.

• • •

When we finally beat the Friday dinner rush and the last few diners were finishing up, Henry came out of the kitchen and gulped down three of the pre-poured glasses of water Sloane had set up on the counter.

"Already setting up for the after-movie slam," Henry said. "Good thinking."

"Don't kiss my butt. I'm still mad," Sloane said. But clearly she felt Henry had learned whatever lesson she needed to teach and the two of them were back on the road to Sweethearts-ville.

"Wait. The what?" I said. I mean, it had been maybe a little therapeutic to get out of our heads for a while but the idea of having to deal with yet another room of people who thought *server* and *servant* were the same thing . . .

Sloane saw my face and said, "I keep telling Henry to tell his parents to sell this place and buy a pizza franchise instead. It's more money, less work, and a much easier business to run by telephone from our house in the Hamptons."

"Running a diner's not a bad business, actually," Digby said. "If only the customers were—"

"Not animals?" Sloane said.

"Come on," Henry said.

"Who else orders bottomless garlic bread when they know it's just day-old buns smeared with shortening and garlic powder?" Sloane said. "And what kind of restaurant does that?"

"Lots of places use up their day-old bread like that," Henry said.

"Lots of places that are dumps," Sloane said. "It's tacky. You should get rid of it."

"And let them eat cake instead?" I said.

"Actually . . ." Felix said. "That's probably the most profitable item on the menu after soda." He came over with a copy of the menu. "If you want to streamline, think about things like the moussaka. Why is *moussaka* on the menu?"

"We're Greek, Felix," Henry said.

"You were averaging fifteen minutes between orders going in and orders going up until one guy ordered the moussaka plate. Then everything slowed way down and we never got back up to fifteen minutes after that." Felix took a Sharpie and started crossing out items. "This menu's too big. Too many soups. The Greek stuff's a time waster . . ."

"Hey," Henry said.

Felix said, "And the restaurant's basically a set from a workers' compensation PSA video shoot."

"What?" Henry said.

Felix pointed around the counter area. "The leaking soda machine's flooded the floor and that's a major slip and fall hazard. The electrical tape you used on the frayed wire for the cash register is now frayed too, and it's throwing off sparks—"

"Sparks? I've never seen that," Henry said.

Just then the wire crackled and a small blue spark popped out. Digby carefully unplugged the register.

"And do you smell that? That gasoline smell?" Felix said.

We all sniffed.

"Isn't that Sloane's perfume?" I said.

Sloane gave me a dirty look.

"I told you," I said. "It doesn't matter how much it costs,

Sloane. When you wear too much, it just smells like roach spray."

"No, no. I think it's that." Felix kicked at a pile of rags on the floor under the counter.

"Oh, we use those to polish the metal on the counter." Henry pointed at the ridged metal banding that edged the entire length of the diner's lunch counter and all the diners' tables.

"Metal polish is highly flammable," Felix said. "Safety first. You need to make changes."

"Flood or fire, Felix?" Henry said. "Which is it?"

"I didn't really see it as an either-or situation," Felix said.

"Whoa," Henry said. "You have really been thinking about this."

Felix sighed and closed his eyes. "Anything to keep my mind off the fact that we stole confidential government information this afternoon," he said.

"You what?" Henry said.

Sloane turned to me and said, "I couldn't find you at lunch but I just figured you cut and went to the mall."

"Um . . . you guys." I pointed at a nearby table of college frat guys who were obviously trying to eavesdrop.

Henry clapped his hands and said, "Okay, everybody. The diner's closed. If you leave right now, your food's on the house."

We watched the last few tables empty out. I was relieved. I wouldn't have wanted to let down Henry but I couldn't imagine having to deal with a second round of grumpy diners.

Digby said to the eavesdropping frat guys, "The food's free

but the service isn't. Don't forget to tip your server." All that got him was a round of jeering.

"Ugh. Ungrateful creeps," Sloane said.

"Why do you think I prefer working in the kitchen?" Henry said. "Speaking of which, I should go tell Jorge he can go home. I'll call my parents to let them know we're closing early."

After Henry went to the back, one especially douche-y frat guy yelled, "The service here sucks balls." And then he raised his glass of water and poured it all over the table.

Digby glanced at me, silently asking for permission to deal them a little instant karma.

I put my hand on his arm. "The things we did today . . . if that's the worst we have to deal with, then we are solidly in the win column."

It was Sloane who noticed the lone customer huddled up in the corner.

"Sorry, sir. We're closed," Sloane said.

The guy stood and slowly slithered up to us at the register, giving me enough time to see the tracks that hard living had run all over his face. He was thin in an unwholesome way and the way he tucked his chin down and talked to us in an insinu-ating, I-know-things hiss didn't help either. He creeped me out.

"Great place you got here," Sir Hiss said. And then he started looking at Felix, Sloane, Digby, and me in an assessing and memorizing kind of way.

After a long beat, Sir Hiss finally got that we thought he was being weirdly attentive and he snapped out of staring at us. "And what a bee-yoo-tiful bunch of do-gooding kids. Real upstanding citizen material. Your parents must be proud."

"What makes you think we're do-gooding?" Digby said.

"Oh, I don't know," Sir Hiss said. "I guess that's just something people say." He reached into his pocket for some money. "You sure I can't pay you?"

Henry and Jorge came out of the kitchen and joined us. "On the house, man," Henry said.

"Oh . . . that's mighty nice . . ." Sir Hiss slid a bill across the counter toward Sloane and said, "But here's a little something for you. Add it to your college fund."

Sloane looked confused and didn't touch the money. "It's a five."

"She's new." Henry picked up the bill and tucked it into Sloane's apron. "What she means is thank you and good night."

Sir Hiss tipped the brim of an imaginary hat and walked away. Henry locked the front door after Jorge and Sir Hiss walked out.

"That was weird," I said.

"We get a lot of ex-cons coming here straight after they're released," Henry said. "I had one guy tell me that our steak's a popular get out of jail meal."

"What did that guy have?" I said.

"Coffee," Sloane said. "Just coffee."

"He seemed super grateful for getting just free coffee," I said. "Not normal, right?"

Digby looked lost in a thought and only muttered, "Why did that guy look so familiar?"

"So the frat guys were ungrateful but this guy was *too* grateful?" Henry said. "You two might not have much of a future in the restaurant business."

"*You* might not have much of a future in the restaurant business," Sloane said. "I mean, seriously, once you graduate college, are you even going to work here? Work a diner after you play college football . . . maybe even play in the NFL—"

Henry knocked on the counter, covered his ears, and hummed "America the Beautiful." "Don't jinx it, Sloane," Henry said. "I don't want to think that far ahead right now. We don't even know if we have a season come fall."

"Do the guys on your team know what to do?" Digby said.

"Yeah . . . Principal Granger told us about the plan to just let the lawyers appeal the positive drug tests until the steroids work their way out of the guys' systems," Henry said. "I told them to double the mileage on their runs for the next month to sweat that crap out faster."

"That won't work," Felix said. "Their bodies won't metabolize the drugs any faster."

"*I* know that and *you* know that but those guys don't know that," Henry said. "But now they can run eight miles a day and meditate on why they should just say no to drugs." Henry thought for a long second and then said, "There's something twisted about that guy. Principal Granger, I mean."

Digby grimaced and nodded. "Yeah, there is. But stick to

the story and you'll have a season. Just promise me that when you're up in the bigs, you'll speak out against kids putting this steroid junk in their bodies?"

"That's the plan," Henry said. "Okay, now, what's up with you guys? When Felix said . . . did he mean . . ."

Digby nodded. "Yeah. My mom's research. We took it today."

"Whoa," Sloane said. "So that's . . ."

"Treason," Felix said. "Yup. I betrayed my country. And I feel like I betrayed my parents."

"Because you did. And I made you do it for me," Digby said. "Now we both have to live with that. And Henry. Remember when you asked me the other day if you should worry about Silk or Coach or whoever else they were working with coming after you and I said, *Relax, these guys aren't the mafia*?" When Henry nodded, Digby said, "Well, the truth is you can't ever say never and you'll always wonder and be a little paranoid. You'll have to live with that too."

I put my hand on Digby's arm. "You're starting to scare people."

Henry sighed. "No, he's right. It'd almost be better if he just came after me and we could get it done already."

"'Get it done already'? Yikes," I said. "Be careful what you wish for."

"Yeah, look at Felix," Digby said. "He became the soccer team's manager to be more social and . . . what did you say to me last night, Felix?"

198

"That job is destroying my life," Felix said.

"Why?" Henry said. "Isn't it scheduling and budget and all that stuff you like?"

Felix said, "It's those girls. I can't take them anymore."

"Oh, the virgin thing?" Sloane said. "They're still teasing you about that? Get a new joke already."

"They have a pool going to see who gets to do it with me first," Felix said.

"Those girls are just kidding, Felix," Sloane said.

"Wait a second, though. Hold on," I said. "Would we say that to a girl? If she had an entire team joking about having sex with her?"

"That's different," Sloane said. And then she looked less sure. "Isn't it?"

"Uh-oh . . . we are too tired to go down this hole tonight," Digby said.

"Is this the erection argument? That it'd be physically impossible to 'make me'?" Felix said. "Because there are ways around that. I heard them talking. Why do you think they were trying to pickle me with all that tequila?"

"Just tell them to stop," Henry said. "Say you're not interested."

Felix looked at Sloane and me and said, "Does *that* work?"

"Yes, Henry. *Does* that work?" Sloane said. "And if just saying 'not interested' *does* work, then should I assume that I found Maisie doing Pilates on your lap because you *didn't* tell her you aren't interested?"

"I'm out," Henry said to Felix.

"Seriously, Felix. This keeps coming up with you. You need to learn to say no to people," I said. "Same thing with your parents and the apartment. You need to tell them not to buy that apartment."

Felix looked at me, super nervous.

"What apartment?" Sloane said.

"Felix's parents are buying a place in Boston so they can live with him when he starts college," I said.

"Boston?" Sloane said. "Why Boston?"

"Well, MIT," Felix said. "Or, if something goes horribly wrong, Harvard's my backup."

I mean, it was a fact that Felix was smart enough to consider Harvard his safety school but it was still quite a thing to hear.

Sloane put her hand on her chest and inhaled sharply. "I think I finally understand what it's like for normal people when I tell them what I pay for my clothes," she said.

"*Anyway,*" I said. "I'm serious, Felix. The bullies, these girls, your parents . . . you don't want to be doing this your whole life. You really just have to tell them no." He still looked unconvinced. "Felix, you straight-up defibbed a dude with a gun. In the *face*. What can still scare you after you've done *that*?"

"My mom is *not* going to take it well," Felix said.

"Oh, come on. You're doing a start-up security company. It's not like you're quitting school to . . ." I struggled to find a ridiculous example but couldn't. In frustration I flailed my arms and knocked a dirty soup ladle out of its spoon rest and onto Digby's jacket, where it left a huge smear before hitting the floor. "Oh, no . . ."

"It's okay. I'll be back," Digby said. And then, out of nowhere, he kissed me. "We did it, Princeton." He gave me one of his rarely seen unironic smiles and went into the kitchen.

NINETEEN

I was feeling a little embarrassed about the unexpected PDA when I turned back to face Henry and Felix, but whatever shyness I felt was replaced by confusion when I saw them staring at me, unsmiling. Henry looked downright angry at me.

"What?" I said.

"Be careful with Digby," Henry said.

"Yes," Felix said. "Don't screw him up even more."

"I don't believe this. After all the crap he's put me through, I'm the one getting the warning?" I said.

"Because you're leaving this summer," Henry said. "You started up with Digby when you know you won't even be here that much longer?"

"That is kind of messed up," Sloane said.

"I haven't even decided if I'm going yet," I said.

All three of them said, "Of course you're going."

"Why are you still pretending you aren't?" Sloane said.

"Digby has liked you for so long that he doesn't care how bad he's going to feel when you leave," Henry said.

Felix pointed his finger at me. "But we care. So, please. Be. Careful."

I wasn't the only one who noticed Felix's weird intensity, because Henry said, "Felix, are you okay?"

"Yeah. I know you're worried about Digby but . . ." I said. "That was kind of next level."

"So you guys aren't fighting anymore?" Sloane said.

"Fighting?" I said. "Oh, you mean that Bill thing? Yeah, Digby and I worked it out . . . I guess. It still bothers me that I let Bill get to me, though. I feel like she might've won that one."

"You think Bill won?" Sloane snorted. "People have finally realized she's just a user and everyone's ditching her. What's she going to write about now?"

Digby walked out of the kitchen, still wiping his jacket. It took him a second to notice the weird vibe in the room and when he did, he said, "Now what?"

We all said, "Nothing."

Digby said, "Well, *obviously* nothing's up."

And then Felix slumped facedown onto the counter.

"Felix?" Digby said. "Are you all right?"

Felix stayed facedown in his folded arms but gave us the thumbs-up.

"Are you sure, buddy?" Digby said. "Can I get you anything?"

And then I realized. "Oh . . ." I said. The agitation, the

sudden bursts of hostility, the sweatiness . . . "Do you think it's the coffee?"

"Should've stuck to your rule, man. 'If it's brown, turn it down'?" Digby said. "You're a Sprite man for a reason."

"I think you're having a caffeine crash, Felix," I said.

Felix straightened up and took his pulse. "Hm. I'm exhausted and I feel worthless and unbelievably sad."

"Sounds about right," I said. "You need more coffee."

"So, the answer is more coffee?" Felix said.

"Always the answer," Sloane said.

"I think I'm starting to understand the Starbucks business model," Felix said.

"That's why I never touch the stuff," Henry said. When he saw me starting to pour Felix a cup, he said, "*No*. No, no, no. Don't do that. What he needs is a nap." Henry gestured at Felix and said, "Come with me, man. You can nap on the couch in my dad's office."

"Is that the famous Petropoulos family couch?" Digby said.

"Famous?" Felix said. "Why famous?"

"The Petropouloses have eight kids but they work in this diner basically nonstop. Where do you think all the magic happens?" Digby said.

"What?" Felix said.

"Ha-ha, very funny," Henry said. "The magic happens in the old-fashioned way. In a bed, in the dark—"

"After they say their prayers?" Digby said.

Henry put his arm around Felix and said, "Ignore him. Digby's just being a jackass as usual."

"A nap does sound good," Felix said.

Henry and Felix went into the back.

Sloane waited until the door to the kitchen swung shut behind them before she said, "I am *this* close to just burning this place down." She made a condescending pointing motion at the counter. "*This* is not going to be my life."

"Then you are going to have a problem, my friend, because Henry loves *this*." I mimicked her condescending pointing motion.

"That's what I mean. He'd never quit," Sloane said. "But all I need is a match."

Suddenly there was a loud knocking on the front door's glass. We all turned to see Sir Hiss standing outside. When he saw us looking, he yelled, "I need to get something I left behind."

Sloane smirked at me. "Maybe he's back for his five dollars." She hopped off her barstool and said, "I'll get it." She took Henry's keys from the register and walked to the front. Sloane unlocked the door, saying, "Sorry. We're closed, so you'll have to make it quick—"

Digby and I couldn't see exactly what was going on because Sloane was standing at an angle that completely eclipsed our view of Sir Hiss, but the way she suddenly froze in her tracks and put her hands in the air told the whole story anyway.

Sir Hiss came in, pushing along Sloane in front of him until he'd corralled the three of us behind the counter. I guess we'd all been staring at the knife in his hand because Sir Hiss said, "You're all thinking . . . probably only one of us will get stabbed before some other one of us gets that knife away from him and you'd be right . . . except . . ."

The kitchen door swung open and Silk came out holding a gun. "I'm baaack." He pointed the gun at us. "Did you miss me?"

Sloane stepped closer to me when Silk leered at her.

"What's the plan, Silk?" Digby said. "A little fun before leaving town? I'm sure they won't look long for a two-bit drug dealer but they'll never stop if you add five counts of murder to your hot sheet."

Silk turned his gun to Digby. "Maybe I just kill *you*, then."

"Hey," Sir Hiss said to Silk. "You need to *focus*."

Angry that Digby had obviously shaken him, Silk said, "I ain't afraid of jail. All my friends are there."

"Oh, yeah? Your partner looks a lot less excited about the prospect." Digby turned to Sir Hiss. "And how long before the money runs out? What's the split?"

Sir Hiss's smile dropped. "What money?" Sir Hiss walked toward Silk. "You didn't say anything about this place having any money."

"I didn't know about any money," Silk said. "Where's this money?" He poked Digby with the gun.

"Don't you remember what I've been telling you about

planning? Stick to the plan," Sir Hiss said. "Anyway, the kid's probably lying. Look at this place. How much money can they have here?"

Digby smirked at Silk and said, "I know for a fact that they put at least ten grand in the safe this afternoon because their meat supplier only takes cash."

"You see what he's doing?" Sir Hiss said. "Ask yourself why he's being so helpful. What's he up to?"

"We sure could use that money," Silk said.

"Let them go and I'll open the safe," Digby said.

"Don't do it," Sir Hiss said.

"We need it. You can open the safe?" When Digby nodded, Silk said, "Come on."

I was frightened, no doubt about it. But when I saw Digby had on his bored face, I was filled with the totally irrational and completely unjustifiable feeling that everything was going to be all right.

"Hey, Princeton," Digby said. "You'll be all right here?" When I nodded, he said, "Remember, Princeton. Safety first. Don't do anything I would do." And then he let Silk push him through the doors into the kitchen.

What *would* he do?

Safety first. Felix had said that. What else had he said? The metal polish on the rags? No. The leaking soda machine? No. Maybe? But I didn't know how. The frayed wire. Yes. How? It plugged into the register. The register full of money. Yes. *That's* what he'd do.

Sir Hiss opened up the pie display and gouged out a handful of cherry filling with his fingers.

"Do you want a plate for that?" Sloane said. I had to give her credit. Even under stress, she was 100 percent Sloane.

Sir Hiss glared at us. "Say what?"

"Look. You should just know now . . . neither of us knows how to open the register," I said.

Sir Hiss turned to the register and thumped on the open button a few times. "It's not plugged in," he said. He pointed at me and said, "Plug it in."

As I edged toward the plug, I thought about everything that had to happen in the next couple of seconds. I plugged it in and just as I thought he would, Sir Hiss opened up the register and immediately got caught up in the task of emptying the cash from the drawers.

What I hadn't foreseen, though, was how far he would be from the part of the wire that was exposed. But then he started rummaging around under the register, muttering, "Where's the cash drop box . . . ?" and I knew I had to get ready to take the chance that was starting to open up. For a moment, I worried that maybe not all metal could conduct electricity but when Sir Hiss put down his pie and put his hand on the counter so he could dip down low for a look, I decided the best way to find out was to just do it.

I touched the sparking wire to the metal banding that skirted the diner's lunch counter. At first, it wasn't clear that anything at all was happening. Sir Hiss jerked up from his crouch and stood poker straight, gripping the counter in front of him with both hands, and looking straight ahead with a grimace. But after a few more seconds of watching him frozen like that, I noticed the steam rising from the soaked canvas of his shoes and the puddle of soda machine leakage that had pooled around his feet.

And then, finally, the register itself started to smoke and sizzle, and with a loud pop, the spell was broken. Sir Hiss slammed face-first into the register's keyboard before slumping down onto the floor in a heap.

"Is he . . . ?" Sloane said.

The smell of burning hair wasn't a good sign. I unplugged the register and kicked Sir Hiss in the ribs. Nothing.

Sloane said, "Did you—"

If you'd have asked me a second before we heard the gunshot in the kitchen if I thought my heart could beat any faster than it already was, I would've said no. But apparently, there was a whole nother level of panic I hadn't even known about. Sloane and I took off for the swinging doors.

We ran into the kitchen, where we saw Digby and Silk wrestling over Silk's gun. They were in the narrow aisle between the prep counter and the grill and had the gun high up in the air between them. They turned when they heard us walk in and I saw their gun-wielding arms drop.

I could see what would come next, so I pulled Sloane down under the prep counter next to me. Just as I did, the gun they were fighting over fired. A shelf of stacked plates shattered right over our heads. Silk and Digby were still dancing around when I popped back over the prep counter for a look. I grabbed a saucepan, threw it at Silk, and watched as it hit Silk in the head and then bounced off to hit Digby too. Both of them went down. I heard the gun hit the floor and skitter away.

From the other side of the room, we heard a dull banging noise and muffled yells coming from the walk-in freezer.

"That's Henry and Felix," Sloane said. "I'll let them out."

While Sloane did that, I went to the other side of the prep counter we'd been cowering under and found both Silk and Digby lying on the floor, dazed. I'd just bent down to check on Digby when he suddenly sat up and his forehead smacked right into my face. Pain bloomed from my nose and wrapped around my head.

Digby and Silk both set off crawling for the gun that had slid to the end of the aisle. I grabbed Silk's ankle and got a sharp kick in the wrist.

Just as both Silk and Digby got within lunging range of the gun, a hand reached around from the other side of the grill and picked up the gun. It was Felix. He pointed the gun at Silk.

TWENTY

"Do you even know how that thing works, short stack?" Silk said.

Felix raised the gun and fired a shot into the ceiling. I guess either the sound of the bullet or the recoil from the shot surprised Felix, because he screamed a little and then whooped. "I am *not* going to college!"

"What?" Silk said.

Digby, still standing behind Silk, brushed off the ceiling plaster that had showered down onto his jacket and said, "Careful with that, Felix."

Sloane and Henry came over. He had a huge cut on his cheek.

"Oh, my God, Henry," I said. "You're bleeding."

"I'm okay," Henry said.

"Where's the other guy?" Digby said.

"Zoe killed him," Sloane said.

"What?" Digby said.

"You killed a guy in the restaurant?" Henry said.

"You killed my father?" Silk said.

"Your *father*?" I said.

"Ohhhhh . . ." Digby said. "*That's* why he looked so familiar."

"What guy?" Henry said.

"The grateful tipper from earlier," I said. "Remember? With the coffee?"

"What happened?" Digby said.

"Zoe fried him with the defective register plug," Sloane said.

"You *what*?" Digby said. "You could've gotten *yourself* killed. Why did you do that?"

"What do you mean?" I said. "You told me to."

"I *what*?" Digby said.

"You said, 'Safety first. Don't do anything I would do,'" I said.

"And from that . . . ?" Digby said.

"I thought it was code," I said.

"I said 'Don't do it' but you thought I meant 'Attack the armed and dangerous criminal'?" When I nodded, Digby said, "Wow. I have driven you crazy."

"We should call 911," Henry said.

"Wait," Digby said. "Let's figure out what we're going to say first. How do we explain this to the police?"

We looked at one another, waiting for someone to blurt out

the answer but after a long minute, it was clear everyone was stumped.

"So does that mean there's a dead body out there?" Felix said. "Wait. Are we sure he's dead?"

"I actually didn't check," I said.

"Well, what exactly happened?" Felix said.

"I put the stripped wire against the metal on the counter while he was leaning on it," I said. "He kind of just froze and then . . ."

Sloane sighed. "I'll go look," she said. "But I smelled burned hair. Pretty sure he's dead."

Felix still had the gun pointed at Silk while Henry rifled through a drawer of aprons muttering about finding one to tie up Silk.

"Too bad you didn't fry this one too." Felix poked the gun in Silk's direction. "He'd be easier to explain away dead than alive."

"Whoa whoa whoa . . ." Digby said. "Felix, watch where you point that."

And then I realized that Felix was on his own at the end of the kitchen, cut off from the rest of us by Silk. And Silk was starting to move closer to Felix.

"Felix, you want to give me that?" Digby gestured at the gun.

But Felix was distracted and thinking aloud. "You know, it's not the volts that kill. It's the amps. Hmmm . . . the counter's rimmed in aluminum . . . that has what? Thirty-six?

Thirty-seven percent conductivity?" Felix snapped to and said, "Where's Sloane?"

"She went outside," I said.

"Someone go get her," Felix said. "I think that guy *isn't*—"

The door slammed open and Silk's father came in, wild-eyed and bloody-nosed, dragging in Sloane behind him.

"I told you these kids weren't going to be easy to get rid of," Silk's father said.

Felix reasserted his grip on the gun and said, "Don't move."

Silk's father pushed Sloane toward us and said, "Son, go get your gun back." He still had his knife.

Felix reasserted his grip on the gun once more as Silk stalked closer to him. The rest of us, standing in a cluster stuck behind Silk and his father, couldn't effectively back up Felix if Silk got close enough to make a play for his gun.

But Digby tried anyway. He jumped onto Silk's back just as Silk got into grabbing range of Felix and the gun.

Meanwhile, Henry, Sloane, and I turned to Silk's dad. Henry struck first, using the apron he'd been holding to swipe at Silk's father's hand. The move caught Silk's father by surprise and the knife flew across the kitchen.

Sloane and I were boxed in behind Henry. The aisle was too narrow for us to get in position to help, so all we could do was watch as Digby and Felix fought Silk on one end of the aisle and Henry and Silk's father had a tug-of-war over the apron on the other end.

And then, suddenly, the gun flew out of Felix's hands,

sailed past Sloane and me, and landed on the grill. After one hop and skip, though, it plopped right into the deep-fat fryer. Immediately, we started to hear a loud sizzling noise.

We all gasped. The two separate fights screeched to a halt. All seven of us ran and ducked down on the other side of the prep counter.

But then. Nothing.

Finally, Digby relaxed and said, "Huh. I guess *that* myth's bust—"

That's when it started. The first two shots hit the shelves with the already shattered plates. During the brief lull that followed, the kitchen door swung open and Art and Jim ran in, their own guns drawn.

Art saw all of us cowering on the floor together and said, "What the . . . ?"

"What took you guys so long?" Digby said.

And then the kitchen erupted with the loud rat-a-tat of the rest of the gun's bullets all igniting. Art and Jim ducked down beside us until Silk's gun emptied itself.

But because on Planet Digby, it's never really over, we stood up to find fire dancing on the surface of the grease in the fryer. Even worse, the fryer was now perforated with bullet holes that were leaking hot cooking oil onto the floor. Within seconds, the oily fire had oozed out onto the grill and started to spread across the other worktops. Henry ran to the fire and tried to put it out with the apron he was holding. But it was obvious that he wouldn't get anywhere doing that.

Sloane left the room while Felix got out his phone and called 911. Silk and his father tried to run off but Art kicked them back down. Jim took off his jacket and tried to smother the flames on the counter near him.

"Princeton," Digby said.

Digby threw me a box of salt and he took a bag of flour. We tried throwing handfuls of each onto the flames but the fire was moving fast. It really wasn't until Sloane came back with the chemical extinguisher that we had a chance of beating it.

Finally, Sloane got the fire mostly out and the small flames that sporadically erupted from the smoldering appliances were easily doused by bursts from the extinguisher.

Art pointed at Silk and his father with his gun and said, "These two idiots stood on the street corner yelling at each other about coming to kill you."

"And you waited fifteen minutes before coming to see if we were all right?" Digby said.

"We were about to come in but . . ." Art pointed at me and smiled. "Looked like she had it all under control."

When we heard the fire engines' sirens approaching, Digby said, "What? You dialed 911 less than five minutes ago."

"The station's around the corner from here," Henry said.

The sirens were getting louder.

"Digby," I said. "Do we let them go?" I pointed at Silk and his father.

"Let them go?" Art said. "Why would you do that?"

Digby thought for a long beat before saying to Art, "If I give de Groot what he wants, can he give these idiots money and walking papers to get out of town and stay gone?"

"Instead of finding out what happened to your sister?" Art said. "That's not the original deal."

"I know," Digby said. "I'm asking to change the deal."

"So, you're saying that you're going to give up on finding out about your sister if we get these two out of town, then?" Art said.

"That's right."

"Digby!" I said. "Do you know what you're doing?"

"Wait, no. You can't do that!" Henry said.

"Henry, listen to me," Digby said. "Unless I get rid of them, they'll never stop trying to get at you. Their tiny little lizard brains will never let it go. And you can't spend the rest of your life looking over your shoulder."

"Digby . . ." Henry said. "You can't."

"Sure I can. When you asked me what you should do, I'm the one who told you that you shouldn't let them get away with it," Digby said. "I did this to you. So let me do this *for* you. I'm changing the deal."

Art and Jim traded looks that I thought were suspiciously happy. My feeling that there was something off about the whole thing increased further when Art smiled and said, "Deal."

"Deal? You don't have to make any phone calls? Ask your supervisor?" I said. "Just like that? Deal?" I turned to Digby. "Are you hearing this?"

Art looked at me and said, "He likes the deal." He picked up

Silk by the scruff and said, "Or would you prefer to talk about it when the police get here?"

"Deal." Digby prodded Silk's dad to his feet and said, "Let's go."

Art pulled the car around to the diner's back door and we forced Silk and his father into the trunk of the sedan. After Digby and I got in the backseat, Art drove around to the front of the diner.

"Slow down," Digby said.

Art pulled over and we watched Henry talking to the firemen for a moment.

"Okay. Let's go," Digby said.

Sloane and Felix were standing next to Henry and as we passed, Sloane raised her hand at us on the sly. She mouthed, "Thank you." The Ice Queen understood exactly how much Digby had given up. Maybe there was hope for her yet.

TWENTY-ONE

Silk and his father banged on the trunk and hollered for a little while but things got a lot quieter after Art pulled over, popped the trunk, and Jim shushed them with a few bone-crunching punches. After that, we got on the freeway on-ramp and settled in for a peaceful drive to de Groot's hilltop lair. Or so we thought.

"This isn't the way to Bird's Hill," Digby said.

"We need to make a stop," Art said.

"Excuse me?" Digby said. "I'm not giving it to anyone but de Groot himself."

"Just relax, kid," Jim said. "This won't take long."

"Stop the car," Digby said.

Art sighed but pulled over. He turned in his seat and said, "Digby, I know you don't have any reason to trust us. But like I said . . . I'm the friend you didn't know you had. We're taking you to exactly where you need to go. Can you be patient?"

"We're in the middle of nowhere in a car I'm not driving," Digby said. "I don't have much of a choice."

And so Art pulled back onto the road.

I leaned over and whispered, "Digby? Are you sure?"

Digby kept his head turned steadfastly toward the window as he took my hand and squeezed it.

Art looked at us in the mirror and said, "So, uh . . . are you two . . . together now?"

"Finally," Jim said.

"Excuse me?" I said.

Jim said, "He means, is it official, because you two hook up all the time—"

"How long have you been watching us?" I said.

"We've been watching your little drama playing out since Digby got back into town. But today was the first time we saw you kiss in front of your little gang," Art said. "Who did *not* look happy to see it, by the way."

"Yeah, why *is* that?" Jim said.

"Probably because Zoe's leaving next year. She got into a really good school. In New York City," Digby said.

"I haven't even decided if I'm going yet," I said.

"What? Of course you're going," Art said.

"And you shouldn't string him along saying you won't go when you know you will," Jim said.

"I'm not comfortable having this discussion with you two," I said. "Especially since I don't even know yet if I'm being kid-napped right now."

"I'm just saying you shouldn't string him along if you already know you're leaving," Jim said. "Like you strung along that last guy."

"Austin," Art said.

"Yeah. Austin," Jim said. "That poor guy."

"Excuse me. 'That poor guy' ran off with my supposed friend," I said.

"I could've told you that was going to happen," Jim said.

Art laughed. "Oh, yeah? Then how come you didn't tell yourself it was happening when your own wife was cheating on *you*?"

"That's my point. Austin took up with Allie because you were running off with Digby. And now you're with Digby, you're running off to New York," Jim said. "Like I was with my wife, you're emotionally unavailable."

"Boy," Art said. "Divorced Jim knows all the big words."

"You two are creeps. You feel good about your job? Spying on high school kids?" I said.

"We do what the boss says," Art said. "But you two are a soap opera. You can't blame us for getting caught up."

"And why *is* he having you watch us? If he already knows I'm getting him what he wants?" Digby said. "Were you supposed to snatch it from me so he can welch on his end of the deal? I'm here now—why don't you take it from me?"

Art and Jim just shared a look.

"The boss didn't send us to watch you. In fact, it'd probably be better if you didn't mention that we talked before today, okay?" Art said, "Just please. Listen to what he has to say."

"He knows we're coming?" Digby said. "I didn't see you make a call or anything."

"He knows we're coming," Art said.

We drove on in silence for another little while before Digby said, "I need the bathroom."

Digby poked me in the ribs repeatedly until I also said, "I need the bathroom too." I actually *did* need the bathroom.

"It's only another twenty minutes. Can't you hold it?" Jim said.

"Look, all the excitement rearranged a bunch of stuff inside," Digby said. "I need to make a stop *now*."

"I have an empty water bottle you could use," Art said, and then laughed.

"It ain't that kind of stop," Digby said.

We got off at the next exit.

• • •

We pulled into a gas station and got out of the car. "Wait. This place is closed," I said. "How will we get the keys for the—"

Both Art and Jim pulled out lock-picking kits. "That's why we carry our own keys to everywhere," Art said. "Hey, Digby. Where's yours? I *know* you carry one."

Walking slightly ahead of us, Digby patted his pockets, said, "Oh, shoot, I think mine fell out—" and abruptly did a 180 and collided with Art. Digby staggered backward, apologizing. And then his hand came out of his pocket, holding his own lock-picking tools. "Oh, sorry. I moved it to this pocket."

When we got to the restroom doors, Digby started working on the lock to the ladies' room. Jim got the men's room door open in a heartbeat and laughed when he saw Digby was having problems getting mine open.

"Come on, kid. Don't you want to impress your girl?" Jim said as he and Art pushed open the men's room door.

"Yeah, yeah," Digby said. "I almost have it."

As soon as the men's room door shut behind Art and Jim, though, Digby abandoned the lock and ran toward the row of gas pumps.

"Now what are you doing?" I said.

I watched him take apart the metal frame of a stand-up curb sign advertising gas prices. He came back with two of the thicker poles and slid them through the bar of the men's room door handle so they spanned across the door jamb. Art and Jim wouldn't be able to pull it open from inside.

"It's an old trick but it's a good one," Digby said.

"What are we doing?" I said even though I already knew.

"Come on," he said. Digby walked back to the car, pulled out Art's car keys, and unlocked the car.

"You pick pockets now?" I said.

"Felix taught me," Digby said.

"But I really do need to pee," I said.

"That's not going to hold them for long." Digby pointed at the bathroom doors.

And it was true. Art and Jim were already pulling on the door, trying to shake the poles loose. And so I got in the car and Digby drove off.

• • •

The winding road going up to de Groot's Bird's Hill estate was downright terrifying at night. Not only were there no street-lights, but spring had sprung and the newly leafy trees blocked the curves up ahead so all our headlights could illuminate was just the few feet in front of the car. But, of course, that didn't stop Digby from stepping on it anyway.

I would've argued with him about going so fast but I was afraid of breaking his concentration. By the time we got to the final straightaway to the mansion's main gate, my hands were sweaty and squeaky against the leather of the seat.

"Um, Digby . . ." I said. "Shouldn't you slow down?"

The guard post was unmanned, none of the lights in the front of the main house were turned on, and the gate was a solid fifteen-foot wall of iron.

But Digby kept up our speed and said, "Make sure you have your seat belt on, Princeton. We're going in hot."

I braced myself but as I did, I glanced down and spotted an unmarked orange passkey sitting in the center console. I held it up and screamed, "Digby!"

He stood on the brakes and we stopped with our headlights

dramatically close to the fence. The agony of the seat belt suddenly tightening across my ribs as I flew forward made me so damned grateful we hadn't tried going head-on through the gate.

Beside me, Digby gasped and clutched his ribs. "Are you okay?"

"Yeah," I said. I handed him the card. "Try this first."

We'd gotten so close to ramming the gate that Digby actually had to back up to get to the gate's access control card reader.

When the gate whirred open, Digby turned to me and said, "Well, that turned out a lot easier than I thought it would." When after a while I still hadn't responded, he said, "What? That scared you so bad you're not speaking to me?"

I shook my head and waved my hand. "I'm okay. Just . . . my chest hurts . . . and I still need to pee."

We got to the top of the drive, pulled up to the main house, and Digby turned off the engine. The lights were on in some of the other auxiliary buildings but nothing was going on in the main residence.

"I thought Art said de Groot knew we were coming," Digby said.

"What do you want to do?" I said.

"Well, I thought about leaning on the horn and waking these morons up," he said.

"Maybe we should build up to that level of aggression," I said.

Digby and I got out of the car and went up the steps to the door. After looking for a while, he said, "I guess why *would* they have a doorbell if there's security out front during the day? Should we knock? It's late but it's not that late."

The word *late* triggered my realization that I hadn't told my mother I wasn't coming straight home after I'd texted her from the diner. "Yeah, but who knows what time that guy goes to bed. He looked pretty sick." I texted my mother "c u soon." My mother texted right back: "Your father wants to talk about Prentiss tonight. What time will u b home?"

"Ugh, damn it, I'm not in the mood for this," I said.

"What?" Digby said.

"My mother. Pretending she isn't interfering by pretending she didn't tell my dad about Prentiss so *he* can be the bad guy and make me go," I said. "Don't say it. It's getting annoying."

"Of course you're going," he said.

"So annoying," I said. "Oh, my God. I just thought of something."

"What?" he said.

"Silk and his father are still in the trunk," I said. "You know, we probably would've killed them if we'd gone through that gate."

Digby looked shocked. "It's funny how one minute, those two guys were life-and-death problems and then the next minute, they're potentially just bodies in a trunk," he said. "I feel like that's a metaphor for life or something."

"Literally no normal person would ever benefit from that metaphor," I said. "Do you think we should check on them?"

"Not unless you want to run around in the dark chasing down the two homicidal criminals who jumped us and escaped when we opened the trunk," Digby said. "Remember what *we* did to the last guy who shoved us in the trunk and then made the mistake of opening it?"

"Fine," I said. "Let's find someone to let us in the house."

Digby and I went back down the steps and started walking until we found a slightly open window on the other side of the building.

"Aha," he said.

"Aha what? You're probably going to set off the alarm," I said.

"Well, officer, I would've rung the *door*bell, but they didn't have one," Digby said. "I had to settle for the sweet ring of the security alarm."

"Maybe leave the talking to me when they arrest us," I said. "This time."

I helped Digby move a concrete planter under the window so we could climb into what turned out to be the formal dining room we'd passed through the last time we were in the house. Digby took a bunch of grapes and two apples from the enormous dining table's center display.

"Are those real?" I said.

"Classy place like this?" Digby bit off a grape but immediately

227

shot it out of his mouth at the wall with such force I had to duck so it didn't hit me in the head on the rebound. "They are not."

We walked along the carpeted corridors and retraced our steps to the white spaceship hospital annex where we'd found de Groot the week before. When we got to de Groot's bedroom antechamber, I stopped Digby and said, "Wait. I need the bathroom."

"Seriously, Princeton? *Now?*" he said.

"Actually, I needed it an hour ago but you didn't let me pee," I said.

"This isn't going to take long," Digby said. "And, honestly, I don't know what kind of mental trauma it would be for me if they caught us on a bathroom break and dragged us away before I got to talk to de Groot."

"What exactly are you going to say?" I asked him.

When he gave me one of his looks, I said, "I just don't think you should go in there and have a random freak-out, that's all."

Digby took a deep breath and said, "Okay. I'm going to say . . . here is what you've been after all these years . . ." He took out the magnetic tape copy Felix had made him from his suit pocket. "And what I want in return . . ." I honestly didn't know if he had the strength to say the next bit. "I need you to give two people new IDs and money to get out of town," Digby said.

"Are you okay with that?" I said. "For Henry? Instead of Sally?"

"I am," Digby said.

I needed to make sure. "You're telling me that you are a hundred percent okay getting this far and *not* finding out what happened to your sis—"

"You're killing me, Princeton," Digby said. "Whose side are you on?"

TWENTY-TWO

Digby opened the door and as we walked into de Groot's bedroom, it occurred to me again that it was marvelous what money could do. De Groot's suite of machines were whiter than white in the glow of the various LED monitor panels in the room. Everything was curved and edge-less and designed to look like an egg. Eggs being the design aesthetic, I suppose, at the exact opposite of the spectrum from what's happening to de Groot, which is death and decay.

But old de Groot's body, lying propped up on a pile of pillows and sleeping with his mouth hanging open, did not look like it was fooled by his machines' promises for a moment. The man was not looking very good.

"He . . . looks . . ." Digby said.

"Like a smushed raisin," I said.

Digby nodded.

We watched de Groot sleep, only knowing he wasn't dead

because his machines told us so. But after a while, I couldn't take it anymore.

"Sorry. I know this is kind of a big moment but I'm gonna pee my pants, man." I pointed at the en suite bathroom. "Wait here."

The bathroom's decor was consistent with the bedroom's aesthetic. White on white, grab bars and safety strips everywhere, and what can only be called a white marble throne in the middle of a shower stall the size of a normal American guestroom. Even the toilet went out of its way to be complicated but I'd seen that particular contraption before because, like much of America, I secretly keep up with the Kardashians.

I'd just used the bathroom and washed my hands when my phone rang. My father. Maybe I was feeling a little bulletproof after having had the day I'd had, or maybe the high from the awesome mirror selfie I'd just taken had formed a toxic combination with my exhaustion—I don't know—but for some crazy reason, I decided to hit accept instead of reject.

"Hi," I said.

"Zoe? Where are you?" my father said.

"Um . . ." By this time, I'd climbed onto de Groot's marble shower throne and shut the stall door for some privacy. "I'm in a bathroom."

"Why aren't you home yet? It's almost eleven o'clock." But his belligerent tone changed right away. "Celebrating, I guess. Anyway. Congratulations." He cleared his throat. "I suppose Shereene and I will be seeing a lot more of you next year."

I didn't need to do the I-haven't-decided-of-course-you're-going dance with him right then, so I just made a non-committal sound and let the moment pass.

"You'll be living with us, of course," he said.

Now *that* I couldn't let pass.

"Actually, I think I'll be boarding," I said. I heard a weird gurgling noise. "Did you just . . . growl?"

"Growl? *No,*" my father said. "Why would I? Oh, you mean because you're going to pour fifteen thousand dollars down the drain so you can sleep on a plastic mattress and . . ."

I didn't actually hear much of the rest of my father's angry speech because by this time, I'd opened the shower door and realized I could still hear the gurgling sound. It was coming from the bedroom. I put my phone on mute and opened the bathroom door to see . . .

Digby had his hands around the now-awake de Groot's throat. De Groot was bug-eyed and gasping for breath.

"Digby!" I somehow had the presence of mind to take the phone off mute, stop hyperventilating, and, in a weirdly calm voice, say, "Let me call you back, Dad."

And then I hung up and ran across to Digby to pry him off de Groot. "What are you doing? Digby, you don't want to do this." But then I noticed that the room was very dark because Digby had unplugged de Groot's various life-supports. Digby absolutely *did* want to do this.

"He's basically dead already. It'd only be half a murder,"

232

Digby said. "What happened to my sister? *What happened to my sister?*"

"*Digby.*" I finally got Digby to let go after I said, "He's trying to answer."

De Groot's mouth really did look like it was moving to form words and after he'd recovered enough from Digby's assault, de Groot started to talk.

"I . . . I . . . I need . . ." de Groot said. He flailed in the direction of his wheelchair until I worked out that he needed to use the oxygen tank strapped to it.

I passed de Groot the mask and flipped on the switch. After he'd taken a few breaths, I took the mask from him and said, "Now tell him."

"Bad cop, bad cop, I see," de Groot said.

I'd pushed Digby to the back of the room to keep him from attacking de Groot again but some of the wax grapes he'd taken from the dining room sailed over my shoulder and peppered de Groot's face.

"He has wax apples too," I said. "Talk before he starts throwing *those* at you."

"Do you have it?" de Groot said. "Your mother's work?"

Digby held up the data tape.

"She's dead. Your sister is dead." De Groot looked so gleeful saying it that I wondered why we even had to coerce him into talking in the first place.

I didn't dare look at Digby's face but his voice was shockingly even when he followed up by asking, "Tell me how." Digby approached the bed, took the oxygen mask from my hand, and turned it back on so de Groot could gulp down a few deep breaths. "Tell me everything."

"I tried to get the research from your mother the legitimate way. But of course . . ." De Groot took another hit of oxygen and waved his hand to indicate *I failed.* "So, I had my men break into your house that night—"

"They did something to me," Digby said. "I've never been a deep sleeper. Why didn't I wake up?"

"Yes. All of you . . . your toothbrushes were dipped in a powerful tranquilizer . . . just enough for all of you to sleep deeply . . ." De Groot laughed. "They were meant to take you, do you know? But you were moving around and they panicked."

Digby did know he was supposed to be the victim. Ezekiel had told him so months ago. But hearing it again was like a new blow to Digby and his voice was small and sounded younger than I'd ever heard it when he said, "How did she die?"

De Groot took more oxygen. "One of my men accidentally smothered her while he was trying to stop her screaming," de Groot said.

"Where?" Digby said. De Groot looked confused, so Digby said, "Where did they put her body? There was a huge search. They never found anything."

"She is here. On these grounds," de Groot said. "Atop a

beautiful grassy knoll overlooking the herb garden." He said it like he was selling us a timeshare in Tuscany.

"Sounds great. Is that where they're planting you when *you* kick it?" Digby said. "Which is fairly soon, by the look of it . . ."

De Groot's skeleton hand reached toward the data tape in Digby's. "That is what I want *this* for," de Groot said. "What is in here will change our understanding of life and death . . ."

"Nothing in this tape can help you now," Digby said. "It's too late, old man."

"They have been saying that to me for over a decade," de Groot said. And then he gathered up his energy and pushed off the bed to make a lunge for the data tape.

And de Groot would've gotten it too, if I hadn't snatched it out of Digby's hand first.

"No," I said. "To get this data, we're going to need a few things from you."

For the first time, I saw de Groot have a real emotion besides contempt and the enjoyment of cruelty. He looked at me, sputtering and outraged. He took two hits of oxygen and said, "You are a cheater. He and I had an agreement."

"No, I'm not," I said. "He got that information out of you by force. Gratis. For this . . ." I held up the data tape. "You will have to trade with me."

And then suddenly, the sound of clattering metal scared the crap out of all three of us.

I was blinded by the lights coming on but I assembled the series of snapshots my blinking eyes took and worked out that de Groot's nurse had come in with his nighttime medication and found us.

"Oh, my God." The nurse plugged de Groot's machines back in and immediately, the screeching alarms of the monitors drowned out her screams of "Who are you?" She hit a button on the wall and a house-wide alarm sounded.

Digby grabbed me and led me to a window that he opened. We were climbing out when he stopped me and said, "Hey, Princeton, in case I forget later . . . I just want to say . . ."

At this point, I heard a bunch of yelling men coming down the hall toward us. Digby and I jumped down onto the lawn and took off running.

"I don't think I've ever been more attracted to you than I am at this moment," Digby said.

"Shut up. Not now," I said. I made a note to maybe put in time at the gym because I'd only been running for a little bit and I was already out of breath. I stopped running when we got to the front of the house. "The gate's this way. But Digby . . ."

Digby took out his phone and turned on his compass. "You heard him. Herb garden. Herb gardens need sunshine." He pointed in the opposite direction from the gate and said, "Southern exposure."

But Digby didn't make a move until I said, "Okay. Let's do it."

And then we ran across the front lawn to the other side of

the house, hiding behind bushes and trees to avoid de Groot's security men as they ran from their living quarters into the main house.

Finally, we got to a cleared patch of the garden that looked as though it had recently been plowed and readied for planting.

Digby turned, checked out the location, and said, "Behind the kitchen. Makes sense." He pointed at a shed and said, "Shovels."

We ran over to the shed and finding it padlocked, I said, "Can you open it?"

I'd imagined him picking the lock open but after Digby said, "Yeah," he simply backed up and kicked the door.

And then we took turns kicking at the door until the padlock broke apart.

We took two shovels to the garden and tried to figure out what de Groot meant by *knoll*.

"He said, 'On top of a lovely grassy knoll,'" Digby said. "What even is a knoll?"

"Like a hill?" I said.

Digby surrendered and looked it up on his phone. *"Another term for a small, low, round natural hill or mound."*

We looked around. Nothing really fit that bill.

"That thing?" He pointed at a small grassy incline to one side.

"That just looks like a big pile of dirt they made to shield the garden," I said.

"His guys might've told him it was a knoll. I doubt he spends a lot of time looking at his backyard dirt piles," Digby said. "For all he knows he has Mt. Everest back here."

I looked at it again. It was smaller than a hill but it was most definitely much bigger than any dirt pile I would ever want to dig up in the middle of the night. But I didn't want to be a party pooper.

"Where do we dig?" I said.

"He said the top," Digby said. "So let's start at the top."

We trudged up the slope and without having any other clues to tell us where to start, we just started digging where we stood. Within five minutes, my arms were tired. The second after I acknowledged that, I felt blisters starting to form on my palms.

I was just debating whether I should take off my hoodie and wrap it around the shovel handle when I noticed Digby standing perfectly still, staring at the ground. He dropped his shovel. And then I realized. There he was, standing at the end of his insane nine-year odyssey. I wondered what he was thinking.

TWENTY-THREE

"So this is what closure feels like," Digby says.

I don't know what to say to that, so I just stand next to him.

"Closure sucks," Digby says. "Now what?"

He isn't asking for suggestions. He is telling me something I already understand. I've often wondered what he would do once it was over.

"What did I expect, right? It's like they say. The truth is almost always disappointing." Digby turns to me. "But . . . now what? Other than me, talking in clichés."

I wonder what this means for Digby and me. At the heart of everything, he and I are partners in crime, and now the crime spree is winding down.

"This isn't the time to think about what's next," I say, putting the shovel back in his hand. "Now we keep digging."

We are about to get going again when a pair of flashlight

beams comes out of the main house's back door and bobs toward us.

"Do we run?" I say.

By now we can see that Art and Jim are the ones holding the flashlights. Digby and I push our shovels into the dirt, and lean on them while we wait for Art and Jim to climb up to us.

"Are you kids going to dig up this entire knoll of dirt?" Art says.

I jump when I hear him use the word *knoll*.

"So it was you?" Digby says. When Art is silent, Digby picks up his shovel, pushes the cutting edge of the shovel's blade against Art's chest, and says, "It *was* you."

"It was both of us," Jim says, then he pauses. "But, technically, it was neither of us."

Digby raises the shovel to neck level and points it at Jim. "I'm not in the mood, man."

"She isn't dead, kid," Art says. "We were taking you to the boss because he thought it was time to let you know that. He was going to explain that your sister didn't die nine years ago."

Digby gets in Art's face. "What are you talking about? De Groot just told me she was dead. He told me that her body is buried right here." Digby uses the shovel's handle to poke Art in the chest. "This is *not* a knoll, by the way. It is a dirt pile."

"We don't work for de Groot . . ." Jim says. "I mean, we do but we get our instructions from his lawyer, Mr. Book. *He's* our boss."

"That's who we were taking you to see," Art says. "When you locked us in the bathroom."

"Wait. Sally Digby isn't dead? Sally Digby is *alive*?" I say. "Then where the hell is she?"

"That's why Mr. Book needs to talk to you." Art turns to Digby and says, "If we drive you to Mr. Book, can you please not murder us in the car?"

Digby stares at him, stunned. After a while, he says, "The night is young. I can't make any promises." He body-checks Art as he walks down the incline, and says, "I'm driving."

• • •

Luckily, when we get to the car, Digby is sensible enough to hand me the car keys. Partially, though, he lets me drive because it allows him to keep a hold on his shovel handle—which he does while angrily glaring at Art and Jim in the backseat.

Finally, Digby can't stand it anymore and he says, "Just tell me where she is."

Art sighs. "You're going to want to hear the whole story from the boss. Context is going to matter *a lot*."

"And this 'context' will help me understand why you people destroyed four lives with kidnap, murder, and extortion?" Digby says. "Now *that* is some context. I do need to hear *that*."

"You'll get it when the boss explains," Art says. "He has a way with words."

"Book. The lawyer," Digby says. Art nods. Digby says,

"We're going to his office? At that office park?" When Art nods at that, Digby says, "Well, since I know who Book is and where he'll be, I don't really know why I need to keep you two around."

"Um, Digby?" Half of me thinks he wouldn't actually do anything crazy, but the other half is uncertain enough to make me nervous.

"I could just give myself a mental wellness treat and ask you to get out so I can run you over with your own car," Digby says.

"Kid," Art says. "Don't force me to use my—"

"Your gun?" Digby takes out a gun from under his jacket and points it at Art in the backseat. "*This* gun? Why don't you give me yours too?" Digby motions at Jim, who does as he says.

"Hey. Be careful where you point that. If she hits a bump . . ." Art says. "You're going to have a huge mess to get rid of."

"Well, at least I'm prepared," Digby says, and pats the shovel's handle with his free hand.

"Put it away, Digby. What are you doing?" I say. "Put it away or I'm stopping the car and this party is *over*."

Digby puts the two guns away and says, "You're lucky she's here."

"I don't know why you're so sore, anyway. This is good news," Art says. "Aren't you happy your sister's actually alive?"

"No, no." I make eye contact with Art in the mirror. "Don't do that."

242

"Too soon?" Art says.

"Be-yond too soon," I say.

• • •

Only one room is lit up in the whole office park and Book's shiny black monster of a Bentley is the lone car in the lot when we drive up. We park and all four of us walk into the building in a loose who-goes-first huddle because really, it isn't clear who's in charge of whom.

"Princeton," Digby says. "I'm nervous."

"It's okay to be nervous," I say. "But since you *are* nervous . . ."

"Give you the guns," Digby says. "Yeah." He nods and then hands both guns to me.

I don't like the feel of them—cold and dense and slippery in my hand—so I drop both guns in the small pond by the building's entrance.

Jim curses.

"Oh, *man*," Art says. "That's my personal carry . . . and it's a fifteen-hundred-dollar piece."

"Fifteen hundred dollars for a gun? A man with his priorities so far out of whack doesn't deserve to even *have* fifteen hundred dollars," I say, even though I'm secretly appalled at having wrecked something so valuable.

Book is sitting in his chair, staring at the door with a stony-faced expression that I recognize from my father. It is the

243

displeased frown of a man who believes time is money and has been kept waiting.

"I've been here for an hour and a half," Book says.

Dead-eyed and as lifeless as the marble bust they'll put up outside whatever college library he'll donate to, Jonathan Garfield Book has the silver-fox, old-boy, school-tie arrogance my father's been trying to fake all his life. This Book guy definitely knows where all the bodies are buried. Or *not* buried, as it now turns out.

Digby takes one of the bottles of mineral water from Book's desk and says, "Am I supposed to say sorry?" And then Digby knocks down Book's very full penholder before walking over to peruse one of Book's shelves of file folders.

I can see from the way he's frowning at the mess on his desk that it really bothers Book. He desperately wants to right the cup and put the pens and pencils back in place but controls himself.

Digby sees this too, clearly, because he starts knocking down picture frames and chamber of commerce–type crystal doodads from the shelves.

"Please. Do not do that," Book says. "You are being a child."

"Oh, I'm sorry, what?" Digby tucks the shovel under his arm so that it sticks out behind him and then abruptly turns so that the shovel's blade scores an angry black scar into the wall before smashing into and knocking over a fully loaded drinks cart. Broken glass everywhere. "My little baby ears didn't catch that."

Book closes his eyes and takes a deep breath. I'm sure he has done this to calm down but I don't see how it could work, because the smell of alcohol from the broken liquor bottles is so strong that I have started to cough.

"Do you have your mother's research with you?" Book says.

"Do you have my sister?" Digby says.

Book smiles and says, "Well, I didn't keep her for a pet if that's what you mean."

"Then where is she?" Digby says.

"I don't know exactly," Book says. "But she isn't dead. Or, at least, she wasn't dead when I last saw her. Who knows what she's been up to since. Nine years is a long time."

Digby uses the shovel to sweep off all the stuff on Book's desk and perches on the top so he's looming over Book. "Yes, nine years *is* a long time." And then he punctuates that by thrusting the shovel sideways so that it shatters the window behind Book.

Through gritted teeth, Book says, "If you would just calm down, I can explain everything to you and you will see that, in fact, I have done you and your sister—"

I see Digby start to tense up again and realize I should step in since we are running out of inanimate objects for Digby to deflect his anger onto.

"No, no, no," I say. "Don't try to bright-side him. Just tell him what happened." I take the shovel out of Digby's hand and say, "But. If you don't stop trying to make yourself look like you're somehow the good guy, I will give him back his shovel."

Book nods at Art, who moves to pat Digby down.

"Hey," Digby says. "What? Are you checking if I'm recording?"

Book somehow finds a way to arrange his already funereal face into a darker grimace.

"I committed treason today," Digby says. "We are way past recording devices and gathering evidence for the prosecution."

"All right," Book says. "The first thing you should know is that by the time these two called me nine years ago, things were already in motion. They had already taken your sister and had her locked up in a warehouse—"

Digby says, "So your defense is that you didn't have anything to do with *planning* the kidnapping—"

"Nothing," Book says. "That was one hundred percent the product of Hans de Groot's fevered imagination."

"You're an accessory after the fact. You're a lawyer. We know you know that," I say.

"The old man heard about what your mother was working on about six months after his doctor told him he was sick," Art says. "Jim and I were worried when he had us follow her around town. But we did it anyway . . ."

"You were stalking my family?" Digby says. "Is that what you mean when you said you were like the friend I didn't know I had?"

"We didn't know what else to do," Art says. "And I haven't had a good night's sleep ever since. Hand to God."

"Trust me—some of the other guys de Groot has working

for him . . ." Jim says. "Things would've turned out even worse."

Digby turns back to Book. "What exactly does he want with my mom's research?"

"Hans de Groot was diagnosed with a rare form of an already uncommon neurodegenerative disease ten years ago. The doctors had never seen his variant of the disease before and so they couldn't give him a clear prognosis. And that uncertainty sent de Groot down the yellow brick road," Book says. "He thinks your mother's work will allow him to live forever. Some fantasy about her tiny robots rewiring his DNA."

"And it wouldn't have . . . ?" Digby says.

"Of course not. Ridiculous," Book says. "Nine years ago, your mother was in the very earliest conceptual stages. Timothy Fong is only now working out the practicalities. It took more than two hundred million dollars to get him this far, and Dr. Fong's timeline projects fifteen more years before they even produce something they can test in a human body." Book laughs. "It will *not* happen in Hans de Groot's lifetime."

"How do you know so much about Dr. Fong's funding and timeline?" Digby says.

"Because as of three months after my employer took it upon himself to commission your sister's kidnapping, I started the boring but legal process of buying a controlling chunk of Perses Analytics for the de Groot family," Book says. "If only he had asked, I could have gotten him what he wanted without all this fuss."

Digby is silent but I can tell from his neck muscles twitching that he is having the same cascading thoughts that I am.

"Wait. But if he already owns the company, then why did de Groot make us steal this data?" I say. "What was all this for?"

"He doesn't know," Book says. "With Hans de Groot's niece, I arranged to buy Perses from behind an impenetrable stack of corporate identities. And we have kept that fact from him ever since."

"What for?" I say.

"Because the fact remains that all the king's horses and men will not be able to put old Humpty together again," Book says. "His niece feels—and the doctors somewhat agree—that believing the answer is still out there has extended his life well past all expectations. He has even outlived the doctor who told him about his disease."

"So that's it?" I say. "You'll never tell him?"

"Well, as long as he is alive, his niece possesses his votes by proxy on the board and I report to her, so, no, if she and I have our way, I do not think Mr. de Groot will ever find out," Book says.

"And so, what? You people just run around behind these de Groot morons picking up after them while they ruin innocent people's lives?" Digby says.

Book, Art, and Jim share a pained look.

"I'll tell you, kid, I don't want to be doing this anymore either," Art says.

"And you? Is this what you thought your life would be?"

Digby says to Book. "You sat in your Harvard classroom and thought, Yeah, when I grow up, I want to be a bag man flunky."

"Of course not. But spending thirty years living on circuit court wages waiting for one of nine seats to open up and be handed to you . . ." Book says. "It seemed like a bad bet to me."

"And how's this working out for you?" Digby says. When Book doesn't answer, Digby says, "Where is she?"

"I have already told you. I don't know," Book says.

"What did you do with her?" Digby says.

Book says, "Well, clearly, we could not just put her back." He points at Art and says, "I had him find her a good home."

Digby stares at Art. "And?"

"I had a contact. A phone number from a guy I was in the service with. I think he said it was someone inside the local PD," Art says. "I never got a name, never heard a voice, never saw a face, never knew what the plan would be. It was just fixed one day."

"How?" Digby says.

"He told me to put the money in a safety-deposit box in a downtown bank and told me to put the key on a necklace that your sister wore," Art says. "Then, one night . . ."

Art and Jim look at each other.

"You're kidding," Digby says. "They kidnapped her away from you idiots."

"We went into the room the next day and she was just . . . gone," Jim says.

"You've got to understand. It was all happening so fast and even while it was happening, all we wanted to do was get ourselves out of the situation," Art says. "When she disappeared . . . we were just glad it was over."

"Excellent," I say. "And that's the end of the trail?"

No one says otherwise. Digby and I stand there, silent. All the old questions have been answered and we can't yet put into words the new ones.

And then, like a man in a dream, Digby walks to Book and slowly puts his hand in Book's pocket. "I'm taking your car. You will not report it missing for one week," Digby says. "If you report it before next Sunday, I will turn in this recording." Digby pockets the keys and pulls out his phone to show Book that it has recorded the entire conversation.

"But . . ." Book says. "The treason you've admitted to—"

"I'm a minor. Who was coerced." Digby points at Book. "By you, baby."

Book points at his keys in Digby's pocket and says, "But that's a Mulsanne. How are you going to explain suddenly having a three-hundred-fifty-thousand-dollar car?"

"Oh, I'm not keeping it," Digby says. "I'm giving it to a couple of strung-out drug dealers who need cash to get out of town." When that makes Book go pale, Digby claps him across the shoulder and says, "Oh, cheer up. You can get your insurance to buy you a new one next week. This one should be on a cargo ship to Dubai by then."

TWENTY-FOUR

We walk out of the building.

"Digby, what are you doing?" I say when Digby reaches into the shallow pond and fishes out one of the guns I'd thrown in.

Digby wipes off the gun with his sleeve and says, "Relax. It'll just be a prop."

When we get to Art's sedan, Digby tells me to step back. He points the gun and is about to pop the trunk when a gush of water comes out the barrel. He wipes it off again and says, "It's okay. This is why we rehearse."

I tighten my hold on the shovel and steel myself for a fight. Digby opens the trunk and is about to yell something when we both realize . . .

"Are they asleep?" I say.

We watch Silk and his father pretzeled together and snoring in the trunk.

"How can they sleep? They've been stuffed in a trunk

against their will," I say. "Is extreme relaxation a side effect of stupidity?"

"I would mock them, except I haven't slept in forever," Digby says. "I would seriously trade a couple of IQ points for that kind of chill."

When it becomes clear that Silk and his father aren't going to wake up on their own, Digby has me bang on the trunk with the shovel. Finally, Silk and his father stir and sit up.

Silk sees the gun and cowers. "Please . . ."

"Get out of the car," Digby says.

Digby listens to Silk's and his father's incoherent begging for a while before saying, "Stop crying." And then he throws Silk the keys to the Bentley.

"What's this?" Silk asks.

"Press the remote start," Digby says.

Silk does and jumps when the Bentley's engine comes on. He turns to Digby, incredulous.

"Do you have a guy?" Digby asks Silk's father.

Silk's father smiles, finally understanding. "Yeah. I got a guy."

"Don't take less than a hundred for it. That car's your get-out-stay-out money. Start fresh. Brand-new street corner," Digby says. "On some other Main Street far, far away. Where you will forget all about River Heights."

Digby looks nauseated to do it but when Silk's father stretches out his hand and says, "Deal," Digby takes it and says, "Far, far away."

"I've been feeling a little tropical lately," Silk's father says.

"You have a week before people start looking for this thing," Digby says.

"Plenty of time," Silk's father says.

Silk still looks confused. His father takes the keys from him and says, "Just get in the car."

"What about this guy?" Silk says.

Silk's father says, "You mean the guy who's giving you a hundred grand to completely forget him?"

When Silk still doesn't get it, his father smacks him upside the head. Finally, Silk says, "Oh . . . right." And they get in the Bentley and drive away.

"Just like that? You really think they'll stay away?" I say.

Digby waves me off. "Meh . . . at least one of them will get the other killed and then spend the rest of *his* short life running away from the person they double-crossed."

Art and Jim come out in time to watch Book's Bentley pulling out of the lot. Digby hands Art the gun.

Art sniffs the end of the barrel and groans. "Chlorine . . ."

"Aw . . . did we ruin your gun?" Digby says. "Oh, also, we're taking your car now." Digby's already walking to the sedan when an idea occurs to him and he comes back to say, "I'm sending someone to you next week. His name's Aldo and you're going to hire him as a driver."

"What?" Art says.

"He needs a job. I don't care if you pay him to drive your

farts into the wind. He needs a job. Benefits. Place to live. Understand?" Digby says. "Start working off some of that nighttime guilt, *friend*."

"Are you kidding me?" Art says. But he sees Digby is a hundred percent serious, so Art says, "Fine. I'm sure there's something we can use him for."

Digby unlocks the door and we start to climb in.

"Wait a minute, you put the money in a safety-deposit box? Downtown?" Digby says.

Art nods.

"Which bank?" Digby says.

"First Union Atlantic," Art says.

"Which branch?" Digby says.

"Third and Catherine," Art says. "But that branch is gone now. I went back last week to look—"

"At the time, you never went back? Asked around? Looked at CCTV to see who was picking up the money?" Digby says.

"At the time, all I could think of was that I just wanted it all to go away," Art says.

"You don't even know if that person did what they said they would. They could've taken the money and drowned her in a lake," Digby says.

"Don't you think that's the thought that's haunted me all these years?" Art says. "I even stuck my neck out to get a copy of the police files to see if I'd recognize something that'd help me find who took her."

"And?" I say.

Art shakes his head. "I'm sorry."

I see Digby wants to say a million angry things to Art but he eventually just sighs and takes the data tape out of his pocket. He throws it at Art and says, "Tell Book it's done. I'm done with all of you." He stops and realizes, "I'm done with all of this."

"Wait," Art says. "Will I get my car back?"

Digby throws him a nasty look, gets in the car, and starts the ignition. But then we just sit in the parking lot, engine idling. He doesn't put the car into drive until Art and Jim finally turn and walk back into the building.

"I didn't trust myself not to yank on the wheel and run them over," Digby says.

"I can't believe you didn't," I say. "I would've."

Digby is silent for a long time. "No one came out of this happy, Princeton. De Groot's been sitting in that white bubble of his, thinking about death for ten years. Book buys himself insanely expensive cars so he doesn't have to deal with the fact that he's just a gopher for a half-dead maniac. And then those two idiots . . ." Digby waves at the office park receding in our rearview mirror to indicate he means Art and Jim. "What we have here is a bunch of people trying to outthink each other when, really, we're just all living the same sick cosmic joke . . . but nobody gets to laugh."

"There's Sally," I say. "She's still out there."

Digby sighs and says, "I don't know, Princeton. When I said back there that I was done with all this, it felt pretty true."

• • •

There is no question of his driving himself home and when we get to my house, Digby follows me into the living room and collapses onto the sofa. He stares at the ceiling and laughs.

"Are you okay?" I say.

"I haven't been this okay in nine years," he says. "Why? Don't I look okay?" He turns to face me. His eyes are red and they're clearly having trouble focusing. The skin on his face is gray and he looks clammy.

"Um . . . let me get you a glass of water or something?" I say.

Digby makes a vaguely grateful sound.

When I get to the kitchen, I suddenly remember that besides the small bites of food I'd managed to steal while serving food in the diner, I haven't eaten in a really long time. I am starving. It starts with taking a few bites from the leftover pizza in the fridge, moves on to finishing off a bowl of pasta salad, and ends with my eating straight out of the peanut butter jar as I fill a bottle with water for Digby.

I get back to the living room and I am not surprised to find Digby is fast asleep already. All I want to do is crawl into bed but I catch a whiff of myself and drag myself through the shower. As the layers of adrenaline-tinged sweat roll off me, I contemplate the image of Digby, standing in de Groot's garden, telling me that the truth is almost always a disappointment.

And then I realize that I am having a problem accepting it really is over for the same reason I haven't stopped thinking about Digby's telling my mother that he planned to go to college and become an actuary. In all my subsequent googlings of the field of actuarial science, I have yet to find a way to think this is not the saddest surrender to banality ever. I can't handle thinking Digby could be the peak-in-high-school guy that everyone mocks in the "remember when" game during class reunions. That thought is so tragic, I start to cry and I fall asleep, my wet hair still wrapped in a towel.

• • •

I wake up the next morning with a headache, a mouthful of unbrushed teeth, and eyes bloodshot from crying. I've never had a post-alcohol hangover but I doubt it could be much worse than this feeling.

I look at the time and marvel that I am as alert as I am after only three hours of sleep. I try to fall back asleep but can't, so I get dressed and decide to do something about my headache.

Downstairs, I'm surprised to find an almost-full pot of fresh-made coffee in the kitchen. My mother is still asleep in her room and Cooper is still not back from his shift, so I wonder if maybe Digby is already awake. And then I notice the jar of peanut butter is gone from the cupboard and I know he is.

"Digby?" The couch is empty. I wonder if he's gone home but then I hear the whirr of my mom's printer. I head to the study and find Digby printing off something from Cooper's laptop. "*Hey.*" I close the door behind me and say, "Hey, man. What are you doing?"

Digby looks up at me, eerily bright-eyed and fresh. "Oh, I bought some new kicks. I'm just printing the receipt," he says.

"Oh." It feels weird to be disappointed about that but there it is. "What color?"

"What color?" Digby gives me a weird look and hands me a piece of paper from the pile he's printed. "Did you really think I was buying shoes? Are you okay, Princeton?"

It takes me a while to register that I'm in fact looking at a River Heights Police Department document. The header says PAYROLL and the rest of the page is a long list of names and addresses in a tiny font.

"What is this?" I say.

"If we assume that Art's police department contact chose to ask for the First Union Atlantic safety-deposit box at Third and Catherine specifically because it was either on their beat or that they lived near there . . ." Digby says.

"I thought you said you were done," I say.

"What?" he says.

I say, "Last night, you said you were done looking for Sally—"

"I hadn't eaten in hours and hadn't slept in two days," he says. "Temporary madness. Why did you even listen to me?" He gets up to look over the list with me. "See a name you recognize?" When I don't find it fast enough, Digby points at a name halfway down the page. "Michael Alphonse Cooper."

"Whaaat?" I say. It's too preposterous to contemplate. "That's ridiculous. Cooper? *Our* Cooper? He thinks even free-range eggs are too cruel. And you've heard him talking about the fricking bees . . . he couldn't kidnap a kid."

"Maybe that vegan crap is his way of repenting," Digby says. When I roll my eyes, Digby says, "I mean, it makes *some* sense. Why else would he let us get away with everything he does?"

"Digby, the man saved up for six months to buy a fruit dehydrator. He does *not* have a box of money lying around," I say. "It must be someone else." I go back to reading the names on the sheet and suddenly, I see something that trips a switch in my brain. "*This* name."

"Rosetta Pickles? Early retirement," Digby says. "What about her? She wasn't on the case. Her name's not on any of the reports . . ."

"You don't remember her? The lady with the big mole on her lip?" I say. I know I sound crazy and there's really no better way to explain what I'm thinking, so I run over to Cooper's computer and go down the Google hole until I find the news footage I'd watched months ago.

"She was the sweetest little girl," Rosetta Pickles says on the news footage.

"She used the past tense," Digby says. "That's weird. Cops are trained not to do that when they talk to media."

"Weird, right?" I say, and then I google again and show him the real estate listing for the Central Park–adjacent apartment

259

that Rosetta Pickles had bought after she'd left the River Heights police force.

"When did you see this?" Digby says.

"Last year," I say.

"*Last year?*" Digby says. "And you never said anything?"

"I'd just met you," I say. "I was snooping around, trying to figure out what your deal was . . ."

Digby goes back into the police pension database and starts looking into Rosetta Pickles's record.

"I can't believe you've been sitting on this," he says.

"It didn't seem like it was anything . . ." I say. "I just thought it was strange . . . how she sounded on the news."

Digby stops at a screen.

"Wait," I say. "Does that say 'deceased'?"

Digby presses the down arrow and sees a name and address in Cherry Hill, New Jersey. "Her sister's the beneficiary."

"No mention of a kid. I guess that'd be too much to ask," I say. By the time I turn to him and ask, "What do you think?" Digby has already opened a new tab and is looking at flights to Philadelphia. "When are you going?" I say. I see him click today's date. And then I see him click "2" passengers. "I'll go get dressed."

TWENTY-FIVE

"Ah, Cherry Hill," I say.

"You've been there before?" Digby says.

"My mother went to college in Philadelphia and she used to go to Cherry Hill to bowl and eat Chinese food," I say. "She took me during one of her class reunions."

"Great schools, bad traffic, insane property taxes—first-world problems," Digby says.

"That's good, right?" I say. "That she's probably in a good situation?"

"Is it?" he says. "I don't know what to hope for."

We print out our boarding passes and go through security. We stop at the Hudson News, where I read some of the more embarrassing gossip magazines before buying a copy of *The Economist* to redeem myself. I finish paying and join Digby as he stares, unmoving, at a rack of Disney princess junk.

"She's thirteen, Digby." I point at the rack of lip balms and tampons. "This is probably more her deal now."

"Nine years is a long time," Digby says.

We board the plane and I try to relax, but Digby is sitting rigid and staring straight ahead in the seat next to me. I read and reread the same article on something I immediately forget about mere seconds after I look up from the page. After a half an hour of this, I give up and put away the magazine.

"Hey. Are you okay?" I say.

He nods.

"Digby, you have to take a breath," I say.

"I mean, there was no mention of a kid or anything," Digby says. "So we might get there and . . . nothing." He sounds weirdly relieved by the thought.

"Is that what you want?" I say.

"I don't know what to hope for," he says again.

• • •

"Well," Digby says. "It's a bakery."

Skolnik's looks like a pillar-of-the-community kind of family joint. "Since 1945," its masthead announces.

"Is this the right place?" Digby checks the piece of paper with the details of Rosetta Pickles's benefits payout over and over. "It can't be the right place."

"So they have a bakery. Why not?" I say, even though I can't quite make the conceptual leap myself. I think about the kidnapping, the extortion, the running, the screaming, the lying. And then I look at the old-timey bagel place going through a hipster gentrification. Nothing about it makes sense.

But, to be sure, I Yelp it and find that: "Yeah, it says here, *Owned and operated by the original founding family, the Pickleses.*"

"What else does it say?" Digby says.

"Please don't make me read Yelp. The comments on it are just so absurd . . ." I say, but I can't physically stop my eyes from seeing the words. "Like this. Two stars because the plain bagel is *too* plain. And then this one says the salmon is too fishy. . . ." I can't stop.

"Okay, okay, I'm sorry I asked. May I?" Digby takes the phone from me.

He scrolls through and reads out, "*The service is awful. When I asked for the manager, the aggressive counter girl told me her family owned the place and then threw a bagel at me. Also, the bagels are really hard.*" Digby thinks for a second. "Sally?"

"Wow. So you're saying your rudeness is in there at a genetic level?" I say.

We stare at the shopfront for a few seconds more.

"Are you ready?" When he nods, I set off toward the door. But then he pulls me back.

"What?" I say.

"Hit me," he says.

"*What?*" I say.

"I'm nervous. I need you to hit me," he says. "As hard as you can. Take your best shot."

"Are you kidding me? No," I say. "You're *nervous*? Aww, poor little nervous baby. Is little baby nervous?" I tickled his chin to really sell the condescension. "It's okay, baby. You'll be okay, baby—"

Digby snaps out of it. He straightens his suit and gives back my phone.

"Emotional brutality. Thank you. Works as good as a slap," he says, and strides to the door.

• • •

Digby opens the door with a huge flourish that flings off the cluster of bells attached to the frame. Everyone in the store turns to look and watch the two of us struggle to reattach the fallen bells to the door.

We finally get the damn bells back on their little mount and Digby and I take a look around.

Digby says, "It's very charming . . ."

The food is stored in wood-and-glass display counters that are obviously original to the store. There's a huge ball of twine hanging from the ceiling that the busy counter girl pulls from to tie up boxes of pastry. No wonder the hipsters love it.

The line is long, and to a person, the customers look irritated but are generally well behaved. I watch the counter girl. It's clear that her surly demeanor is the key to controlling this crowd. The fear of what might come out of her frowning mouth is the only thing keeping this powdered sugar keg from blowing up.

A heavenly buttery smell has saturated the place. It's been a very long time since I've had anything this anti-vegan. And I haven't eaten since the bags of nuts on the plane.

I am walking to join the end of the line when I hear Digby say, "Excuse me, miss?"

And then I hear the entire room explode in various angry versions of "Get back in line."

Digby is about to justify himself, saying, "I just have a ques—" but the crowd starts to really roil.

The lone counter girl says, "Hey. Get back in line. People have been waiting."

I can't tell if the girl at the counter is as pretty as her heavy makeup insists she is. She's obviously a citizen of the post-YouTube world of painting the face you want on top of the face you have and I can't see her bone structure clearly enough to determine whether she looks like Digby. Figuring out whether she's in the right age range is even more complicated. With her mink eyelashes, tight top bun, and bleached platinum hair, she could be anyone, of any age within a twenty-year range, from anywhere that has a Sephora and Internet access.

"Really, I just want to ask a question," Digby says.

"They *all* have questions," Counter Girl says, and points to the crowded room.

"Digby," I say. "Psst. Get over here."

But he ignores me and says, "I don't even want to buy anything—"

"Then what the hell are you doing in my store?" Counter Girl says.

I hurry over and hustle him away. As I walk him to the back of the line, Counter Girl holds up two fingers and says, "That's strike two."

"What?" Digby says. "What was strike one?"

I physically turn his head away and shush him. "Are you crazy? You don't cut in line in places like this," I say. "This is *New Jersey*. Do you want to die?"

"She said 'my store,' so that's her, maybe," Digby says. "What do you think?"

"I don't know," I say. I stare at Counter Girl but every time I think I see a similarity, she steps into different lighting and my confidence vanishes. "She's kind of in disguise a little."

"The blond hair is throwing me off," Digby says. He holds up his finger and squints, trying to edit the living image as he stares at her.

"The hair? It's the eyes for me, I think. I can't tell what their real shape is under that cat-eye," I say. "And her cheekbones and jawline are shaded in. I once saw an Asian woman use makeup to turn herself into Drake. This is what we could be dealing with here."

Digby raises his phone and takes a picture of Counter Girl right as she turns in our direction and catches him doing it. Her frown deepens and she stares at him for a pointedly long beat before continuing to ring up the customer she'd been helping.

Digby zooms in on different parts of the picture and

compares it with an old snapshot of Sally that he's brought along. We do this for the entire fifteen minutes we are in the line but we never get to a decision.

Finally, it is our turn. Counter Girl looks ready for a fight when she says, "Can I help you?"

"Um. Maybe?" Digby says. "Can we get a rhubarb pie and a Fresca?"

"Rhubarb pie? What is that even?" Counter Girl says.

"So . . . you don't know what *rhubarb* is?" Digby says.

"Next customer!" Counter Girl says.

"Wait, wait." Digby shows her Sally's snapshot. "Have you ever seen this kid?"

Without looking at the picture, Counter Girl rears up and crosses her arms. "Are you going to buy anything? Because there's a whole line of people behind you I need to help if you aren't."

I push Digby aside and say, "Actually, may I have a half dozen cream cheese kugels and two deluxe salmon schmears on everything bagels, please? Extra onions." Digby looks at me like, *How can you eat at a time like this?* and I say, "And *you're* paying. You never take me anywhere." I look at Counter Girl to see she's nodding.

"Yeah," Counter Girl says. "He looks like a cheap date."

I force a laugh and say, "Oh, sweetie. You don't even know. He made me drive two hours today so he could track down some girl he went to kindergarten with who he's gotten obsessed with lately . . ." I pause so Counter Girl's disgust can develop more fully. "Watch him find her and get engaged right in front of me or something trashy like that."

"What a winner," Counter Girl says. "You're better off with someone else, honey. Get your hair did, get a spray tan, get your revenge body on, and upgrade your man. You deserve better."

I am just thinking to myself that I have to somehow get Sloane in the same room as Counter Girl when Digby says, "Oh . . . *the bells* were strike one. But that was an accident." Counter Girl ignores that and tells him how much we owe for the food.

Digby hands over his mother's credit card and tries to give her Sally's picture again.

"Please," Digby says. "Can you just take a look?"

Counter Girl runs the credit card and leaves Digby hanging with the photo in his outstretched hand until I take the bags of food from her. She takes the picture and the moment she sees the image, her face drops. With her muscles slackened this way, I can finally see that under her makeup, she is in fact very young.

A twenty-something guy in an apron comes out from the back, sees Counter Girl seemingly standing around doing nothing while the shop is full of customers starting to rebel, and yells, "Hey. What are you doing? There's people here."

Counter Girl tries to show Apron Guy the picture and says, "He asked if I—"

Digby, emboldened by Counter Girl's dramatic reaction,

says, "Wait. Please. Tell me. Is that your real hair color? Are you a natural blond?"

Apron Guy hasn't yet seen the photo and in the absence of any kind of context, he is immediately enraged by Digby's question and says, "*What* did you say? Did you just ask my sister if the carpet matches the drapes?"

'A collective gasp echoes in the bakery.

"Hey, Tasha, has this guy been mackin' on you? I told you to stop making up your face like that." Apron Guy points at Counter Girl and says, "She's only thirteen years old, buddy."

Without thinking, Digby says, "Thirteen?" He smacks his hand on the counter. "That's *perfect*."

And then Apron Guy runs out from behind the counter, grabs Digby by the collar, and wrestles him out of the store. I take the snapshot and the credit card from Counter Girl, say something dumb like, "Have a nice day," and follow Digby outside.

TWENTY-SIX

"Princeton. Was that her?" Digby is wild-eyed. "It must be her. The way she reacted to the picture . . ."

"Well, that's not really definitive proof of anything," I say.

"No, but she's thirteen and she obviously knew that picture was of her . . . it fits," Digby says. After a long stunned pause, he says, "In all the ways I imagined this moment would play out, I never imagined it like this."

"Like what? A bakery in Cherry Hill? I mean—"

"No, I never imagined that I wouldn't like her," Digby says. "I prepared myself for finding out she's dead, mostly . . ."

"That would've been the most likely thing," I say.

"A tiny, tiny part of me fantasized that I'd find her and we'd see each other and immediately just *know* . . ." Digby says.

"Right. Happily ever after," I say.

"But I spent exactly zero minutes preparing myself for *that* . . ." Digby says, ". . . mean little turd."

He stares at me, stunned. And then, one of us emits some gut gurgles. Both of us put our hands on our stomachs, not sure whose it was. I hand him one of the bagels and we go around to the shady side of the building to sit on a low wall near the bakery's back door. We eat. We look around. It all seems so surreal.

"Good schmear," Digby says. "So this is New Jersey. My first time."

"Well, this is a parking lot, to be fair," I say.

"No, no, I like it here. The food is good . . ." He points at his sandwich and then points at the bakery. "And the people are absolutely delightful."

A delivery van drives past us and backs into a spot right by the back door. The driver toots the horn. The bakery's back door opens a minute later and a girl runs out to meet the driver slowly climbing out of the van. She's dressed in black jeans, big black boots, and a rumpled blazer two sizes too big for her slight frame.

"Hey, jag-off, you're *late,*" the girl says. "We don't have any blintzes today because of you. I should take our loss from that off this payment—"

The delivery guy hears this and immediately gets in her face, screaming back at her. It's a heavily uneven match, though, because he has at least a foot and a half on her.

"Whoa," Digby says. "That's . . ."

I think so too, and I walk over to the fight with Digby.

"Excuse me," Digby says. "Is everything okay here?"

271

"Yeah, thanks pal, it's under control," the girl in black says.

Digby says, "Are you sure?"

"Yeah. What's your problem?" the girl in black says. "We're talking here."

"Yeah, back off, moron. Mind your own business," the delivery guy says.

"And *your* business is what? Beating on little girls?" Digby says.

Simultaneously, Delivery Guy says "beating?" and Girl in Black says "*little girl?*"

And then both of them turn on Digby and berate him as I drag him away, saying, "Sorry. Our mistake. Excuse us . . ."

We retreat to our spots on the wall and resume eating our sandwiches.

"New Jersey, man," Digby says.

"Digby," I say. "You know . . . *she* . . ." I nod to the girl in black.

It takes him a shockingly long time to catch on but when he does, he looks relieved.

"Oh . . . that would make more sense," he says.

We watch the girl in black wrap up her argument with the delivery guy. It's hard to say who is the winner but the delivery guy slams every door and every box he comes in contact with as he transfers the van's contents into the bakery in that sore loser kind of way. The girl in black stands beside the van while it's being unloaded. I catch her looking our way periodically.

"She looks like my father," Digby says.

"But she reminds me of you," I say. "Even though her face doesn't exactly look like yours."

"She might just be an employee with a bad attitude, though," he says.

The delivery is done and the van squeals away.

"Well, I guess now we can ask her because here she comes," I say.

The girl in black walks toward us and stops a few feet away as though she hasn't decided to commit to actually having the conversation.

"Sitting around waiting for more people to rescue?" she says. "What's your deal?"

Digby is staring at her, not saying anything.

It gets awkward, so I say, "It looked like he was going to attack you. Sorry."

The girl in black says, "He's our flour supplier. He pushes my aunt around, so she let me take over dealing with him. Today was my first day. That's why I was pissed when you stole my thunder."

"We were just worried," I say.

The girl in black pulls out some brass knuckles and says, "I would've been fine."

I whisper to Digby, "There's two of you now." It really is uncanny how much she reminds me of Digby. Beyond the weird jerky way their arms move and their similar taste in business-casual Johnny Cash clothing is the look of impending anarchy in her eyes that I've seen in Digby's so many times. I like her already.

"Sorry," I say. "I'm Zoe, by the way."

"I'm Shelley," the girl in black says.

"Shelley," Digby says. "They kept your name close. Smart."

"What?" Shelley says. "Kept my name close? Close to what?"

"Shelley, could you look at a photo for me?" Digby says.

"Oh . . . you're *that* guy. Showing photos in the bakery. Anthony's inside saying you're a pervert but you've got my cousin Tasha all upset and she deals with perverts all day long, so I know that's not it . . ." Shelley says. "Let's see this photo, then."

Digby hands it to her.

Shelley sees the picture, takes a deep breath, and says, "Is this me?" Shelley holds up the picture next to her face to give us the side by side. "I think this is me."

I cannot help myself. "Ho . . . ly . . . crap. It's happening."

"Am I adopted, dude?" Shelley says. When Digby doesn't answer, she says, "I knew it."

And then I realize Digby is no longer standing next to me and that Shelley is yelling at his back as he walks to the bus stop.

"Hey, dude. *Am I?*" Shelley looks at me and says, "Am I?"

It isn't for me to say, so I just shrug like a dumbass and walk away too. "I'm sorry."

I reach for the photo but Shelley snatches it away and says, "Are you kidding me? Get back here."

A bus rolls up and Digby gets on.

"I'm sorry, but I have to go," I say, and run.

The bus driver closes the door behind me and as we pull away, I watch Shelley standing at the bus stop staring at the picture. I sit next to Digby and watch him tap away at his phone for a minute until I can't take it anymore and say, "That was weird." He doesn't answer me. "I mean, you literally ran away."

"I didn't run away," Digby says. "I stepped away to figure out the situation." He continues typing.

"Ummm. You can rephrase all you like but you still left your *sister* standing on the side of the road, not knowing what the hell is going on except that the people she thought were her parents have probably been lying to her," I say. "You need to explain yourself. Also, you need to tell your parents." But he doesn't answer and just goes on typing into his phone. "And what are you typing?"

"I'm telling my parents I found Sally," he says.

"You're *texting* them? You can't text this kind of thing," I say.

"Which is why I wrote an email," he says. "I mean, I'm not an animal."

"I guess I know what to expect when we break up," I say.

"Break up?" he says. "Princeton . . ." Finally, he puts away his phone. "Are we . . . *together*?"

"Aren't we?" I say.

275

"I don't know," Digby says. "I was going to bring it up, but . . ."

"Okay, you know what? This isn't really the time to talk about it," I say.

"You brought it up," he says.

"Well, now I'm dropping it," I say. "Can we talk about it later?"

"What's the matter with right now?" Digby says.

"While we're on a New Jersey Transit bus headed to Camden?" I say.

"Which part bothers you?" he says. "That it's a bus or that we're going to Camden?"

"Digby." I know what he's doing. He'd rather talk about anything besides the fact that he's found Sally.

After a while, he says, "Yeah. I know." The jokey smile drops from his face and he stares out the window in silence. I let him be and he is sad and quiet until a fight between the bus driver and a fare dodger cheers him up again.

The next time we talk, we are both careful not to bring up anything really meaningful. We stay like that all the way back to River Heights, gliding on the surface, pretending that if neither of us looks down, Digby won't fall into the new bottomless pit that's opened up beneath his feet.

TWENTY-SEVEN

We'd taken Art's crummy sedan to the airport and are driving it back to Digby's place when he says, "I hope you don't mind, but I feel like taking a walk. Is that okay?"

I'd been so good up to this point. I hadn't complained when we'd missed the flight out of Trenton we'd been booked on because Digby just *had* to stop for a real Philly cheesesteak. Comfort eating, I'd thought, and if anyone needs comfort, it's Digby right here, right now. And then I didn't complain when the next flight we'd gotten on was delayed and then had non-functional toilets. But now a walk? On top of the ten hours of travel hell since leaving Cherry Hill? Nope.

"I'm exhausted, dude," I say.

"It'll be a short walk, don't worry," he says.

When we are a few blocks away from his house, Digby pulls over onto the side of the road that's right above a slope leading to the river and gets out.

I climb out after him and say, "Here?"

Digby looks around. "Looks good to me."

"Are we just going to leave the car here?" I say.

"Nope." And then he leans into the car, puts it in neutral, and starts pushing it toward the slope.

"Digby?" I know what's coming but I still gasp when the car slides down and comes to a crunching stop halfway in the river. He and I stand watching the car for a while.

"Well, he probably knows he had that coming," I say.

• • •

It is already past midnight by the time Digby and I get back to his street.

"I guess my mother got the email." Digby says this because his house is the only one on the block that is lit up. "Oh, great. He beat us here," Digby says.

"Who?" I say before I notice the silhouette of a man standing to the side of the front door, leaning on a car and smoking. "Who's that?"

And then the guy steps out of his lean and lopes over toward us and I recognize the way he moves.

"Princeton. Hang on to your hat," Digby says. "My father is here."

I run back over the few stories Digby's told me about his father and prepared myself for Air Force Colonel Joel Digby. Engineer. Strict. Speaks in short, angry bursts.

"Are you her?" Digby's dad says to me.

At first, I flatter myself with the notion that Digby has told him about me. And then I realize what he's really asking. "Oh . . ." is all I manage to say.

"This is my girlfriend, Zoe," Digby says.

"But you *have* found your sister?" Digby's dad says. "That email wasn't some pathetic cry for help?"

"Yes, I've found her," Digby says. He notices his father's clothing. "You're wearing your gym clothes. You came straight here?"

"Where is she?" his father says. "Is she all right?"

"New Jersey. She doesn't know she was kidnapped," Digby says. It's odd to hear the change in the way he talks. All the joking around that usually laces everything he says is gone when he's talking to his father.

"Your mother told you everything? About what happened?" his father says. When Digby nods, his father says, "So you know it's not something we discuss in the open." His father's eyes flick over to me. "You're excused. This is a family matter."

This annoys Digby and he squares up to his father and says, "Zoe knows everything, Joel. And she's the reason I know where Sally is, so, in fact, you should maybe thank her instead of dismissing her."

Digby's father nods, looks at me, nods again, and says to Digby, "It's fine if you don't want to call me dad. You're your own man now. But address me as 'Colonel Digby' or 'sir' until I tell you otherwise."

The door flies open and Digby's mother comes out to join us.

"You found her," Val says. She is cry-laughing. "I knew you would . . . and I knew she was alive."

Digby nods. I can see him struggle to return his mother's happiness without breaking the cool façade he's put up for his father.

Val kisses Digby and then surprises me with a kiss too. "I called Fisher," she says.

"I told you not to," Digby's father says. "What do you need to call that fraud for?" Sparks fly when he throws his cigarette against the wall.

"Fraud?" Val is outraged. "Fisher was the only one who believed Sally was still alive when everyone else—including you—"

"Oh, here we go again with *this*," Digby's father says. "It's not hard to have hope when you're getting paid six K a week to care."

Six thousand dollars a week? I play back Fisher telling me I should think about going into that field and think, Hmmm.

"Well, *this*, Zoe doesn't need to hear," Digby says. "Let me drive her home. I'll debrief when I get back."

"That's fine. I have to take a shower anyway." Digby's father is about to walk away when he stops and says to Digby, "You know . . . I always wondered if maybe *you* did it."

Digby nods. "I know."

"I need a drink," Digby's father says.

When he is gone, Digby says, "I hope he likes chocolate milk, because that's all we have."

"Zoe, won't you come in?" Val says.

"No, thanks, Mrs. Digby. It sounds like you have a lot to talk about," I say. "I can call a cab."

"That's crazy," Digby says. "Come in. Have a drink while I get the keys and use the bathroom real quick."

"No, if it's okay, I'll wait here . . ." I say. "I'm just going to fall asleep if I sit down on the couch and get comfortable."

Before Val follows Digby into the house, she grabs me and hugs me tight. "Thank you, Zoe. For bringing both my children back to me." Thankfully, she hurries back into the house so neither of us has to deal with the emotions that kicks up.

I jump up on the hood of Digby's father's rental car. The engine is still warm and even though I know it's a bad idea, I let myself close my eyes.

• • •

I don't know how long I sleep, but I wake up feeling vulnerable. It takes me a second to work out that it's because I feel myself being watched. I sit up and see I really am being watched by someone standing on the paved walkway to the house.

"Digby?" I say before the sleep haze lifts and I realize my voyeur is far too short to be Digby. And is female. "Shelley?"

Shelley says, "Zoe, right?"

"How did you get here?" I say. "We just arrived like, two hours ago."

"What?" Sally says. "Why? You left the bakery hours before I did."

"Ugh. I know." I don't feel like telling her about the cheesesteak idiocy, so I say, "How did you find this place?"

"I called the credit card company and told them we were reconciling our books. They gave me the billing address for the credit card he used in the bakery." Shelley abruptly shifts gears. "I'm not adopted, am I? The way my aunt freaked out . . . Anthony said something to me about not calling the police."

"I don't think I'm the right person to have this conversation with you," I say.

"Shelley?" Digby walks out of the house. He and his sister stare at each other.

"Tasha said you came in asking for rhubarb pie and Fresca," Shelley says. "What was that?"

"Your favorite snack. Instead of a cake, we had rhubarb strawberry pie for the last birthday you had here," Digby says. "I wondered if you'd remember."

"When I was in kindergarten, I had an imaginary best friend named Rhubarb TiscaFresca. I never understood why I made up that name," Shelley says. "Who are you?"

"I'm your brother," Digby says.

"You found me?" Shelley says.

"Yes . . ." Digby points at me. "She and I did it together."

"Are you my sister?" Shelley says.

"No," I say. "He and I are . . ."

Shelley nods at Digby and says, "Mazel tov." She looks up at the house's façade and says, "I used to have nightmares about a place I called the 'screaming house.' I had trouble sleeping for years. I even got hypnosis. I think it might have been this place."

"Our father is a recovering alcoholic and our mother is still recovering from a breakdown," Digby says. "'Screaming house' sounds about right."

"Digby . . ." I say. "That's a little bleak."

"She should know what she's walking into," Digby says.

"That's okay," Shelley says. "It wasn't exactly heaven where I was. It's not like I was Tasha and Anthony's Cinderelly or anything, but I always felt . . ." Shelley says. "Not at home."

Digby struggles to suppress something but it gets the best of him. "You know . . . your cousin Tasha's stealing from the business."

"When she rings people up on the back register?" Shelley says.

I vaguely remember thinking it was odd how one of the registers was on the rear counter facing the wall so that Tasha's back would block the customers' view of the screen while she rung them up.

"Like, she tells people seven dollars for a dozen bagels, and then rings up four-fifty for a half dozen so she can keep the two-fifty difference for herself?" Shelley says. "Yeah. Why do you think my aunt wants me to start taking over? Also, Anthony gets kickbacks from the suppliers."

"My God, there really *are* two of you now," I say.

"What happened to me?" Shelley says.

"You should come in. We need to talk," Digby says.

"What's your name?" Shelley says.

"I'm Philip," Digby says. "Philip Digby."

Shelley nods. "Then I *am* Sally Digby. The kid who was kidnapped."

"Googled the name on the credit card we used? That's our mother's name, by the way," Digby says. "Yes, you are Sally."

"And my parents are in there?" Sally points at the house.

Digby nods. "They're divorced but they're both in there right now. They know I found you."

Sally stares hard at the front door of the Digby house. "This was a mistake. I'm not ready for this. I need to get out of here."

Digby is momentarily taken aback but when he recovers, he says, "What if you stayed here without them knowing you're here? Just so you can adjust at your own pace?"

"How . . ." And then I realize what he means. "Oh, my God, are you seriously going to stick your sister in the garage?"

"I lived in there for three months myself," Digby says.

"Sounds great to me," Sally says.

"You know there isn't a bathroom in there," I say. "You'll have to pee in a sink."

"Actually," Sally says, "people are grossed out by pee but it's sterile—"

"As your brother has explained to me. In great detail," I say. "Maybe you guys should put it on your family sigil. House Digby. Pee is sterile."

Sally starts walking to the garage in the back. "Hey, am I Jewish?"

"No," Digby says.

She thinks about that for a long while. "Maybe later, can you take me for a bacon cheeseburger?" And then Sally goes inside.

"I'll call a cab," I say.

"You don't want to come in?" Digby says.

"I think she wants to talk to you," I say. "In private."

"Don't call a cab." Digby throws his mom's car keys to me. "I'll talk to you tomorrow?"

"Are you going to be okay?" I say.

Digby shrugs. "I don't know . . . but at least my problems are about to change." He smiles. "And change is good."

TWENTY-EIGHT

Not going to lie, I am relieved when I pull Val Digby's car into my driveway without having fallen asleep and crashing into anything on the way home. I fight the temptation to sleep where I sit and lure myself out of the car with fantasies of rolling into my soft warm bed and sleeping straight through until Monday morning.

I lock up Val Digby's car and turn to see Sloane, Henry, and Felix climbing out of Sloane's SUV. My exhausted brain takes an age to remember that I'd texted Sloane something about finding Sally right before I'd fallen asleep on the hood of Digby's father's car.

"Well?" Sloane says. "Where is she?"

"Sally?" I say.

"Who the hell else?" Sloane says.

"Yeah, I thought about putting her in the car and bringing

286

her over here for a show-and-tell with you, Sloane," I say. "But weirdly, she wanted to readjust to her parents first."

"Parents?" Henry says. "*Joel* came back?"

I grimace and nod.

Henry whistles. "Joel's back in town."

"Bad?" Felix says.

"You think *you* had a bad afternoon with your mom? Pray you never have to give Digby's dad bad news," Henry says. "When I was nine years old, I told him that I'd spilled some juice in his car, and he turned around and gave me this one look that he has . . . and I just sat there and wet my pants. Luckily, he couldn't tell because there was already juice all over the seat."

"Felix, why'd you have a bad afternoon with your mom?" I'm afraid to ask but I do anyway. "She didn't find out about what we did, did she?"

"No, no, she doesn't know," Felix says. "Wow. That would be bad. But I did tell them they shouldn't buy that place in Boston."

I suck in my breath. No wonder he looks so worried.

"How did *that* go?" I say.

"Well, my father hasn't spoken at all since I told them," Felix says. "My mom, on the other hand, said *plenty*. And then she took a Xanax and went to bed."

"Then how are you out now?" I say. "Aren't you at least grounded?"

"Oh, you bet I am," Felix says. "I climbed out the window."

"You've probably been hanging out with us too much," I say.

"How's Digby?" Henry says. "How's Sally?"

"Sally is *exactly* like Digby. I mean *exactly*. Like, spookily so," I say. "And Digby is . . . I don't know. He seems like he's okay but . . . you know."

"Who can even tell with that guy?" Sloane says.

"Right," I say.

"What about Silk and his father?" Sloane says. "Did they leave town?"

I nod. "All taken care of."

"Taken care of, like . . ." Henry says. "*Taken care of?*"

"No, no. Not like that. They got a lot of money to forget all about you," I say. "What about the police? The fire department?"

"We told them those guys tried to rob us," Henry says. "So far so good. We'll go give a report and my parents will file the insurance claim afterward."

"Hey, Sloane. I saw you with that fire extinguisher," I say. "I thought you said you wanted to burn that place down—"

"If that place burns down, it'll be because *I* lit it on fire," Sloane says.

"So now what?" Felix says.

"I have no idea. But I have *got* to get some sleep," I say. "I feel like a zombie."

Sloane reaches over and surprises me with a hug. "Yeah, you look awful," she says.

"We really need to work on your phrasing, Sloane," I say. I am just finishing my hug with Felix when the front door of my house opens and my mom steps out, communicating her fury with the way she plants her feet and crosses her arms. I groan.

"Say good-bye to your friends," my mother says.

I walk past her into the house. "I already did," I say.

$$\bullet \bullet \bullet$$

She shuts the door behind us. I want to walk straight up the stairs and pass out but I don't want to start a fight when I don't particularly feel any hostility. And so I lean against the wall and get ready to soldier through the next few minutes.

"I'm trying to be cool because I know trying to tell you who you can and can't be friends with—or more than friends with—would just drive you away but . . ." Mom throws up her hands. "This is ridiculous."

"Where have you been, Zoe?" Cooper says. I guess the indignation I feel flares up and shows on my face, because he very quickly adds, "I'm not going to Dad you around, but we're at least roommates, and even a roommate would worry if you just disappeared like that."

"I didn't disappear," I say. "I texted."

Mom holds up her phone and reads me back my text. *"I'm in New Jersey. BRB."*

Hearing it aloud, I know it's indefensible and I don't have

289

the energy to try to find a way to rationalize it, so I just mumble, "Sorry."

"You didn't have to go all the way to New Jersey, you know," Mom says. "They have plenty of motels right here in town . . ."

"O . . . kay . . . now you're being crazy." I can see she's about to really go off the rails, so I say, "Can we talk about this after I get some sleep?" I start going up the stairs.

"And maybe we should also talk about what to do now that your father's threatening not to pay *any* of your tuition if you don't live at his place next year?" Mom says.

"Just tell him I'll live with them until he pays the balance in June and then we'll submit the housing request right after his check clears," I say. "If that doesn't work, then we should file papers and get them served at his office during business hours." I lower my voice and continue, "Or maybe I should just cut through the crap and ask him whether he's visited his secret bank account in the Caymans yet this year . . ."

Cooper whistles. "That's hardboiled . . ."

I climb the stairs, my entire body a slow-moving collection of aches and pains.

"Zoe? Are you sure you're okay?" Cooper says.

The easy way out would be to say a simple "I'm fine" but for some reason, I instead say, "We found Sally Digby. She's alive. She's been working in a bakery in New Jersey." And then, before Mom and Cooper can recover from the shock, I go back to stumbling up the stairs.

"You what?" Cooper says.

"Oh, my God," Mom says.

"Is Digby all right?" Cooper says.

"He's fine," I say. "Sally's in River Heights now but she's living in the garage because she can't cope with her crazy parents." Mom and Cooper stare at me openmouthed. Clearly, they are going to need a moment to digest what I've just told them, so I continue up to my room.

"Zoe, wait." Mom runs up the stairs and hugs me.

The hug goes on for a longer time than I want it to. "I'm okay, Mom," I say.

"You did a good thing. Digby is lucky to have you." She strokes my cheek. "You're still in trouble for taking off, though."

TWENTY-NINE

I wake up several times after I collapse in bed fully clothed. The first time I rouse, I have enough energy to take off my coat and shoes. The second time, I'm able to take off my jeans and sweater. By the third time, the sun is up and I am actually able to propel myself out of bed and shower.

At no point did I look at my phone, so when I wake up the fourth time and find Digby sitting at my desk, throwing my wasabi peas in my face, I say, "Go away . . . why do you never let me sleep?"

Digby laughs and says, "It's four thirty in the afternoon. You've been asleep all day."

"I have?" I tell myself I should be rested, but my body begs to differ. I flop back onto my pillows. "I don't care. I'm exhausted." And then I remember. "Hey. How's Sally?"

"We're all talked out for now," Digby says.

I think back to Friday night and say, "Wow. Just two days

292

ago, we were digging around for her dead body and now . . . she's hiding out in your garage."

"Yeah. It's a damn miracle, no doubt about it," Digby says. "You know, Sally wants to stay . . . like, effective immediately. She doesn't want to go back to New Jersey again."

"You're kidding," I say. "What about her family?"

"Well, technically . . ." Digby says. "That's us now. *We're* her family."

"I know," I say. "But you know what I mean."

"No Stockholm syndrome with that kid. It took me hours to talk her out of calling the cops on the Pickleses," Digby says. "I told her how we found her . . . de Groot and Book. There's a lot to figure out. The last thing anyone needs is for all this"—he makes a general waving motion with his hands—"to come out."

Excellent. More lies to juggle. They're really starting to pile up.

"Speaking of which. I just talked to Henry. He's going to file a police report," Digby says.

"Yeah, he told me he would," I say. "I need coffee, I think." I get out of bed and feel weirdly self-conscious in my tank top. I throw on a sweatshirt. "I'm glad I'm not the one who's going to have to sell *that* lie. The *gun*? And the bullet holes everywhere?"

"Henry's going to say two guys tried to rob the place and that the gun fell in the fryer . . . blah, blah, blah . . ." Digby says. "The empty register and blurry CCTV footage the cops got from the ATM across the street will help the story stick."

"Let me add that to the stack of lies I'm going to have to remember when Cooper starts grilling me later," I say. I notice he's eating my stale study snacks and since I know he only forages in my drawers when he bypasses the kitchen and climbs in through my window, I ask, "You want anything from downstairs?"

Of course he does.

• • •

The kitchen is empty and when I look out the window, I see that both my mother's and Cooper's cars aren't in their spaces. The realization that Digby and I are alone in the house suddenly makes me nervous. On the way back to the room, I stop at my bathroom and brush my teeth. This is a dumb thing to do, since the first thing I do right after is take a big sip of coffee. I walk back into my room and hand him the grocery bag I'd filled with his various food requests.

"Thanks, Princeton," he says.

"You know, you didn't have to climb in my window. Nobody's home," I say. I hope he hadn't noticed how weird that came out. But alas.

"Princeton. Are you . . . *blushing*?" Digby laughs. "Are you having 'thoughts'?"

"No," I say. But I'm immediately sorry that I've closed that door. "I mean . . . maybe? I don't know what I'm saying." I cover my face because I can't take his staring at me. "I don't know where we stand."

Digby gets out of my chair and sits next to me on the bed. He peels my hands away from my face and says, "I think we are both attracted to each other and have wanted this to happen for a long, long time but there was always something getting in the way. Am I right?" When I nod, he says, "It really bothered you when you thought that I might've slept with Bill."

I nod again.

"I swear to you, I didn't. Do you believe me?" When I nod again, he says, "But it bothers you that I've slept with two other girls—"

"But I'm trying not to let that bother me," I say.

"How's that going?" When I don't say anything, Digby gets up and says, "That's what I thought."

My heart sinks when he grabs his jacket from the back of my chair. "No, don't go," I say.

But instead of putting on his jacket, Digby takes out a tiny spray can from a pocket.

"I hope you don't think I was being presumptuous but I thought we might have this conversation today, so . . ." He raises the can above his head and starts to spray.

"Is that hairspray?" I say. But then I get a whiff of the toxic-smelling cloud. "What the hell is that?"

Digby tosses the can onto the bed next to me. I pick it up and I'm just beginning to realize why on earth he'd spray NEW

CAR SMELL all over himself when he says, "Brand-new, just for you . . ." Which is what it says on the New Car Smell can.

Digby takes my hand, spins me around, and dips me down low. He says, "Seriously, Zoe. As far as I'm concerned, there's never been anyone but you."

He kisses me but just as I feel my thoughts slipping into an incoherent chain of fantasy world gibberish, I give in to an intrusive thought that's been following me around for the last little while.

"Digby, stop. Wait," I say. "I have to ask you something."

"Okay . . ." Digby laughs. "What would a real Princeton romantic moment be without the awkward questions. What is it this time?"

"Did you really mean it when you told my mother you wanted to be an actuary?" I say.

Before I even finish asking, Digby lets me go and flops onto my bed, laughing.

"Oh, my God, Princeton. Have you been walking around worrying about that since I said it?" He looks at me and laughs harder. "Look how *upset* you are . . ."

"Don't laugh at me. I'm serious. I can't even imagine . . . you in some office . . . filling in time sheets . . ." I say. "I'm just having trouble picturing it."

"No, you can picture it, all right. You're picturing it right now. What you can't do is find it attractive," Digby says. "And you're right, who *plans* to sell out?"

"Well?" I say.

"Well . . . I'm ambushed by your mom one day. I'm trying to date her daughter. She already doesn't like me," Digby says. "Am I supposed to say I want to be broke and possibly get murdered working to bust human traffickers?"

"Is that what you want to do?" I say.

"Help people who've been taken and held against their will?" Digby says, "What do you think?"

"Well, why didn't you just say that?" I say. "Mom would've loved that."

"First, no, she wouldn't have loved hearing that. Not from her daughter's boyfriend. She would've loved hearing it on CNN from some dude making amends for being born rich. And, also, I didn't say it because I didn't think I needed to explain myself to her like that," Digby says. "Honestly, I didn't realize I had to explain myself to you, either."

And I realize he's right. "No. You don't." I look at the can of car air freshener in my hand. "Digby . . ."

"Princeton."

"I'm not ready . . ." I say.

"I know," Digby says.

"I'm scared," I say. Admitting it feels like throwing off a heavy burden from my shoulders.

"I'm terrified," Digby says. "You're my best friend. For a while, you were my only friend. I don't want to let you down."

"Do you think it would be weird?" I say. "Because we're friends?"

"I think it'd be weirder if we did it with our enemies," Digby says.

And then the thing that's really bothering me bubbles up. "Digby, I'm going to Prentiss next year," I say.

Digby laughs. "Of course you're going."

"But what about . . ." I cannot bring myself to say "us." "Would we still be . . ." I cannot finish that sentence either.

Digby kisses me and says, "Zoe. I spent nine years looking for a sister everyone else had given up for dead. Do you think I'd give up on you just because you're moving to New York?"

With the pressure off, the vibe between us is different when we kiss again. When my eyes blink open for a second, I spot my neighbor Mrs. Breslauer giving us dirty looks from her window. I give her a small wave.

And then Digby pulls away. "Okay, Princeton, it's my turn now," he says. "There's something I have to tell you."

Oh, no, I think. There is an earnest look on his face that fills me with the anxiety that he's about to tell me something I'm not ready for, like, *I love you.*

"What?" I say.

Digby reaches into his jacket and pulls out a sheet of paper, which he hands to me.

"What is this?" I say.

I open it to find a spreadsheet with a list of some River Heights High School students' names and rows of test scores.

"I took that from Principal Granger's desk drawer," Digby says. "Princeton. He's manipulating standardized test scores to defraud the school district of performance bonus money."

Here we go again.

Acknowledgments

I am so lucky to have written my first three books with Kathy Dawson. SO lucky. I came into this process knowing very little about myself as a writer, and Kathy had to be a lot more than an editor to me. She taught me about the process, the business, the audience, and gave me priceless on-the-job training I couldn't have gotten from anyone else. Kathy taught me how to work and got me past the blocks, past the fear, past the false plots that went nowhere . . .

Three books in the three years we've known each other. That's a big deal for a sloth like me. Thank you, Kathy.

And thank you to my agent, David Dunton, for taking the time to get to know me and my writing quirks before choosing whom to put me with. Thank you also to you and Nikki Van De Car for your consistently outstanding notes.

I also want to thank Claire and Regina at Penguin for their

patience (I'm always late) and the care they take going through my books. I'm always impressed when they find inconsistencies because it's in those moments that it becomes clear to me how much mind-space they've given me over the years. Thank you also to Anna and the many other generous Penguin team members who vet my work and then turn around and put it in the world.

I've had amazing luck with my foreign language translations and I'd like to especially thank Sylke in Germany for caring so deeply about capturing Zoe and Digby. Thank you also to Veronica Taylor for your killer narrating skills. So many people have come up to me to praise your version of the book.

LT and HB don't want cheese of any kind, so I'll limit myself to saying a simple "Thank you" and a blanket "I'm sorry." You know what you've done for me and I'm aware of what I've done to you boys. Hey, SCPY, guess what? It is nice. To my brother, Steve: Sorry in advance for being a bad influence on Sabrina. And, finally, to my parents: Thank you so much for not insisting that I be normal.